Cowboy In My Pocket

Kate Douglas

Hard Shell Word Factory

This story is dedicated, with much affection,
to all romance authors, especially those whose editors have
admonished them to "write the book of your heart."
(With the caveat, "so long as it has a cowboy hero, an amnesiac bride
and a marriage of convenience. Oh, and a secret baby wouldn't hurt.")
Friends, this one's for you.

ISBN-paperback: 0-7599-0126-0
Published May 2001
ISBN-ebook: 1-58200-634-2
Published April 2001

Hard Shell Word Factory
PO Box 161
Amherst Jct. WI 54407
Books@hardshell.com
http://www.hardshell.com
Cover art by Kate Moore Photo

Prologue

"MICHELLE, DARLING, it's good to see you. How've you been?"

"Cut the crap, Mark. You, of all people, know how I've been. Forget the pleasantries. Why did you reject my story?"

"Let's order first, sweetheart." Mark Connor, never one to make eye contact in the first place, studied the oversized menu in front of him. Michelle Garrison seethed and drummed her freshly manicured fingernails on the damask tablecloth. Suddenly she realized she was tapping the toe of her left shoe in the same staccato rhythm. She took a deep, struggle-for-some-semblance-of-control breath that ended in a frustrated sigh.

The waiter appeared, leather-bound notepad in hand, to take their orders. "Michelle?" Mark smiled at her.

"I'm not hungry. You order." Michelle glared at him, imagining large winged crows pecking his eyes. No, buzzards...buzzards made a much more impressive image.

"We'll both have the luncheon salad...Roquefort for me, the low-fat house dressing for the lady." Mark returned Michelle's glare with an innocent look. "Well, you have put on a few pounds, darling. You need to exercise more."

"I haven't had time, darling. I've been sitting in front of my computer without a break for the past six weeks, finishing a manuscript for you to reject. The same manuscript I wrote following your 'suggestions,' using your ideas for plot and characterization. Now, before my healthy, low-fat lunch arrives, would you so kindly tell me why you aren't buying my western?"

Mark smiled beatifically, the smile Michelle had once thought attractive until she realized he used that ubiquitous expression to hide everything going on behind those pale blue eyes of his. She waited for what seemed hours for his answer, returning his smile with a scowl. Finally he tapped his fingertips together in a little steeple, pursed his lips, opened his mouth, shut it again, hmmmm'ed as if pondering a new amendment to the Constitution, then said, "Well, you have to understand..."

"No, Mark. I don't understand. I did everything you asked. 'Put a cowboy on the cover, it'll fly off the shelves,' he says. 'Marriages of convenience are always popular, the readers love them,' so it's got a blasted MOC. Mark, I did it all, right down to the baby. Remember telling me, 'If it's got a baby in it, the story's gonna be a gold mine?' Well, it can't be a gold mine if it doesn't get published. I want to know what gives!"

Mark unfolded his napkin and spread it across his lap, ignoring Michelle and smiling politely at the waiter while the young man placed their salads on the table and departed.

"I'm waiting, Mark." Michelle picked up her fork, thought briefly how it would look imbedded in Mark's impeccably white shirt somewhere in the vicinity of his breastbone, then stabbed a large section of tomato instead.

"Sweetheart..."

"Don't give me that 'sweetheart' crap."

"Michelle."

Michelle swore silently. She practically heard the gears engaging in the gray matter behind his high forehead. Mark always considered every word so carefully. Another irritating editorial trait, she thought. Right up there with rejecting her western.

"Michelle, you have written forty-three books for us, and almost all of them have had an impressive return. All, that is, except the last three." He paused, resting his lips against his forefingers. "How can I say this without being blunt?"

"Go ahead, Mark. Be blunt...it suits you."

"Yes, well, it's my job to be honest. So, to put it bluntly, your ideas are tired, darling. Your characters all sound the same. That's why I wanted you to try a western."

"Well I did, dammit!" Michelle impaled a large piece of lettuce. How dare he find more fault with her story? "I worked hard on that western. My hero is a tall, dark and sexy cowboy; my heroine is an even sexier single mom with a disgustingly adorable little baby girl. They live on neighboring ranches, they ride horses, they chase cows around the field, they..."

"They don't know a thing about being cowboys, they've obviously never been in Colorado, where your story is supposedly set, and I might as well have been reading about an insurance agent as a cowboy. Our readers aren't stupid. When you write a scene about saddling a horse and you don't know that the pommel's at the front and the cantle's at the back, or how to tighten the cinch so the saddle won't slip, well your reader is going to laugh—at you for writing it, and us for publishing it. Look at the stupid name you gave your heroine! Lee Stetson? Come on. I'm sorry, Michelle. Westerns are hot right now, and you don't have a clue how to write them. You even have the hero make love to the heroine while they're riding a horse. That's physically impossible, darling. It hurts merely to think of it." His pained expression might have been funny under other circumstances.

"But it's a really sexy scene...it's..." Mortified, Michelle stared into her perforated salad. Mark loved her stories, he loved everything about her writing. Now he was saying it was awful? Worse than awful, embarrassing? She thought Lee Stetson was a really cute name.

The hefty advance that was going to pay off Michelle's VISA bill suddenly dissolved into a puff of smoke and faded away. She gazed longingly after the imaginary cloud.

She blinked and the cloud disappeared. "Wait a minute," she said, leaning forward. "How do you know the difference between a pommel and a, um, kettle?"

"It's a cantle, Michelle. That's what I'm trying to explain, if you'd only pay attention." He waved a glossy magazine under her nose. "I spent two weeks at a dude ranch. It was a terrific experience. All these western manuscripts suddenly started making sense. I want you to go. Just two weeks at the Columbine Camp in Colorado. That's all. You'll learn everything you need to know about horses and cows and cowboys and the great outdoors. Trust me on this, darling. It'll be good for you. You need a break, it's not that expensive, and besides, you can write it off. We want to keep you in our stable, Michelle..." He grinned, obviously impressed with his play on words.

"You want me to go to a dude ranch? I don't think so." Michelle jabbed her fork in Mark's direction, inordinately pleased when he backed away. "I don't even like horses, and I'm certain I'd like cowboys even less. I imagine they're both smelly, ill-tempered and impossible to control. I'll just do a little more research, maybe watch an old John Wayne movie or two. Trust me, Mark. I'll have my revision to you in, oh, about two weeks." She pushed away from the table. "Now, thanks for lunch, and have a really nice..."

Mark reached across the table, lightly grabbed her wrist, and stopped her. She sat back, stunned. Mark was never forceful, not ever.

There wasn't a trace of humor, or even sarcasm in his voice. "No revision, Michelle. This comes down from the senior editor, and we all know she takes her orders from marketing. Either you spend two weeks at Columbine Camp, which includes riding instructions...yes, dear, don't look so surprised...on a real horse, and an authentic dusty trail ride following authentic, smelly, dusty cows, or you find someone else to buy your stories. Competition's too steep, and there're a lot of hungry writers out there willing to take a lot less money. My advice is to jump through the hoops and learn what you can. Then write the freshest, most knowledgeable romantic western ever."

"You're not my agent, Mark. You're my editor. I thought you were my friend."

"I am, Michelle. That's why I bought you this issue of Western Horseman to read on the plane." He held the thick magazine up in front of her and smiled broadly, his blue eyes sparkling and his dimples dimpling until he looked more like a cover model than a book editor. Michelle thought seriously of telling him the effect was totally wasted on her.

A dude ranch...cows and flies and dust, and waking up with the chickens, and more charges on the VISA bill....

"I can't do this Mark. It's impossible. I..."

"You'll do it, Michelle. Call me when you get back. Don't forget your magazine." He flipped the brand new issue of Western Horseman open to a glossy spread of photos and text. "Read it, sweetheart. Besides a great article about Columbine Camp, it's just full of information about rodeos and barrel racing and horses and cowboys and cowgirls...you're gonna love it. Have fun. Think western. I expect you to come home with a drawl." He winked and smiled, flashing perfectly straight, white teeth.

Michelle stared at the photos in the magazine. Her breath caught in her throat. "That's him," she whispered. She pointed at a photo of a dark haired cowboy with a devil-may-care smile. "That's my hero, the one you rejected." She glared accusingly at Mark. "That's exactly how I described him, tall, dark and handsome with broad shoulders and a sexy grin, and you tell me I don't know what I'm writing about? This should prove to you that I wrote about a real cowboy. How could you reject my story?" She slapped the magazine down on the table, but couldn't take her eyes off the man staring back at her. Actually, she hadn't pictured her hero as quite so, well, elemental, but Mark didn't need to know that.

Mark glanced at the photo, then grinned at Michelle. "His name's Taggart Martin, and according to this article he lives right next door to

Columbine Camp, on a huge ranch called the Double Eagle. Go, Michelle. Meet a real cowboy. Maybe you'll be able to write a real western for a change."

Mark tipped an imaginary hat and sauntered out of the restaurant. Speechless, seething with resentment, Michelle glared at his retreating figure.

Then she glanced at the table, littered with the remnants of their lunch. Damn him! He'd left her with the check.

Chapter 1

TAG MARTIN slammed the telephone down on the table with enough force to rattle the windows in the tiny ranch office, took a deep breath, then counted to ten in Spanish. When that didn't work, he tried Japanese, and he was practically shouting his numbers in French by the time his foreman stepped into the room.

"You start countin' in German, son, I'll pack my bags and leave. I ain't seen you get all the way to French in a long time."

"That's because I haven't talked to my dear grandmother in a long time." Tag swiveled around in his worn leather chair and stared at his foreman. Old Coop...he knew the man had a real name, but there'd never been much need to use it. Other than when Tag wrote out Coop's weekly check, which he'd been doing for over twenty years.

Something he might have to stop doing if his bullheaded grandmother had her way.

"I hate to chance it, but we need to set Operation Betsy Mae in gear, Coop. She back from Austin yet?"

The old man grinned. "She's due back today. Saw her brother yesterday. Will thought it was a brilliant idea. Of course, I didn't tell him all the details." He polished his stained fingernails against his skinny chest with an air of great superiority. "As I recall, you laughed when I suggested it."

"It's a hare-brained scheme, but for both our sakes, it damned well better work." Tag scowled at Coop, who was still grinning like an idiot. Didn't he realize how serious this was?

"I told you. It's my idea," Coop said smugly. "Of course it'll work."

Obviously he didn't have a clue. Tag rounded on the old cowboy. "Don't get so cocky, old man. You wanna move into one of those little tin can mobile homes in the seniors' park? Get chased around the recreation hall by some old widow woman with blue hair? 'Cus that's exactly what's gonna happen if I'm not married within the next couple of weeks. You know my grandmother. She's hard-headed enough to go through with it."

Coop's grin disappeared. He shuddered visibly, slapped his dusty

Stetson against his skinny thigh, and straightened as much as his bowed legs would allow. "I'll head over to Columbine Camp and fetch Betsy Mae." He shot a level gaze at Tag. "I don't understand your grandmother," he muttered. "Lenore Martin is a beautiful, kind and generous lady. I can't imagine her taking this ranch away from you. It just don't seem right."

"It's not right, dammit. Now go get Betsy Mae."

Tag watched the old man climb into a faded blue pickup truck as weathered and scarred as its driver. He couldn't believe it had come to this, faking marriage to a woman he didn't love just to appease his grandmother.

It was either that, or watch Gramma Lenore donate the Double Eagle Ranch, the only home he'd ever known, to the Foundation for the Preservation of Wild Horses.

It wasn't fair. Not fair at all. So what if his grandmother felt guilty because her late husband had captured and sold the last wild horses off his land? Should Tag have to bear the punishment for his grandfather's mistake?

Right or wrong, Lenore Martin had given Tag an ultimatum when he was barely twenty. Marry or lose the Double Eagle. He raked his fingers through his hair and stared forlornly out the window. "I never thought you'd do it," he said quietly. "Didn't Dad's marriage teach you anything?"

Obviously not.

It had certainly taught Tag.

He didn't plan to marry, never had...and if he had things his way, never would. He had everything he needed here, the land, the cattle, the towering mountains, and occasional visits from Betsy Mae Twigg.

Except he was just about ready to lose the land, the cattle and the towering mountains.

Thank goodness Betsy Mae had agreed to this stupid idea of Coop's.

For a price.

Well, it was worth every penny.

A marriage of convenience, Coop called it.

A quick wedding, all for show, of course, even a nice little reception. That should make his grandmother happy, enough so that when he turned forty at the end of the month she'd do as she'd promised and deed the ranch over to him. Once that was accomplished, he and Betsy Mae would conveniently decide they didn't really love each other and go their separate ways. He knew he could count on Betsy Mae, especially now. She'd said she needed a break from the rodeo circuit. Barrel racing took a tremendous toll on a woman's body, and hers wasn't getting any younger.

Tag briefly allowed himself a moment to contemplate Betsy Mae's body. She wasn't half bad for a woman who'd spent as many years as she had following the rodeo. They'd been...well, friends, for a long time. It shouldn't be difficult to convince Gramma Lenore they were a loving couple.

Good Lord, he was actually preparing to go through with this damned charade. His father'd always said it was the sign of a desperate man, when he started taking desperate measures. Coop's plan was about as desperate a measure as Tag could imagine.

Where did that man get his schemes? Tag realized he was actually smiling as he went over the list of arrangements he and Coop had made. He placed a few calls, then settled back to wait for Betsy Mae to arrive. At least with Betsy Mae, he knew there was always the chance of fringe benefits.

The shrill ringing of the phone jarred him out of his contemplative daydreams of Betsy Mae's assets, but it wasn't enough to wipe the smile off his face. "Double Eagle Ranch, Tag Martin here."

Coop's frantic voice, however, was. Tag listened and forgot to breathe, listened and saw his entire future go down the drain. His only response to Coop's call was an expletive that would have sent Gramma Lenore running for a bar of soap.

Betsy Mae the barrel racer had run off with a rodeo clown. His buddy Betsy Mae, his one ace in the hole, had found true love with a guy in a fright wig and a dress.

How could she?

He let his gaze slide about the ranch office, lingering on the framed photos of himself as a youngster astride a horse, the bulletin board covered in ribbons and awards for his 4H projects through the years, and the efficient computer center with the equipment essential to running a modern cattle ranching operation.

This room was a time capsule of his life, the Double Eagle his heart and soul. In less than a month, it would all be gone. Tag dropped the phone on the desk, buried his face in his hands and fought the urge to weep. Only Coop's insistent caterwauling over the line snapped him back to reality.

A few minutes later, Tag silently placed the phone back in the cradle and stared out the window at the freshly mowed field beyond the barn. The clean scent of bailed hay filled the air; the distant bawling of cattle soothed his soul.

"Damn you, Betsy Mae, this better work." She hadn't completely abandoned him, he had to give her that. She'd left instructions with her brother, Will. She had a friend, another barrel racer who even did community theater in the off season. The gal had taken one look at Tag's photo in the current issue of Western Horseman and decided she wouldn't mind pretending to be Tag Martin's wife.

For a price.

"I sure hope you explained we were just gonna play at marriage," Tag muttered. That was all he needed, some danged woman looking for a husband. He'd noticed they tended to get a little desperate once they hit a certain age.

Unlike men like himself.

He'd make sure she knew the score the minute she arrived. In the meantime, he had two days to pull off a wedding and reception. Coop said he'd take care of the preacher, but the rest was up to Tag. He thought of his rapidly dwindling savings account. Then he considered the alternative. Tag figured, if Coop's scheme worked, it would be worth every penny. Whatever it took to convince Gramma Lenore.

Colorado, somewhere east of Montrose

ACCORDING TO the tattered map spread out on the seat next to her, Columbine Camp was still miles up this godforsaken road. Michelle glared through the rental car's rain-swept windshield and solemnly considered the pros and cons of murder. Actually, she thought, there weren't any negatives. All she need concern herself with at this point were methods.

Mark was going to die. There was no doubt at all in her mind. He deserved worse than death for suggesting, no, ordering her on this stupid trip. That was, if she didn't die first. Up to now she'd been too angry to be frightened.

Not any more. A brilliant flash of lightning split the Colorado sky. A vicious gust of wind swirled through the narrow river canyon, carrying a twisted branch that bounced and skittered across the hood of the car.

Fear replaced anger in a heartbeat.

Lightning shattered the cliff, above and to her left. Huge rocks and boulders pitched and tumbled across the road just ahead of the car. Michelle screamed, slammed on the brakes and yanked the steering wheel to the right. The tiny rental car fish-tailed and slid into a two-wheeled spin toward the edge of the road. She screamed again. Her world tilted, shifted.

Stopped.

Then slowly bounced up and down like a boat on the ocean.

Slowly, carefully, Michelle raised her forehead from its contact point on the steering wheel. It took a conscious effort to focus her eyes when all they wanted to do was close. She stared at, then through the cracked windshield. Comprehension dawned gradually...she looked out into...nothing. The car continued swaying, the gentle motion almost lulling Michelle back into her benumbed state.

A loud crack shocked her into awareness. Another sound, the roar and tumble of rushing water, filled her ears. Then more crackling and a few short jerks of the car.

Another crack. The car jerked.

Her world tilted. She slid forward. Her breasts smashed against the steering wheel, her head wobbled closer to the windshield. The leafy canopy of whatever bush she'd hit, parted, and the chocolate brown froth of a storm-swept river filled her view.

The car shuddered again. Michelle's befuddled mind kicked into overdrive. She hadn't hit a bush, she'd flown off the road and landed smack-dab in the top of a tree growing up from the steep canyon below. From the groaning, crackling and lurching, it was obvious the tree was not going to support the weight of the car—or Michelle—much longer.

She tried the door...jammed. "Oh no-o-o-o..." Sobbing, panting with fear, pain and shock, Michelle rolled the window down, eyed the small opening dubiously, shoved the stupid cowboy hat Mark had insisted she wear firmly down on her head, and tried to squeeze her jeans-clad butt through the open window.

Damn those extra pounds! She grabbed both sides of the window frame and grunted, wriggling and twisting her hips through the opening. What was holding her back? The car lurched and Michelle moaned in abject terror, then realized the issue of Western Horseman she'd practically memorized on the flight out was still in her back pocket, hung up against the frame. She slipped back, yanked the magazine free and threw it in the back seat. It landed next to her carry-on bag, the one stuffed with all those expensive western clothes she'd bought at the airport. The receipt was in the bag, blast it.

The image of her tax accountant glowering at her when she tried to explain a write-off of a bunch of fancy western clothing without a receipt was all the incentive she needed. Michelle snagged the handle. Grunting, she dragged the bag along behind as she squeezed through the window. She thought longingly of the matched set of luggage filled with the rest of her clothes, locked securely in the trunk.

One of her boots tangled in the twisted seatbelt.

Her priorities suddenly shifted.

"Oh, God," she sobbed, scrabbling to free herself. "Please...?" Frantically, she kicked and twisted her foot.

Suddenly she was hanging onto a bowed limb like a monkey on a branch, the bulging suitcase tucked against her chest. She gasped for breath against the driving rain and stared, trembling, as her car slid slowly through the leaves until, with a tiny twist and a flip it tumbled into the raging water below.

Released from the substantial weight of the car, the thick branch whipped back to its original shape. In the process, it threw Michelle Garrison, wearing her brand new Stetson cowboy hat, her pointy-toed cowboy boots, yoke-fronted shirt and tight fitting Lee jeans half-way across the rain-slick road. She landed next to her suitcase, a crumpled heap of humanity tossed against a wall of rocks and mud.

A few tiny pebbles dislodged by the impact skittered across the asphalt. Unrelenting, the rain continued its assault on the motionless figure lying in the road.

"BLASTED DAYS are going by too fast," Coop muttered. He shifted the old truck into gear, hit the gas and headed through the storm, searching the road that ran from the Double Eagle to town. Everything was set for Tag's wedding and reception.

Everything but the main attraction. Tag's bride should have been here by now.

"You promised Betsy Mae you'd be on time, dang it." Coop didn't need this kind of aggravation. Tag was already pacing, the decorations were up, and the woman was nowhere in sight.

She must have had car trouble, or maybe she'd taken a wrong turn. It was easy to miss signs in this kind of weather. Coop didn't want to imagine the alternative, that she'd changed her mind.

No, that was too awful to contemplate.

She was out here, and he was gonna find her.

He wondered what she looked like. Lord almighty, he hoped she was good lookin', especially considering what he was planning to do. Would Tag ever forgive him?

Rain bounced off the windshield and ran in rivulets across the highway. Coop thought of Lenore safely tucked away in her little house in town, and wished she were the one waiting for him to make it safely home.

He'd thought about offering to bring her out for the wedding, thought about walking her into the house, hanging on his arm like she belonged. But she'd told Tag she had a ride, and Coop knew better than to say anything. What would Lenore want with an old saddle tramp like him, anyway?

"Damn you, woman," he muttered, wiping the condensation off the windshield. It didn't seem right, after all these years, that she still be so strong in his mind...and his heart.

It definitely wasn't right, what she'd confided in him just last week. She shoulda told Tag, not Coop. For a man who didn't like secrets he sure seemed to be dragging the weight of everybody's problems around with him. Trying to keep the stories straight was wearing him out.

Tag pretendin' to fall in love and marry was a bit farfetched, but it was the only solution Coop had come up with. It woulda worked perfectly with Betsy Mae. Now, well he just wasn't quite so sure anymore.

Coop carefully navigated the narrow strip of highway bordering the river, his thoughts tangled in memories and remorse. He did hate the lying. Lying to the two people he loved the most. Lying to Tag, lying to Lenore...lying to some woman he'd never even met.

Of course, with his brother's help....

No, he didn't even want to think about that. The stunt he and Buck were planning might even be considered illegal, could maybe put him—and Buck—behind bars.

Of course, when Tag found out, he'd probably kill them both anyway. Coop switched his thoughts back to Lenore.

Poor, sweet Lenore. He'd quietly loved her since they were kids. He hadn't spoken up when she married the boss, much as he'd wanted to, even though Ed Martin was a cold and unfriendly son of a buck. Coop couldn't have given Lenore the life she deserved, not then and not now.

Nothing could give her the life she deserved. Not anymore. If only she hadn't made him promise. But he didn't have a choice, not after she'd sat there in her sunny little kitchen, bright-eyed and beautiful as ever, touched his hand with hers, and told him she was dying.

Her only wish, before she went, was to see her grandson married. "Promise me, Coop. Promise you'll help me get that boy wed."

Like the lovesick fool he was, he'd promised.

It hadn't seemed so bad, what with Betsy Mae playing the bride, but suddenly things had gotten terribly confused.

Tag and Betsy Mae's friend were getting married. Coop figured he could do that much for Lenore. Unfortunately, he hadn't gotten around to telling Tag it was going to be a real marriage. Legal, binding and duly recorded. That had been tricky, but it helped having friends in all the right places and a brother who was legally empowered to perform marriages, another fact Coop hadn't gotten around to telling Tag.

He was doing it for Lenore. Hell, he'd do anything for Lenore, but he sure hated lying to the boy.

Especially since now it was some strange woman, not Tag's buddy Betsy Mae Twigg who was going to be repeating those vows.

Another burden.

Maybe Coop'd manage to be well away from the ranch when Tag and this gal found out their marriage wasn't just an act.

On second thought, maybe he just wouldn't tell them. At least not right away.

More lies.

Add 'em to the load.

Rain nearly blinded him, sweeping across the truck in wind driven gusts that buffeted the old pickup and almost drowned out the sound of the engine. Coop drove carefully, swerving around a pile of rocks and mud partially blocking the highway, and hoped the gal's car wasn't somewhere under the pile. Slides were common along this stretch of road. This one just about blocked the entrance to Columbine Camp and it appeared some lines were down. He'd have to call Will.

"Son of a buck," he muttered, braking to avoid a boulder that rolled across the road directly in front of his wheels. He watched as it bounced over the edge, through the leafy treetops, and disappeared into the rushing river below. Grumbling, Coop continued on his search. Somewhere along this road, he was bound to find the bride.

SHE SHOVED her mud-soaked hair out of her eyes, smashed her Stetson down hard on her head, and fought the urge to sit back down on the side of the road and cry. Her boots pinched her toes and the stupid little wheels on her suitcase kept hanging up in the gravel, but all she could think of was getting to the ranch, taking a shower, and crawling into bed.

But which ranch? Both Columbine Camp and the Double Eagle shared a space in her jumbled thoughts, but there was something about the Double Eagle that drew her the most. She knew she had to be close, though she'd have to be right on top of the place to see the entrance through the pouring rain.

Her head pounded and there wasn't a bone or muscle that didn't feel bruised, but for the life of her she couldn't recall exactly how she'd gotten hurt. Or how she'd ended up sitting on the side of the road in a storm, dressed in her rodeo finest with her little carry-on suitcase tucked under her arm and her best cowboy hat crumpled beneath her.

Of course, with all the years of barrel racing under her belt, you'd think she'd be used to hurting by now. Probably just got thrown from her horse...again. But where was that stupid beast, and why was she carrying a suitcase? Especially this absurd little thing with wheels? Her thoughts were so jangled and confused! Damn, she was getting too old for rodeo. Days like this, she didn't care if she never saw a horse again.

"Well girl," she muttered, tugging the suitcase wheels free of a clump of weeds, "you've been dumped on your butt before and still managed to survive."

But she didn't think she'd ever been dumped in a place as miserable and wet as this.

A rumble and clatter echoed against the steep canyon walls, almost drowning out the rush and roar of the river. Startled, she turned and cocked her head, struggling to identify the sound. She squinted against the pouring rain, then stuck her thumb out without hesitation when a battered pickup rattled into view. She hadn't a clue as to who was driving, but she'd crawl into a truck with an ax murderer if it would just get her out of this rain.

The ancient pickup slid to a halt in a spray of mud and water. She tilted her hat back and swept her muddy hair out of her eyes, but before she could ask for a ride, a cowboy as battered and ancient as the truck climbed out and grabbed her by the arm.

"You Betsy Mae's friend? What are you doing out in this storm, girl? Don't you know weather like this can be dangerous?" The old man shouted at her like he was mad about something, but at least he'd stopped the truck and was helping her inside. "You're a mess, and the wedding's in less than two hours!"

Wedding? That explained it. She must be going to a wedding. That accounted for the fancy western duds. She knew that name, Betsy Mae, even if she couldn't for the life of her remember her own. She had vague memories of Betsy Mae Twigg...she must know her from rodeo. That was the only explanation.

A picture flashed into her mind, of a smiling blond standing next to a beautiful black and white horse, and another crisp image of the same woman racing her horse around a barrel in a huge stadium. She could almost hear the roar of the crowd.

Yep. That was it. Finally, a memory! She almost giggled in relief.

This old man acted like he was expecting her, seemed to know who she was. Maybe, if she just played along, he'd tell her. She shoved her wet hair back out of her eyes once again and looked for a seatbelt.

Obviously, the truck pre-dated seatbelt laws. She grabbed the arm rest and hung on as the cowboy shoved the thing into gear, turned the truck around and rumbled on down the road.

"Lenore's due out in a bit, and we sure can't have her seeing you like this." He sat hunched over the steering wheel and rubbed the foggy window with one gnarled hand, but she knew he looked over at her every chance he got.

He didn't seem impressed with what he saw.

She really was a mess. Her jeans were plastered to her legs and steam rose off the stiff denim. She reached up to smooth her hair, and realized it hung in wet, ratted tangles past her shoulders. Thank goodness there wasn't a mirror on the passenger side...she'd just as soon not know how bad she looked.

"I sure hope Betsy Mae didn't put one over on us," the old guy muttered.

"I know Betsy Mae," she said, fishing.

"Well, o'course you do, gal. She's the reason you're here. If it weren't for Betsy Mae, you and Tag sure wouldn't be gettin' married, and that's a fact."

"Tag? You can't mean Taggart Martin?" She swallowed. I'm marrying Taggart Martin? That sexy, dark-haired hunk? She'd certainly remember if she were planning to marry him! The man was incredible. A brilliant image swam into view, photographic in its clarity, the tall, darkly rugged cowboy with that rakish smile and the midnight blue eyes. "The same Taggart Martin who owns the Double Eagle?"

She'd better do something about that squeak in her voice!

The old cowboy slanted her a suspicious glance. "Didn't Betsy Mae tell you nuttin? She told Will you were lookin' forward to this, that you liked the way Tag looked."

"I do, I mean, he looks wonderful, it's just..."

"There ain't nobody else other'n Tag fit ta own the Double Eagle. Why, he's been runnin' that ranch since he was just a boy."

"Oh." What more was there to say? Eventually, some of this had to make sense. Hopefully before she got to the wedding vows.

She took a deep swallow and grabbed the dash as they bounced through another puddle. "Then I guess you'd better get me to the Double Eagle," she said. An old tune floated through her benumbed brain. Get me to the church, get me to the church, get me to the church on time.

She hummed quietly, losing herself in the familiar melody.

The old cowboy grunted and turned his attention back to his driving. They passed through a huge gate carved with a soaring pair of eagles across the top and festooned with white ribbons and balloons hanging sodden and limp in the storm. Almost a mile farther up the road the old man pulled into an oddly familiar yard which bustled with activity in spite of the rain. Half a dozen mongrel dogs barked and yapped, circling the truck with tails wagging and teeth showing.

She hadn't been here before, she was sure of it, but somehow it all looked so....

"There you are!" Tag Martin stepped down off the porch, shielding his face from the driving rain and almost tripping over one muddy black and white dog. "Ramón," he shouted, "lock these mutts up!" A stocky young cowboy rushed to obey.

Lee knew it was Tag, recognized the thick black hair and the midnight eyes, but she'd never seen him like this, disheveled, impatient...curious?

If only she could remember.

"They've got the front room all decorated and the cake's been delivered. Gramma Lenore's due here any minute. Good lord, is this her?" He stared at her, an almost angry glint in his dark eyes. "What happened to you?"

Without giving her a chance to answer or gather her thoughts, Tag grabbed her by the arm and hustled her across the huge covered porch, through a dark entryway and into a cheerful kitchen warmed by a woodstove in one corner.

All around her women bustled and laughed, carrying flowers through the kitchen doors, stacking glasses and plates on a long table that stretched the length of the kitchen. A few of them eyed her curiously, one or two even smiled.

Before she had a chance to take it all in, Tag shoved a thick towel in her hands and stuck her on a small bench by the stove. He scowled darkly in her direction. "I sure hope Betsy Mae knows what she's up to," he said, spinning around and glaring at the old cowboy.

The old man backed off a bit, then the two of them moved across the kitchen. She sighed, stared at the towel in her hands and wished something made sense. Obviously they'd been expecting her, and obviously she wasn't quite what they expected. She took off her hat, shoved her hair back again, and began wiping the grit off her boots and suitcase.

If only she could figure out what was going on. For a man planning to be married in less than two hours, he sure didn't act like he was in love. She studied him out of the corner of her eye, and felt the old familiar tug beneath her heart.

Had she dreamed of him? She recognized Tag, but he seemed unsure of her. Why couldn't she remember? Had she possibly forgotten knowing him, the way she seemed to have forgotten so many other things? If what the old man said was true, she was going to be Tag's wife before the day was out.

No! I can't marry him. I don't know what I'm doing here!

She bit back a sob. Crying wouldn't solve a thing, dammit. Instead, she blinked the tears away and scrubbed furiously at her muddy boots.

"I don't know, Tag." Coop kept his voice low so the woman sitting across the kitchen wouldn't hear. "She acted a little surprised when I mentioned the wedding. Will told me his sister had taken care of everything, but I'm beginning to wonder if Betsy Mae filled this little gal in on the details."

"I sure hope so. It's too late to change plans now. She's not much to look at." Tag rubbed his freshly shaved chin as he studied their bedraggled guest. "I thought Betsy Mae told Will she was a tall redhead."

"Maybe when she washes up?" Coop didn't sound convinced.

"Washing up sure isn't going to make her any taller." Tag bit his lips then blew out a puff of air. "Um, Miss," he said. "Coop here'll show you to the room we've got ready for you. I mean, I hate to rush you, but people should start arriving within the next hour or so. You don't want them to see the bride any way but at her best, do you?"

She stared up at him, her eyes deep green and as fathomless as a mountain pool. Tag felt a sudden clenching in his gut, and blinked, drawing himself out of those mysterious eyes and back to reality. *No, no, no, no, no! Not that. Definitely not that!*

He took a deep breath and smiled.

She smiled back, masking her confusion and the beginnings of a throbbing headache as best she could. "A shower sounds great," she said, pulling herself very carefully to her feet. She grabbed her suitcase and her badly smashed Stetson, and obediently followed the old man down the long hallway.

The room was lovely, decorated in pale shades of yellow like something out of another era. Coop pointed out the adjoining bathroom, then turned and paused a moment. He cleared his throat, then looked away. She waited, impatient for her shower, anxious for a quiet moment to try and gather her disordered thoughts.

Finally, he tipped his hat and mumbled. "If Lenore wasn't dyin'..."

"Excuse me?" Her head pounded so that nothing made sense.

"Nothin'. Nothin' at all." He stared at her a moment. "We'll be in the kitchen if you need anything," he muttered, then quietly turned and shut the door.

Lenore who? Dying? Later. She'd make sense of all this later. She used the facilities, then looked longingly at the big old claw-footed tub. Every bone and joint in her body ached, and a bath sounded so much better than a shower.

She was definitely getting too old for barrel racing. The thought of soaking away the pain along with the mud and grit tugged at her like a magnet. She turned on the water, then decided to at least wash her face while the tub filled.

She turned on the taps in the small sink and rinsed her hands, then splashed some of the warm water on her face. She grabbed a dark blue towel hanging from a rack under a mirror next to the sink, scrubbed her face dry, then looked up...directly into the startled green eyes of a stranger.

Oh my, she thought, grabbing the edge of the sink for balance while fighting a bubble of hysterical laughter. *This is much worse than I imagined.*

COOP RUBBED his bony old hands together, leaned against the door jamb to the ranch office, and grinned gleefully at Tag. "Relax. Besides, it's too late for second thoughts. Trust me. It's gonna work."

"The last time I trusted you, I folded with a full house and lost to your pair of fours." Tag slipped his feet off his desk and leaned forward. He buried his face against his folded arms, like a kindergartner at rest time.

"That was cards...this is the Double Eagle."

"I don't know, Coop." Tag lifted his head and scowled up at his foreman from under the brim of his hat. "With Betsy Mae we might've pulled this off. I even thought it might work when you told me she'd sent a friend in her place. I did, that is, until you dragged her in. Coop, not only is she a mess, this gal's a space cadet. I don't see her putting anything over on Gramma Lenore. We can't do this. It'll never work."

Coop blanched. "I don't want ta go live in a mobile home park full of blue haired old biddies, Tag. You can't do that to me. Besides, she hired on for the job. Poor kid. She must need the money real bad to agree to something like this."

"Yeah, you're probably right." Tag studied his old friend's weather-beaten face, the bushy eyebrows, the battered hat. Hell, Coop was as battered as the hat. Leaving this ranch, his home for over sixty years, would kill him. But putting one over on Gramma Lenore...damn.

She might be old, but she wasn't stupid.

Coop obviously saw Tag's determination wavering. "All we've done is hired you a cute little gal to play your wife," he said, slapping his palm down on the desk. "A little lie in the bigger scheme o' things. Ya gotta look at the big picture, Tag. This ranch...this ranch..." He bowed his head, as if he'd suddenly run out of steam.

"Tag." Coop's voice took on a hollow, lifeless sound. "Tellin' a little white lie to Lenore ain't gonna kill her. In fact, it'll ease her mind, knowin' you're finally hitched. Hell, more'n fifty percent of marriages fail nowadays, so when you two separate and that little gal goes her merry way, it won't be a surprise to Lenore. We both know there's not a decent woman around who'd put up with you for real anyway."

The old man studied Tag as if weighing his determination, then straightened his shoulders and raised his bristly chin. "You're goin' through with it. Everything's ready. The cake's been delivered, the keg's on ice, and the folks'll be arriving any time now. Besides, this is the Double Eagle we're talking about, boy. This is our life." He stared, long and hard at Tag. "Now, I'm gonna go get myself cleaned up. I suggest you do the same." He turned around and quietly left the room.

Coop shut the door. Tag felt like a six second rider on an eight second bull. His shoulders sagged with the weight of what he was about to do. Coop was right about a lot of things, but most particularly on one point. No decent woman would put up with him, not that he wanted one. Even so, he'd never felt like such a failure in all his thirty-nine years.

THE WATER was cooling. She couldn't hide out in the bathroom forever, so she climbed out of the big old tub and dried herself. The double bed beckoned, so wonderfully warm looking, cozy and comforting. She visualized peeling back the crisp sheets, climbing under the blankets, falling asleep.

Then waking up in a place she remembered.

To a face in the mirror she recognized.

With trembling fingers, she carefully traced the welt on her forehead. There was only one way to explain all this. Somehow she'd been injured. The disorientation she felt must be amnesia.

She'd practically screamed when she saw her reflection. She hadn't recognized a thing about the woman in the mirror, not the dark green eyes, the high cheekbones, not even the wide, full-lipped mouth with the tiny birthmark at one corner.

She'd studied that face, trying to remember, trying to feel something besides a great emptiness.

She didn't recognize the old man, either, though the younger one looked tantalizingly familiar. Her heart literally skipped a beat when he touched her, so obviously her body remembered what her mind had forgotten.

But she had absolutely no idea who Lenore might be, dying or not, and though she remembered Betsy Mae's name and a lot about the rodeo circuit, the information felt vague, unfocused.

It wasn't until she saw her reflection that she'd actually thought about her name. She didn't have a clue who she was.

None of this made sense.

Naked and beginning to chill, she ripped open her battered suitcase and rummaged through the meager bits and pieces of her life. Nothing but brand new jeans and some really fancy western shirts still wrapped in a bag with the tags attached, a few pairs of lacy panties, a brassiere and a nightgown. There was a make-up kit, a toothbrush and a comb and brush set.

But no identification.

She found a receipt for the clothing in the bag, but the signature wasn't legible and the credit card numbers were disguised with little asterisks. There was a leather strip on the handle of the suitcase where a name tag might have been attached.

It wasn't, anymore.

So much for detective work.

It shouldn't be so difficult to remember the basics, like why she felt she knew Tag, why the Double Eagle seemed so familiar, where she was from, if she had any family...her name. She frowned, struggling for the memories.

A sharp pain lanced between her eyes as her headache returned with a vengeance. She sat heavily on the edge of the bed. Maybe it was going to be that difficult.

Practically crying with frustration, she did the only logical thing she could think of, under the circumstances. According to the old man, she had over an hour before the wedding. Sighing with exhaustion, she pulled the tiny wisp of a nightgown out of the suitcase, slipped it over her head, and crawled into bed.

Maybe, just maybe, she'd wake up and realize this had all been a dream. Or even better, she'd know who she was and what was going on, and why she and Taggart Martin, a man she could have only known in her dreams, were getting married today.

Married! She couldn't possibly go through with this until she knew what was happening.

She gathered what memories she could. She was certain she'd been headed to the Double Eagle, but for the life of her she couldn't recall anything about a wedding. Everyone appeared to expect her, even though none of them actually seemed to know her.

She knew she'd agreed to something, but not what, though she thought it involved money. Marriage? For money? To a complete stranger? Her head started to ache again and she snuggled down into the soft pillow. There was something familiar about the man, familiar enough that she recognized not only his name, but his face as well.

And what a face! Not to mention the body it was attached to...she drifted, floating in that enchanted space between awareness and sleep. She imagined him holding her in his arms, felt the gentle touch of his lips on hers...then slipped peacefully into her dreams.

Chapter 2

COOP ROCKED back on the heels of his very best Sunday cowboy boots and tucked his hands in the back pockets of his shiny black western cut suit pants. He grinned encouragingly at Tag, who hesitated uncertainly just outside the woman's bedroom door. "Well, aren't you purty? Ain't seen you in a suit since Big Ed's funeral. You ready to fetch the little woman? She's probably all dressed up by now, waiting for you to make her your bride." He chuckled. Tag frowned at him. Coop was having way too much fun at his expense.

"Cut it out, old man, if you know what's good for you." He practically snarled at Coop.

"There's nothing wrong with a marriage of convenience," Coop said defensively. "Happens all the time."

Tag snorted in disgust. "Oh yeah, every day," he said, running his finger under the tight collar of his best shirt. Lord but he hated to dress up! He hated weddings even more, this one in particular. Even if it was all for show.

"Which reminds me," he said, glaring at Coop. "Where do you get these damned ideas of yours?"

"I read a lot," Coop said. "Now quit stallin'. Go in there and tell your young lady it's time for the show. Be nice, even if she doesn't look like the gal of your dreams. You don't want to confuse that poor little thing. Might make her up and quit. Like I said before, I doubt there's too many women ready to marry Tag Martin, even if it is pretend. 'Sides, she's had a bath. She might just clean up real good. You can't never tell." Coop cast a sideways glance in Tag's direction. "Sumpin' just might work out for real, if you play your cards right...you know, a little conversation, a little..."

"It's those damned romance novels you've been reading, isn't it?" Tag interrupted. At Coop's embarrassed snort, Tag poked him in the chest. "You think I don't know you've got 'em stashed out there in the barn? Filling your head up with all these stupid ideas. You oughta be ashamed."

"I...I save 'em for Lenore," Coop sputtered, straightening his spine and yanking his hands out of his pockets. "They're not mine, they're hers. Never read the things myself."

"Right." Tag ran his fingers through his hair and glanced at the closed door. She'd been in there a long time, and already the few guests they'd invited were beginning to arrive. He wanted to go over the details, make sure she knew what was expected of her.

It was now or never. Tag had a sudden insight into how a mountain lion might feel, trapped, its back against the wall. He felt that way, as if the dogs were closing in and he had nowhere to run. Fight or flight, only flight wasn't an option.

"It's for the best, son." Coop rested his gnarled fingers on Tag's arm and squeezed affectionately. Tag took a deep breath and looked down at the hand that had helped him up so many times over the years. He had to put this plan in to action. He couldn't, wouldn't fail Coop.

An iron band suddenly clamped over Tag's lungs, squeezed his heart. His mouth went dry as dust.

"Coop, I can't go through with this." He stared at the door to his parents' old bedroom and brushed his sweaty palms along his thighs. Even the thought of a fake marriage was giving him the cold sweats. What if this were for real?

Coop glared at him, his bushy brows almost knit together beneath the wide brim of his hat. The affectionate squeeze on Tag's arm suddenly turned into an iron grip of resolve. "Ya got no choice, as I see it. You turn forty in less than a month. You go through with a phony marriage, convince Lenore it's the real thing, and the ranch is yours. Then the two of you separate, you pay off the young lady, and everything'll be fine. Lenore'll be happy and you'll have your ranch." Coop released Tag's arm, took a ragged breath, and stared off down the dark hallway. "You only need to stay together for a few weeks, a couple of months at the most. Then your grandmother'll be...satisfied."

The sadness that flashed across the old man's face startled Tag. He thought of something Coop had said earlier.

This ranch is your life, boy. You lose it, what've you got? Nothing. Nothing at all.

Coop was right. What did he have? Tag stared past the man who'd been more a father to him than anyone else, living or dead. He pictured the miles of taut wire fencing, the barn he'd just re-roofed, the cattle grazing on over a thousand acres of good pasture, and tried to imagine life without the Double Eagle.

There'd been a big article about Tag and some of the other ranchers in the valley in the latest issue of Western Horseman. The writer's flowery prose suddenly filled Tag's mind:

Taggart Martin, one of a dying breed in the great American West. His love for his land is elemental, a piece of the fabric that makes him as much a part of the Double Eagle as the Double Eagle is of him. An honorable but lonely man, battling the elements, the government, and the threat of encroaching civilization.

Tag almost snorted. The guy left out battling Gramma Lenore. She was a bigger threat than everything else combined. Scratch honorable, too, he thought. Considering the current scheme in progress, that description was questionable. The writer had gotten one thing right, though. The part about being lonely. Briefly, Tag wondered what it would be like to share all this with a real wife, a partner in every way, not some stranger who needed a change in her life and a few extra dollars cash money.

Never. He'd never risk having a life like his father's, tied in marriage to a woman who didn't love him or the son she bore, drinking away the best years of his life until he finally had one drink too many before climbing behind the wheel of his truck.

Tag always wondered why he'd been spared, when both of his parents had died. Even more confusing, he couldn't figure out why the grandmother who'd loved him and raised him would want to force him into a loveless marriage.

An overwhelming sense of exhaustion swept over him. Tag closed his eyes, sighed once again, reconsidered his choices, then feeling more tired than he could ever remember, knocked quietly on the bedroom door.

There was no answer.

He glanced at Coop. The old cowboy shrugged.

Tag knocked a bit louder, waited a moment, then slowly opened the door, just far enough to peek inside.

He had to remind himself to take another breath.

Coop was right. She did clean up real good.

The woman slept soundly, lying on her side, the covers tucked up under her chin. A tiny frown marred her smooth skin and her full lips were parted, as if she'd drifted asleep on a sigh. Her hair, still damp from her bath, clung in dark auburn waves to the column of her throat and fanned out beside her on the pillow. Her eyebrows were the same dark color, arched and prominent as a robin's wing, and her thick lashes shadowed dark half moons across her cheeks.

There were a few scratches and bruises, most notably an egg-sized welt across her forehead, partially hidden by her hair.

She hadn't said anything about an accident. She'd been so muddy when she arrived, Tag hadn't even noticed her injuries. He frowned, suddenly aware she hadn't explained why she'd been walking instead of driving to the Double Eagle in a rainstorm.

Well, he'd find out soon enough. Tag swallowed deeply, loathe to disturb her rest but aware of the clock ticking, his future waiting.

He cleared his throat, then stepped into the room with Coop following silently behind. She came awake slowly, stretching both arms above her head. The blankets slipped away from her chin, revealing the full creamy swell of her breasts, the darker nipples achingly visible beneath the silky blue wisp of nightgown she wore.

It took every bit of strength he possessed to focus on her troubled green eyes. "Uh, Miss..."

His tongue felt tied in knots, so much so that he could barely say the words out loud.

In barely an hour, this woman was going to be his wife.

Kind of.

WHAT A STRANGE dream. Tall skyscrapers, blaring taxis, a river of chocolate milk rushing and tumbling by just in front of her face, and a crowd of cheering onlookers, screaming out seconds on a clock.

None of it made sense, including the man walking quietly across her room. He hesitated a moment beside her bed, then eased himself down to sit carefully beside her on the patchwork spread. He'd barely spoken to her when she'd arrived, wet and muddy, in his kitchen. He didn't look threatening now, if you discounted the serious gleam in his eyes and the hard line of his jaw. She scooted away from him anyway, pressed her back up against the headboard, tugged the blankets across her chest and locked them securely beneath her armpits.

It never hurt for a girl to be careful.

He took one of her small hands in both of his, and smiled. His fingers completely encircled her hands within his grasp. She felt rough calluses, the strength of a working man's hands. She glanced down, surprised his fingernails were trimmed and clean.

She looked up and smiled back.

Why couldn't she remember?

He looked so familiar. She must know him.

He reached out and touched a tender spot on her forehead, his fingertips as gentle as if she'd been a newborn. "I wonder how this happened?" he muttered, more to himself than to her. "Did you have an accident? Is that why you were wandering down the road in the rain?"

"I'm not sure...I think I must have fallen off my horse," she said. Barrel racers did that all the time, she knew that, somehow. She didn't remember a car, or an accident. "I don't know exactly when it happened, but I'm okay." At least she hoped she was okay. Her head only hurt when she tried to remember.

"That happens. I've got a neighbor...that's stupid," he said. "Of course you know Betsy Mae." He paused, then grinned, a brief smile that curled one side of his mouth and popped a dimple out in the opposing cheek. She caught herself studying that dimple, staring at his mobile lips, the tiny scar on his chin.

This man was absolutely gorgeous and disturbingly familiar.

She knew him from somewhere, but how? He must know her, or why would they be getting married? Maybe they'd been lovers?

"We haven't really introduced ourselves," he said, blowing that wishful theory. "I'm Taggart Martin, Tag for short. This is Coop, my foreman. You have no idea how glad we are that you've agreed to this." He flashed an indecipherable look at the old cowboy, then turned back to her, still smiling. "But Betsy Mae never mentioned your name. You're...?"

She stared at him a moment and struggled to gather her thoughts. She had to quit thinking about that dimple. It wasn't there now, anyway, darn it. She couldn't remember ever feeling so confused, couldn't remember...anything. It didn't help that he still held on to her hands, rubbing one callused thumb back and forth along her wrist.

His touch had a mesmerizing effect on her, as if she needed anything else adding to her confusion.

Nor did it help that he was the proverbial "tall, dark and handsome." His dark brown western cut suit emphasized his lean, muscular build, and the white shirt with pearl snaps and a bolo tie only added to his rugged masculinity. A dark blue turquoise slide held the cords of his tie closed at his throat, and his thick, dark hair curled just over his collar, giving him a rakish, devil-may-care look. He had the darkest blue eyes she'd ever seen, midnight blue eyes surrounded by thick, silky lashes. Why, he reminded her of the cover model on a romance she'd read.

What was the name of that book?

More important, what was her own name? She had to tell him something, anything. Obviously Betsy Mae had sent her here, and she trusted Betsy Mae, didn't she? Again the image of the smiling blonde, self-assured and strangely familiar, filled her thoughts. Her gaze swept the room, lighting for a moment on the stack of clothes she'd left on top of the dresser. She tilted her head and looked at him out of narrowed eyes.

"I'm Lee," she said. "Lee, you know, like the blue jeans." It did sound familiar...kind of.

"Lee...?" He squeezed her hands and smiled at her. Encouraging her. She knew a moment of panic, until the old cowboy in the doorway tugged his hat off his head and brushed a bit of dust from the crown.

Suddenly, in a burst of what felt like a real memory, she knew. "Stetson. Lee Stetson," she said, mentally crossing her fingers.

"Lee Stetson?" The corner of his mouth quirked up in that perfect grin again. "Good name for a barrel racer, I guess."

So she did race barrels! She'd only said she'd fallen off her horse, not that she raced. He must know something about her. Lee practically sighed in relief...at last, a clue she could use. That much of what she'd remembered must be right.

"I always thought it was a stupid name," she said, tugging her hands out of his light grasp. But it was her name, wasn't it? It sounded right, but it was so hard to think when he touched her. Her fingers felt suddenly lonely, clasped together in her lap. She swallowed back the uneasy sensations bombarding her.

"Your parents must have liked it." He grinned down at her. "I think it's just fine, a fine name."

"My parents must have had noodles for brains," she answered. "Fine for what?"

He grinned even wider. "To tell you the truth, I was so mad at Betsy Mae when I found out she ran off and married that clown after promising to marry me, I thought I'd blow a gasket. But then when she said you'd agreed to take her place, well, Lee, I want you to know how much I appreciate what you're doing."

"Thanks, I guess," Lee said, scrambling mentally for her bearings. What a flake! Her opinion of Tag Martin took a deep dive. His fiancée marries another man, and he just casually switches to another woman? Someone he's never met?

Wow!

"But we have to hurry. People are already arriving, and you're not even dressed."

"Dressed?" He honestly expected her to go through with this?

Betsy Mae must have some terrific powers of persuasion if she'd talked Lee into marrying this jerk.

"The preacher will be here," he glanced down at the serviceable watch on a thick leather band around his wrist, "in about half an hour. Think you can be dressed and ready to play the part of the blushing bride by then?"

"Uh, I, um..."

"Good girl," he said, patting her hand. "Yep, I think it's gonna work. We'll do just fine together."

She glanced wildly about the room, at the old cowboy standing by the door, then back to the dark blue eyes gazing directly into her own. Oh yeah, just fine, she thought. Absolutely, one hundred percent fine._

She really should get a prize for keeping her smile intact. Maybe Betsy Mae was blackmailing her? Maybe Lee'd done something so appalling, she'd do anything not to be caught, up to and including marriage to this guy.

But when Lee tried to remember there was nothing but a huge void where her past should be, and the threat of another headache. "Why don't you fill me in again on the details," she said, mentally crossing her fingers.

"It won't be that difficult." Tag looked back at Coop, as if searching for instructions, but the old cowboy just shrugged his shoulders. "You just have to, uh, do bride stuff. You know, repeat after the minister, look, well, like you're head over heels in love with me. You know, act like a bride." He cleared his throat. "I'd like to keep it simple. Nothing personal, you understand, but I'm really only doing this for my grandmother."

"HIS GRAMMA'S been threatening to..."

"Find me a wife if I don't find one myself before I turn forty," Tag said, interrupting Coop. "It was all Coop's idea. I thought at first it was pretty dumb, but once Betsy Mae agreed, we figured, well, hey, it'll work."

"It's called a marriage of convenience," the old cowboy said. "I've read about 'em before."

Lee wondered what kind of reading material Coop preferred.

Tag picked up the conversation as if he hadn't been interrupted. "Then Betsy Mae flaked out on us. I sure appreciate you taking her place. My grandmother's wanted me hitched for years. Lately she's really stepped up the pressure. Betsy Mae said it sounded like fun, until she fell in love with that clown." He snorted. "Her timing couldn't have been worse, but I think my grandmother will like you a lot, Lee. That's really what's important, isn't it? That's the reason you're here."

He smiled that perfect, lopsided smile at Lee. "Just to make an old woman happy."

"I see," Lee said, though she wasn't sure she saw anything at all. So he hadn't been in love with Betsy Mae after all. Obviously he didn't care who he married, as long as dear Grandma approved. Could he be gay?

Impossible. She'd know that, wouldn't she? "And this wedding is...?"

"Just like I told you." He looked at his watch again. "In the front room, in less than an hour. We've got the preacher and the marriage license and everything." Tag smiled like a man with a winning plan.

"But I don't have anything to wear," she said, perfectly aware there were a lot of other, more important things she should be wondering about.

Like how Betsy Mae had talked her into something as stupid as a marriage of convenience.

Like who she really was and what she was doing here.

Like where the bride and groom were going to sleep.

Tag looked at Coop. Coop shrugged his shoulders. Tag glanced around the room, finally settling on the closet door. "I figured Betsy Mae would have taken care of that. Guess she didn't. My mother was about your size. Maybe something of hers?"

"Okay, I guess." No, it's not okay! But he talked like she'd already agreed to this, so her so-called friend Betsy Mae had to have talked her into it. Why can't I remember?

"Does your grandmother know Betsy Mae arranged this, um, marriage?"

"No," Tag muttered. "That's something we'd rather she didn't find out. The story's gonna be that we met at the rodeo down in Durango, fell in love, and decided to tie the knot. Think you can carry it off?"

"You want her to believe we're in love? We don't even know each other!" *For crying out loud, I don't even know myself!* She sensed another headache beginning, and lowered her voice. "She's going to realize we're pretending, don't you think?"

Tag's grin slipped, and the look he flashed at the old man could only be described as one of pure panic. "You're right, I guess. Like I said, we're, uh, still working out the details." He took a deep breath, then once more grasped her hands between his. "Maybe we can, umm, work on, our, umm, rela...well, get to know each other. Just to make it look realistic," he added in a rush of words.

"I gotta go check the preparations, Tag." Coop suddenly came to life and skittered for the door. "I'll take care of everything for you. You just get to know the little lady." He checked his watch. "But make it quick, okay?"

The door bounced shut behind the old cowboy, leaving absolute silence in its wake. And Lee, alone in a strange bedroom with a devastatingly handsome man she didn't know a thing about except that in less than an hour he was going to be her husband.

But first, he wanted to work on a relationship.

Not a real relationship, of course. He didn't love her, but he wanted a bride to make his grandmother happy? This would be weird even if she did recall what she'd agreed to do!

She fought the urge to tug her hands out of Tag's, and instead looked down at their linked fingers. She quietly contemplated her fingernails. They were perfectly manicured, the polish only slightly marred, each nail a flawless oval. They certainly didn't look like the nails of a horsewoman.

Her hands were so smooth. Tag's hands were rough and work-worn, with deep ridges where the leather reins must pass between his thumb and forefinger. She thought about his hands, their strength and size, and how gentle they felt.

Gentle, strong and warm. A woman would feel sheltered by those hands. Sheltered and protected from just about anything.

She looked up into those midnight blue eyes staring back at her and wondered if he had any idea how confused she felt at this moment. There was no reason to believe she wasn't exactly what he'd said, an ex barrel racer now a bride of convenience he'd lined up with the help of his ex-fiancée Betsy Mae.

But none of it felt right.

Why was her head so full of rodeo, images of such static clarity they might have been photographs? Why did this man beside her look familiar, when she shouldn't even know him?

Why can't I remember?

A teasing image flashed across her mind, tall buildings and crowded sidewalks and a taxi blaring, then just as quickly the image faded.

Leaving another tremendous headache in its wake.

"Are you all right?" He reached out and lifted her chin with one finger. His eyes darkened with concern.

"Just a headache," she replied honestly. "I'll be fine."

"Good." He squeezed her fingers, took another deep breath, and she heard him swallow. "Then kiss me."

"What?" She yanked her hands out of his and scooted away.

"Kiss me. Or I can kiss you. Whichever." The expression on his face was one of grim determination. In fact, she thought he looked like a man facing an IRS audit.

"I don't think so." She glared at him out of narrowed eyes. She really wasn't ready for this. Not yet, anyway. Obviously, neither was he.

"You'll have to kiss me at the wedding," Tag said. "I think we need to practice or we'll look like a couple of fools. My grandmother will never believe we're in love, much less married." He reached up and twisted one long strand of her hair around his fingers. For a moment the look that crossed his face was one of loss and longing.

"That's all, Lee. Just a few kisses to convince my grandmother. You don't have to lie about who you are or what you did for a living, where you come from, anything other than how we met." His gentle words took on a forceful note. "I know you've decided to get out of rodeo. Betsy Mae told Will you really need the money. The simpler we keep this, the better. But you'll have to kiss me occasionally or my grandmother'll guess in a heartbeat."

So many questions, and absolutely no answers. Why did her body respond to his touch, when her mind screamed *beware?*

Everything depended on her success at the Double Eagle. Why did she know that? How would Betsy Mae know she needed money? Lee tilted her head and studied his wary expression. He certainly didn't look like he wanted to kiss her all that much. "So you think we need to practice?" she said, watching his expression and stalling for time. When he nodded his head, she looked down and smoothed the covers across her lap.

"Just a little," he said, dropping the strand of hair to lightly stroke her shoulder. "Just enough to be convincing."

"Oh." She shivered under the light caress, suddenly so aware of him, of his size, his presence, his almost careless sensuality. She had a feeling it wasn't going to be difficult at all to make this convincing.

The hard part would be remembering, not her past, but the reality of the present. This meant nothing to him.

Playacting, to put one over on a little old lady. She'd have to give that some thought as well. Lying didn't set well with her at all. She might not be positive if Lee Stetson were really her name, but she knew she was an honest woman.

She knew she'd been lonely. With that knowledge, came awareness, and an almost shameful sense of vulnerability. How easy it could be to forget this was basically theater to him.

It was up to her to prevent it from becoming a tragedy.

He studied her intently a moment longer, until Lee felt almost preternaturally aware of herself, of the rate of her heartbeat, the sudden dryness to her lips, the essence of the man leaning almost imperceptibly closer.

Suddenly their mouths were touching. Startled by the contact, she jerked away, but his broad hand gently cupped her skull, lightly restrained her, calmed her nervous reaction. He smiled against her mouth, and his lips explored with infinite slowness, his taste every bit as warm and wonderful as she'd imagined a lover's could be. "See," he groaned. "That's not so bad, is it?" He leaned closer and swept his hand through her hair, tangling his fingers in the thick strands.

She tilted her head to fit more perfectly to him. Her lips parted as naturally as if they'd been lovers for ever. Tag cupped her head in both his hands, steadying her as his tongue swept the inner recesses of her mouth. She drew him in, suckling, tasting, needing. Her arms encircled his waist, drawing him down, drawing him closer until he sprawled across her body, weighting her with the hard length and breadth of him.

She whimpered, a soft catch in the back of her throat and her hands slipped beneath his jacket and tugged at his shirt, pulling the crisp fabric free of his dress slacks. Tag's hand swept along her side, then back across the silky gown to cup her full breast in his palm. The tiny nub come to life beneath his touch. Lee whimpered again, and arched her hips against him.

The instinctive return of pressure, the groan she heard from deep within his throat, the hard ridge of his arousal pressed against that sensitive spot between her thighs, jolted Lee's senses as nothing else could.

Her hands, once grasping his hips to pull him closer, now clutched at the leather belt he wore and shoved.

He didn't budge at first, but the sudden restraint in his embrace told her he got the message.

He ended the kiss abruptly, rolled away, and draped his forearm across his eyes. She scooted back up to a sitting position, tugging the blankets with her. His breathing was as ragged as her own, his chest rising and falling with each gasp.

"Okay," he said, a long moment later. "I think that's convincing." He rolled his head to one side and stared up at her, his eyes even darker than before. "Are you okay? I'm sorry. I didn't plan to let that...I mean...." He closed his eyes, took a deep breath, and propped himself up on one elbow. "It wasn't supposed to happen quite like that, Lee. I shouldn't have let things get so out of hand. It won't happen again. I promise."

He brushed his hand over his eyes. "You'll still go through with this...you'll still marry me, won't you?"

*Ohmygod, ohmygod, ohmygod....*She'd imagined kisses like that, but Lee knew she'd never, not ever in her life, experienced anything remotely like this cowboy's kiss. She couldn't possibly let him know how he'd affected her.

"Of course," she lied. "I'm fine." But would she ever be fine again? The man was willing to marry a stranger because he obviously didn't want the commitment of a true marital relationship. The last thing she needed to do was let him think she was attracted to him. He'd have her out of here in a heartbeat, with absolutely no money to her name, no past, and no one to count on.

It wasn't going to be easy. She couldn't believe her body's response! Her lips still tingled, her heart still thudded unevenly in her chest.

Just how real was this marriage to Tag Martin supposed to be? He didn't actually expect to...No! He'd just promised not to kiss her like that again. Darn it! If he expected a more intimate relationship after they married, wouldn't he have mentioned it?

Tag stood up with his back to Lee and quickly tucked his shirt back into his pants and straightened his coat. He finger combed his hair, then turned around with that devilish lop-sided grin back on his face.

"You'd best look for something in that closet." He dimpled up again, as calm and relaxed as if he hadn't just kissed her into oblivion. "I'm sure there's something that'll work."

Suddenly, a cacophonous blast from a loud horn disturbed the quiet moment. Tag raced to the window with Lee right beside him. A bright red, 1959 Cadillac coupe slid into the yard in a spray of gravel and mud, then spun to a stop in front of the porch. It was truly a sight to behold. What wasn't painted fire engine red was covered with chrome, and its fins were so broad the thing looked as if it could take off.

"My Lord, she drove the beast out by herself," Tag muttered. "I thought Gramma Lenore said she was too old to drive that thing." He whirled around and pinned Lee with what he hoped was a convincing stare. "You stay here and get ready for the wedding. I'll send Coop in to fetch you when it's time."

"But..."

"No buts." He grabbed her by the shoulders and tried not to look too closely at the delicate gown she wore or the faint outline of some of the fascinatingly feminine body parts it barely disguised. It wasn't easy, not when the fabric hinted at more than it covered.

He suddenly realized he was no longer grabbing her shoulders, but instead was gently massaging her tense muscles and thinking about kissing her once more before the wedding.

Just to make sure they had it right.

She wasn't looking at him with frightened eyes, with eyes that questioned. No, that was definitely a look of anticipation. He'd bet the ranch on it.

The loud knock on the door reminded him he *had* bet the ranch.

With a muttered curse Tag let go of Lee's shoulders, took a deep breath, turned, took another deep breath, and yanked open the door. A slender, elderly woman about Lee's height with short cropped white hair and dangly turquoise and silver earrings poked her nose through the opening. She smiled broadly, stepped into the room, and stood up on her tip toes to give him a resounding kiss on the cheek.

Then she pushed him aside.

Tag's chin sagged to his chest. The game was over before he'd even gotten it started. He took another deep breath, then turned around to introduce his grandmother to Lee.

"Well, where are you keeping her? Coop said you were in here with your bride. Where is she?"

"She's..." Where was she? "Lee?"

"I'll be out in a minute, sweetheart. I'm just finishing my make-up."

Damned if she wasn't gonna go through with it! And he hadn't even told her what all to do! This gal was a lot smarter than he'd thought.

"She's just finishing her make-up," he repeated, grinning broadly. "She'll be out in a minute."

It was almost five minutes, actually, but when Lee opened the bathroom door, Tag almost choked. She'd been beautiful before, but now, wrapped in his father's old faded blue terry cloth robe with her hair falling loosely around her shoulders and the slightest hint of make-up adding drama and depth to her emerald eyes, she was gorgeous.

She smiled sweetly at his grandmother, holding out her hand in greeting.

Gramma Lenore bypassed the handshake and grabbed both Lee's hands in hers. She held her back for a good, long look. "Why, you're definitely not Betsy Mae. You're a lot prettier than that little twit. I'm Lenore Martin, Tag's gramma, and I must admit when that boy told me he'd found the girl he was going to marry, I was scared to death he meant that Twigg girl. But just look at you! I'm so glad I got here in time."

She wrapped her arms around Lee, enveloping her in a huge, welcoming hug. Absolutely speechless, Lee hugged her back, but she gazed over Lenore's shoulder at Tag with a look of total confusion. Was this the same woman Coop said was dying?

"Taggart, you led me to believe you were planning to marry Betsy Mae, and I was coming out here to talk you out of it. I don't want grandbabies that badly!"

"Gramma Lenore, you know Betsy Mae and I have been buddies too long to ever think of marriage," Tag said, looking down at Lee. "This is the woman I'm going to marry. This is Lee Stetson. I met her at the rodeo down in Durango. She's a friend of Betsy Mae's. From rodeo'n."

"It's a pleasure to meet you." Lee smiled at his grandmother. Suddenly, inexplicably, Tag felt very proud of the woman standing next to him.

He put his arm around Lee's waist and drew her close against his side. She fit perfectly, just under his arm, gazing up at him with the perfect look of adoration a woman should feel for her man. For the first time in days he began to relax.

He felt her hand slip around his waist, just under his jacket, felt the heat of her fingers tucked against the waistband of his slacks. She gave him a light, familiar squeeze.

He squeezed her back. Maybe this dumb idea of Coop's was going to work after all.

Chapter 3

"NOW TAG, you need to let this little gal get ready. Go, shoo. Your wedding's in less than thirty minutes."

Lee practically giggled, watching Tag's grandmother grab him by the arm and run him out of her room, but suddenly the door was closed and she was alone with Gramma Lenore.

"So, where's your gown? Don't you think you oughta put it on?"

"Well, I..." How did she explain there wasn't a gown? How could she possibly go through with this wedding? But Tag had looked so desperate when his grandmother drove into the yard, Lee hadn't even considered letting him down. "My luggage was stolen," she said, grasping at the first plausible thought that entered her mind. "Tag suggested I look for something of his mother's." She gestured vaguely in the direction of the closet door, then before Lenore could stop her, opened it and grabbed the first thing she found.

"How about this? I think it'll fit." The pale blue suit was thirty years old if it was a day, but the classic style was fashionable enough that it might actually look okay on her. It wasn't the wedding dress she'd always dreamed of, but then this wasn't the wedding she'd wanted, either.

Lee knew she'd dreamed of a church bursting with music and flowers, herself dressed in satin and lace with a flowing train. She'd wanted attendants and flower girls...the magic that little girls imagine when they romantically arrange Barbie and Ken on the living room carpet, then get in trouble for picking Mom's miniature roses for Barbie's bouquet.

Lee smiled, knowing she'd just stumbled over one tiny part of her past. She had been that little girl, and her mother had been quite angry at first, until she'd recognized the seriousness of her daughter's make-believe.

Then she'd joined her daughter in play, the two of them totally involved in the elaborate fantasy. Lee opened her mind to remember more, to picture her mother's face, her name, but her head immediately started to pound. The last thing she needed today, her wedding day, was a headache.

Lenore's disgusted snort snapped her back to reality. "You've got to be kidding," she said. She lifted one pale sleeve of the blue suit and spun around with her hands on her hips.

"You're not going to wear that ugly thing, not on your wedding day! Why that suit's been out of style for thirty years. I didn't like it when Maggie bought it in the first place. Too dowdy." She opened the closet door and shoved hangers aside, burying herself deeper and deeper among the racks of clothes until she finally disappeared at the far end of the huge closet.

"Ah ha! I knew it was in here."

Lee peered into the shadows, then jumped aside so the older woman wouldn't knock her down. Hadn't Coop mumbled something about Lenore dying? If that was true, she was the healthiest dying person Lee'd ever seen. Lenore backed out of the closet, dragging a large quilted garment bag behind her.

"Maggie wouldn't wear this, said it was ugly, but I think it would be perfect on you." Lenore gestured in a "no nonsense" manner for Lee to help her, and the two of them carefully stretched the bag out on top of the bed. Then she turned around, and with her hands firmly planted on her hips, glared at Lee.

"Lee," she said, thrusting her chin out in a belligerent manner, "I made a bad marriage to the wrong man and I've regretted it ever since. My son Jim did the same thing when he married Tag's mother, and his unhappiness is what drove him to drink. Seeing you and Tag together, feeling the love you two share...well, it just does something wonderful to me..." She pressed both hands over her heart. "...right here. This was my wedding gown, Lee. I'd be thrilled to have you wear it."

Lee wondered if she'd been an actress in her previous life. She had to be, or she'd have run screaming from the room. Gramma Lenore felt the love Lee and Tag shared? That was a stretch.

How could she possibly go through with this farce?

It's too late to back out now. But was it, really? All she had to do was walk out there and tell Tag she couldn't do it, couldn't marry a man she didn't know. She'd have to tell him the truth, that she couldn't remember agreeing to any marriage.

Yeah, like he's really gonna believe that. Lee rubbed her temples, hoping to massage away the dull ache building in her skull, and tried to pay attention to Gramma Lenore as the older woman carefully opened the garment bag.

All Lee could think of was Tag. She'd been lying to him since she'd arrived at the Double Eagle, letting him think she knew what was going on. If she tried to back out now, he could probably sue her for something.

Then where would she be? For all Lee knew, she was homeless, with a past that, for all intents and purposes, began on a rain swept road somewhere in Colorado.

A past that possibly included something terrible, if Betsy Mae had been able to talk her into participating in this mess.

Lee pulled the old bathrobe tightly around her and concentrated on Tag's grandmother. The grandmother who, according to Coop, might not have too much longer to live. Not only would Lee be breaking a promise, she'd disappoint Lenore in her final days. Lee felt a quick sting of tears. She hardly knew Tag's grandmother but she seemed like a wonderful, loving person. So full of life...for now. Lee swallowed the lump in her throat.

Gramma Lenore slowly tugged the stubborn zipper down on the garment bag, allowing the mass of ivory satin to escape. She shook out the wrinkles and held the gown up for Lee's perusal.

It took her breath away. The design was right out of her dreams, the fitted bodice with an intricately beaded yoke, the sheer lacy sleeves with pearl buttons at the cuffs, and a billowing satin skirt. Reverently she took the gown from Lenore's shaking fingers, held it a moment in front of herself, then brushed the ivory satin against her cheek. Cool, smelling faintly of lavender, it had been perfectly preserved in its sealed bag. It was the gown of her fantasies, right down to the tiny pearl buttons at the low scooped back and the yards of ivory chiffon gathered into a short train.

It was even prettier than Barbie's gown.

Such were little girls' dreams made of. Lee held the gown against herself and looked at her reflection in the mirror on the closet door. Speechless, she turned to catch Gramma Lenore's reaction. There were tears in the older woman's eyes.

Swallowing nervously, Lee stepped out of the ratty blue robe and slipped the dress over her head. She carefully buttoned the row of pearls at each wrist. Lenore silently helped her with the tiny buttons down the back, then hooked the train at Lee's waist and fluffed it out until it trailed about three feet behind her. There was a pair of ivory satin shoes in the bottom of the garment bag. Lee tried to slip them on, but they were too tight. Regretfully, she set them aside.

She turned, and almost gasped aloud at her reflection. She'd never looked lovelier, she knew that. The gown was a bit snug, but it accentuated her narrow waist and full hips, the ivory satin a perfect counterpoint to her fair skin and the dark auburn hair waving softly across her shoulders.

"When Tag sees me in this..." She looked up and caught Gramma Lenore's tearful reflection.

"He'll know he asked the prettiest girl around to be his wife." Lenore stepped closer and rested her hands on Lee's shoulders. "I just know you and Tag are meant to be together. I feel it."

Lee closed her eyes against the truth. She couldn't hurt Lenore, not when it meant so much to her to see her grandson married.

"YOU SURE Buck knows all the words?" Tag glanced out his office window at an exact duplicate of Coop, a solitary figure dressed in black jeans, black coat and wrinkled white shirt, leaning against the porch railing while the rain fell steadily just beyond.

Other than the fact the duplicate was taking regular sips from a small silver flask, every move, every mannerism, was Coop's. The bandy legs and bushy brows, the thinning gray hair slicked to one side, even the slow, careful speech.

"He'll do fine," Coop said, but Tag noticed his foreman's fingers were crossed. "My baby brother always comes through for me. He looks up to me. I'm older."

Tag laughed. "Yeah, by three minutes. How your poor mama stood raising two of you is beyond me."

"I was always good to my mama." Coop glared at Tag. "Don't you forget it."

"Well, let's just hope Buck manages to perform this ceremony before he passes out. Did you remember to water down the booze in that flask?"

"That I did. Don't you worry about Buck. He's played the preacher in lots of community theater. He knows his lines." Coop stared disdainfully at Tag. Tag grinned back. He'd teased Coop about his identical twin for years, knowing Buck was Coop's touchiest subject. The fact that Buck didn't like horses and probably couldn't tell a cow from a steer had brought more shame down on the old cowboy than had his brother's drinking.

It was so much easier to tease Coop than to think about what was going to happen in less than half an hour. He'd be standing next to a woman he didn't know, promising to love, honor and cherish a complete stranger in a ceremony that was nothing more than an act.

He'd never considered himself much of an actor.

But Betsy Mae said Lee had done community theater. She was good, he had to give her that. Why, Lee'd slipped into her role so quickly when his grandmother showed up, she'd even caught him off guard. He wondered what would make an obviously intelligent woman agree to such a thing. Especially one as beautiful as Lee Stetson. He still hadn't had a chance to discuss the details with her. As far as she knew, the reason for the marriage was merely to get his grandmother off his back.

Using her to help him get the ranch sounded so deceitful. Tag figured it was just as well Lee didn't know the full scope of his plan.

According to what Betsy Mae told Will, Lee was one barrel racer tired of all her friends trying to set her up with "the perfect guy." Maybe she figured a temporary but make-believe marriage of convenience would give her a little peace.

Tag understood that. Still, he wondered if that was her only reason for going through with this sham. That or the money. She was certainly costing him plenty.

Betsy Mae had insisted on half again what Tag had offered her. She'd pointed out, in the message she left with Will, that her friend was, after all, a stranger to Tag. A stranger giving up her own free time, doing Tag a very large favor.

So far, Tag had to admit, Lee was worth it. She was smart and beautiful, obviously well-educated from her manner of speech, and probably the sexiest thing to ever set foot on the Double Eagle.

Which could, under the circumstances, create its own set of problems.

It wasn't going to be easy, pretending to marry a gorgeous thing like Lee, then keeping his hands to himself. But if that kiss they'd shared this morning was any indication of the attraction that sizzled between the two of them, he'd be a damned fool to take the chance of kissing her again.

She could just stay right there in his parents' old room, right where she belonged. He'd stay in his.

Tag glanced at his watch and realized the minutes were quickly ticking away. It was almost eleven. Now that Gramma Lenore had met Lee, there'd be no backing out.

He was committed. *Oh what a tangled web we weave...oh Lord, I can't do this.*

He took a deep breath and swallowed, then another, but a huge fist squeezed his lungs, pressed down on his heart. He couldn't do this, couldn't go through with it, couldn't...*uno, dos, tres, quatro....*

Coop's quiet voice interrupted Tag's escalating panic. "It'll be okay, boy. I hope you know how much I appreciate what you're doin'." The old man slowly took his hat off and held it in both hands in front of him. Tag took one more deep breath. Then he noticed Coop's fingers were trembling.

It wasn't often Coop removed his hat.

Tag had never seen the old man tremble. In fact, until now, he'd never really thought of Coop as old. At least not old in the sense of aging. Coop just was. Tag couldn't stop staring at those gnarled, trembling hands.

"Since your mama and daddy died, I guess I al'as felt like you were my responsibility. I know what I'm askin' you ta do is wrong, I know it goes against everythin' you believe. You've always been truthful to a fault, and I...well, I truly appreciate the chance you're takin' for me. For the ranch. I truly do."

"It's okay." Tag exhaled one big calming breath and pushed himself back from the window. He grabbed Buck's bottle of Jack Daniels and poured a shot for each of them, then handed one to Coop. "To save the ranch, Coop. Here's to the Double Eagle. No bird and bunny foundation is going to destroy what my grandfather and my father...and you and I, have worked so hard to build."

He downed the whiskey in one quick swallow, and closed his eyes against the burn. He thought of the woman in the other room and wondered how he'd ever allowed himself to be talked into this mess.

"It's time, Coop. Go fetch Lee and Gramma."

LEE TURNED, dipped, pirouetted, then stopped, caught once again by her reflection. She pictured Tag, the look on his face when she stepped into the front room, and her resolve wavered.

She heard a soft knock on the door, and spun around to answer it, fully expecting Tag, half afraid of his reaction. Coop waited in the hall, but his reaction was more than satisfactory.

"Ahhh," he sighed, his eyes suddenly brimming with tears. "You found Lenore's dress. She was a beautiful bride, you know, but you look almost as lovely, Miss Lee. Just lovely."

"Did you really think I was beautiful, Coop?"

Lenore stepped out from behind the door, and for the briefest of moments Lee thought she could hear the sizzle in the room. *But they're both so old....*

"More lovely than any woman I ever saw, and don't you forget it." Coop stripped his hat from his head and clutched it in front of him, obviously forgetting Lee was even there. "I never told you, Lenore, but I thought you were beautiful the first time I saw you when you were seventeen, and you've only grown lovelier. Many's the time I wanted to..."

"Why Cooperton Barlow Jones, you silver-tongued devil. You watch what you say in front of Lee. You've embarrassed her."

But Lee noticed it was Lenore who blushed and stammered and looked away. Coop's watery blue eyes followed Lenore with such unabashed love it made her heart ache.

She looked down at the full satin skirts billowing out from the trim waist and felt an ache in her soul that threatened to shake every bit of self-control she had. That was what she wanted when she married, that look in her husband's eye that told the world she was the only woman he saw, the only one he wanted.

Instead, she was fulfilling the obligation of an agreement she'd made with a friend she barely remembered. But what option did she have? Without knowing the details, Lee couldn't bring herself to disappoint Gramma Lenore, nor break her agreement with Tag. She touched Gramma Lenore's hand, consciously breaking the silent spell between the two elders. "I'm ready," she said, her voice barely a whisper. "We're late. It's after eleven."

Coop chuckled. "Oh, Tag's not going anywhere," he said. "You're going to really surprise that boy when he sees you, Miss. You are definitely a sight to behold."

He held his arm out to Lee, his smile absolutely beaming. Lenore sniffled behind her, then blew her nose. "Here, put this on first," she said, pulling a fragile lace veil attached to a flowered headband out of the garment bag.

Lee slipped it over her freshly brushed hair, clipped it securely, then curled her fingers around Coop's bony forearm and flashed him a nervous smile. *Well, Tag Martin,* she thought. *Ready or not, here I come.*

TAG STOOD beside the big stone fireplace and nervously slipped the worn gold band off and on his little finger. Thank goodness Coop had mentioned the ring, or he'd have missed that important prop completely.

He raised his eyes in a silent prayer for forgiveness from his parents, more specifically, his father. Jim Martin had loved this ranch with all his soul, and he'd loved his young bride just as much.

Unfortunately, Tag knew it hadn't taken her long to kill that love. Maggie'd never tried to hide her feelings about the Double Eagle or the man she'd married. Even as a youngster, Tag realized his mother had married his father merely to escape an unhappy home. She'd simply brought her own unhappiness with her.

Tag rolled her wedding band between his thumb and forefinger, and thought about slipping it on Lee's slender finger, wondered what it would be like to know the promises you made were real and lasting.

He guessed that was something he'd never find out.

Buck took another long swig out of his silver flask. Tag frowned at him. Buck returned his look with a sheepish grin of his own, tucked the flask in the breast pocket of his suit coat, and belched. Tag did his best to suppress a groan. This was not going to work.

The hired hands, all dressed in their Sunday best, milled around the big front room. A few of the men had wives with them and there were a couple of small children, but for the most part they were single men who kept their lives fairly separate from the boss's affairs. Tag wondered how much they knew, or if they even cared. They had no idea their futures rested on the success of this stupid charade.

They were the only guests he'd invited, other than Will Twigg, who hadn't shown up. There was no point in putting on a show for the entire community. It was going to be hard enough, carrying off this charade in front of his men and their families.

Tag checked his watch and glanced toward the hallway. Almost ten minutes late...had Lee changed her mind?

Tag was silently counting in German by the time she appeared.

A sigh swept across the small gathering, a soft exhalation of awe. Tag knew he wasn't the only one to react, but he was the only one she was smiling at.

She was a vision in satin and lace, every man's fantasy, every woman's secret dream, crossing the room on the old cowboy's arm. Coop couldn't have played his part better.

He held his head high, his old black Sunday-go-to-meeting Stetson neatly brushed and sitting at a cocky angle on his gray hair. His western cut suit, shiny from years of wear, gave him the look of a nineteenth century gambler, and he held his elbow cocked at a perfect right angle to his body. Lenore stood silently behind them, off to one side where she could watch the entire proceedings from an angle.

She looked suspiciously as if she'd been crying.

But Tag's focus wasn't on the old man or his grandmother. It was on the woman at Coop's side, the most beautiful bride he'd ever seen. His bride. A band of satin roses across her forehead held a sheer lace veil that merely emphasized her sparkling green eyes, full red lips and softly waving auburn hair. The gown fit as if made for her, the yards of ivory satin flowing out from her tiny waist, shimmering with each measured step she took.

Bright pink toenails peeked out from beneath the hem. He bit his cheek to keep from laughing. His blushing bride was barefoot.

Tag recognized his grandmother's gown from the wedding pictures he'd seen. This woman, who smiled at Tag as if she truly loved him, was acting exactly as if this marriage was real.

It was more than he could have hoped for. So convincing even he believed her. How could his grandmother ever doubt their love?

He felt like throwing up. But Coop was placing Lee's hand on Tag's arm and she was smiling up at him, the tremulous smile of a nervous bride about to marry the man she loves.

Tag gulped, covered her hand with his, and hoped she didn't notice how badly his palms were sweating.

The ceremony passed in a blur. Other than a slight list to the right, Buck handled his duties as preacher impeccably.

Tag repeated the vows, his voice strong and unwavering, and wondered if the tightening in his gut was the same feeling he'd have if all this were real. With his hands noticeably trembling, Tag placed the ring on Lee's finger. She stared at it for a long, silent moment, as if unable to believe any of this was actually happening.

Then she gave his trembling hand a compassionate squeeze, and smiled at him with so much love in her eyes he wanted to sit on the steps and cry.

Instead, he followed Buck's instructions and kissed the bride.

Lee knew this wasn't real. She felt as if she'd stepped into a fairy tale, but it was someone else's, not hers. She couldn't remember her past, but Lee knew her life had never been this perfect. Obviously, someone had made a big mistake.

She looked down at the simple gold band on her finger, the metal warm from this man's touch, and wished it could be true. Then she gazed up into his dark blue eyes just as he lowered his mouth to hers, and she believed.

It didn't matter, none of it mattered, not when his lips made her heart sing, not when his touch made her feel whole.

Sighing, Lee kissed him back.

She might have stayed lost in his kiss forever, but the hoots and hollers, the ribald cheers and the sound of applause invaded their quiet, private moment. They ended the kiss together.

Buck spread his arms wide, encompassing the small crowd of well-wishers as well as the bride and groom. "May I present Mr. and Mrs. Taggart Martin," he said.

Lee's heart soared.

With their arms around each other, linked as if they'd always been a pair, she and Tag turned to greet their guests.

TAG SHADED his eyes with one hand and watched Lee talking to a small child out near the horse barn. Miraculously the rain had stopped just as the ceremony began. Now the sun shone down on his bride as if she were the focus of all of heaven's attention.

She was leaning over in earnest conversation with the four year old daughter of one of his men. Tag knew the child didn't speak a word of English, but it was obvious Esmeralda and his new bride were conversing without any problem.

One more surprise from this surprising woman...she clearly spoke Spanish as well as English. He wondered what else he might find out in the coming days.

Coop stepped up on the porch beside Tag and leaned on the railing. "Seems to get along with the young 'uns just fine," he said. "Lenore thinks she's perfect for ya, the women seem ta like her, and I think the hands are all half in love with her."

"How can they have an opinion? They don't know her," Tag muttered, turning his back on Lee and the little girl.

"Neither do you, but that didn't stop you from marrying her."

"It's not quite the same."

"Shhh." Coop glanced in all directions then back at Tag. "No one but you an' me knows that for a fact."

"Which reminds me," Tag said, turning around so that he could watch Lee. She'd taken the little girl's hand, and the two of them were walking over to where a couple of kittens played in front of the open barn door. The full skirt of her wedding gown billowed out around her ankles, exposing her bare feet. She'd tucked the train up in back to form a jaunty bustle that bounced with every step she took.

Tag couldn't take his eyes off her.

"Reminds you of what," Coop prompted.

Tag blinked, and dragged himself back. "I wanted to tell you...the license really was a nice touch. I hadn't thought of that, but when Buck pulled it out for us to sign, I swear I heard Gramma Lenore sigh from clear across the room. What made you think of phony'n up a license?"

"Uh, well, I jest wanted to be sure it looked all legal. Your grandmother and I signed it, as your witnesses." Coop stared out across the yard, watching Tag's bride as intently as he did. "Hate to go to all this work and not have it look believable, ya know." He coughed and cleared his throat.

"Yeah, well, I'm glad you thought of it. Now I'm just wondering how long we're going to have to pretend to stay married. Gramma tell you when she's planning to go home?"

"Nope," Coop said. "She brought luggage, though, so she's not goin' home tonight. I'm guessing she'll stay on through round-up, maybe till your birthday." Coop grinned and tipped his hat to Lee as she climbed the steps to the porch, then he turned and headed into the house.

Tag stared at the door as it swung shut behind him.

"Is something wrong? Tag?" He looked as pale as a ghost. Lee stopped just in front of him and rested her hand on his forearm. He drew her into a light embrace. "It was a beautiful wedding, Tag. Thank you. Your grandmother is just wonderful. I feel as if I've known her forever."

He grunted in response. Lee reached up and cupped the side of his face with her hand. His skin felt cold and clammy, like he might be coming down with something.

"Tag, are you all right?"

"Yeah," he said, closing his eyes a moment, then dropping his arms from around Lee's waist. "I'm fine, Lee. Fine and dandy. Couldn't be better."

Without another word he turned and headed to the barn.

What had put Tag in such a strange mood? She'd overheard him and Coop talking about Lenore staying on. Could that be it? It was their honeymoon, after all, and a grandmother might not be a welcome guest at such a time.

Except, as far as Lee knew, they weren't even sharing a room, much less a bed. Tag hadn't made himself completely clear on that subject. It had to be something else.

Something nagged at the back of Lee's mind, something about researching material and finding answers. Then she remembered... the way to find answers was to go to the source. It looked like she was going to have to talk to Tag. Smiling, welcoming any chance at all to get to know her new husband better, Lee headed for the barn.

TAG STROKED the velvety muzzle on the big old bay gelding. Dandy had been a fixture on the ranch for well over twenty years and he'd listened to more of Tag's problems than any friend should have to hear. At least that was what Tag always said to him before he opened up and dumped his worries on the big horse's broad shoulders.

But what could he say? This mess was so huge even Dandy's calm acceptance couldn't help. Lenore was here to stay. Tag definitely hadn't counted on carrying out this charade for more than a few days. Oh, he'd planned on Lee being here, but more as a house guest than a wife, at least until the ranch was his. His grandmother always said she missed being in town, and her visits to the Double Eagle were usually brief.

Of course, she'd never had a granddaughter-in-law to get to know. Damn. Tag saw it all unraveling right in front of his eyes.

If his scheme fell apart before his grandmother turned the ranch over to him...Gramma Lenore would never forgive him, Coop would hate him till his dying day, and if Lee ever learned this marriage was part of a scam to get his grandmother to deed him the Double Eagle, she'd have his hide and then some.

How could he have known his temporary bride and his grandmother would bond like blood kin? No, Lee would never forgive him for using her to fool his grandmother to get control of the ranch.

This was one mess even Dandy's undying loyalty couldn't solve, though running his fingers across the velvety smooth skin around the animal's broad nostrils and stroking his silky cheek never hurt.

"Oh, he's just beautiful."

Tag jumped and whirled around at the sound of Lee's soft voice, thankful that, for once, he hadn't been spilling his guts out loud to Dandy. Lee stood in the dusty barn, a beam of light from the overhead doors shining down on her like a spotlight, casting a golden glow over the ivory satin, illuminating her fair skin with the soft glow of polished marble.

She was so beautiful she made his stomach hurt. Or maybe that was just the ulcer this whole charade was beginning to give him. Lee smiled and stepped closer, holding her hand out with a tentative manner like a woman who'd never even touched a horse.

"Be careful where you step," Tag warned, thinking of those perfectly shaped bare feet.

"I'll be careful," she said. "May I pet him?" She stepped closer, so close Tag felt the brush of her satin gown against his pants leg, so near he smelled the fresh, clean scent of shampoo and Ivory soap.

He swallowed a lump in his throat the size of Colorado. "Of course. Lee, meet Dandy." Tag moved aside so Lee could reach the big horse. Dandy lowered his head and nuzzled her open palm. She giggled when his whiskers brushed across her skin. Giggled as if she'd never experienced this before.

But of course she knew horses...she was a barrel racer, wasn't she? At least that's what Betsy Mae told Will. A barrel racer willing to act like a blushing bride...for a price.

That sure didn't sound like the Lee Stetson he was beginning to know. She lacked the hard edge, the competitive nature of most female athletes, or at least the ones he'd met.

Her smile was too open and honest for her to be a gold digger. Wasn't it?

Hell, even he was confused.

Lee turned and smiled at Tag. At that moment, Dandy decided he needed more attention.

He butted Lee with his nose. She stumbled directly into Tag's arms. He grabbed her and she molded her body against his, giggling when Dandy nudged her again.

"I think he wants me to hold you," Tag said, holding her.

"Really?" Lee's upturned face was only inches from his.

"I'm sure of it." Tag licked his dry lips, imagining the taste of hers. Dandy nudged her again, pushing the veil off her head and tipping it over her brow. Tag lifted the lace away from Lee and carefully untangled the clips from her hair, then hung the entire contraption on a convenient nail. "In fact," he said, "I think he wants me to kiss you."

"Do you always do what Dandy wants?" Lee licked her lips; the tip of her tongue, the tiny cleft between her lips an open invitation as far as Tag could tell.

"Whenever possible," Tag whispered against her mouth. Then whispering didn't make any sense at all, not when what he really wanted to do was hold her and kiss her, taste that sweetness he'd barely sampled earlier this morning.

Her arms went around his waist and her fingers stroked his back. His lips moved across hers, teasing, tasting, searching until he felt her lips part, heard the tiny sigh and whimper of her surrender, reveled in the slick, almost tentative thrust of her tongue against his.

He cupped the back of her head with one hand, with the other held her as close to him as the yards of satin would allow. She arched her back, pressing into the cradle of his thighs, inviting him to touch, taste, explore.

"Tag, are you out here? I'm looking for Lee."

He broke the kiss at the sound of Lenore's voice, leaving Lee with her lips still parted, her fingers curled tightly against his broad back. "We're back here by the stalls, Gramma," he said, gently putting Lee away from him and quickly brushing her tousled hair back from her eyes. "I was introducing Lee to Dandy."

Lee swallowed, struggling to find a sense of calm and control. Tag's stance was easy and relaxed, his arm loosely draped across her shoulders. Suddenly it came to her. The kiss they'd just shared hadn't happened because of any overwhelming passion on his part. He'd just been putting on a show for his grandmother!

She'd been ready to tear at the pearl buttons on his fancy white western shirt and he'd merely been playacting.

She knew that. She'd just have to remember, that's all.

Lenore certainly seemed convinced. She smiled at the two of them as if they embodied young love, completely unaware of their duplicity. "We're about ready out there for you two to cut the cake," she said. "They've set up the table on the porch since the rain quit. Everyone's wondering where the lovebirds have got off to."

"I'd better go wash my hands. I've been petting Dandy." Lee shrugged her shoulders, slipped free of Tag's light grasp, and scurried out of the barn. "I'll meet you on the porch," she said, throwing the words back over her shoulder. Before she could stand up there in front of all those people, she really needed a moment to compose herself.

The phone rang as Lee stepped through the door. She glanced around the large room, but no one else appeared to have heard it. Feeling like an intruder, Lee answered the phone. "Double Eagle Ranch, Lee speaking."

It took a moment for the man's words to penetrate Lee's confused mind. "No," she finally said, amazed when she actually found her voice. "I don't think Tag needs Ms. Anderson after all. It's all been taken care of, but I promise to let him know."

She carefully set the phone back in the cradle, just as her knees gave out. Cushioned by the bustle, Lee sat in a swirl of satin and lace in the middle of the front room floor.

She took a deep breath, then another, then realized she'd better slow down before she hyperventilated. This was one phone message she wasn't quite ready to deliver.

Betsy Mae's brother Will was wondering if it was too late for Annie Anderson, his sister's friend, to head over to the Double Eagle. She'd gotten lost in the storm and ended up at Columbine Camp, but the phone had been out, so Will hadn't been able to call until now. Was Lee positive Tag didn't need Annie's services?

I don't think so. Lee smoothed the billowing skirts, and stared at the gold band on her left hand. She wasn't Betsy Mae's friend after all. As far as she knew, she wasn't even a barrel racer. Maybe Lee Stetson wasn't really her name.

One thing she did know. She'd just signed a marriage license as Lee Stetson, said her vows and promised to love, honor and cherish that handsome cowboy out there, and she'd done it without an escape clause, and without a past.

She didn't even want to think what that would mean to Tag, or Coop, or Gramma Lenore. Especially Gramma Lenore. Coop said she was dying. Lenore said her most important wish was to see her grandson married.

Well, thought Lee. *He's married.*

She fought the urge to giggle, then covered her mouth and realized she might cry instead.

"Are you okay?"

Tag's soft question snapped Lee to attention.

"I'm fine," she lied.

"Then why are you sitting on the floor in your wedding gown?" He hunkered down next to her, smiled that absolutely devastating lopsided smile of his, and held out his hand.

Lee grasped it, aware once again of the strength in his fingers, the hard calluses across his palm. "Just resting," she said, carefully slipping her fingers free of his. She couldn't touch him, not now, when all she wanted to do was throw herself into his embrace and sob against that broad chest of his.

She should tell him the truth, tell him she didn't know who she was or what she was doing on the Double Eagle, tell him she'd signed a marriage license with a name that might be completely made-up, that as far as she knew she'd never ridden a horse in her life.

Who am I? Pain stabbed across her brow, and she swayed with the force of it. Tag immediately steadied her.

"Are you sure you're all right?"

She nodded, unable to speak, unwilling to tell him the truth. "Well, if you're absolutely certain," he said, studying her with obvious concern. "We have to go out and cut the cake." He took her elbow and guided her back out toward the porch. "Everyone expects it, but it won't take long and you'll be able to rest in a little while." He paused, just inside the door.

"I wanted to thank you. You're doing a wonderful job, Lee. Better than I ever expected. My grandmother doesn't suspect a thing." He squeezed her arm and smiled that wonderful, rakish smile of his.

Neither do you, Tag, Lee thought, unwilling to look him in the eye. *Neither do you.*

Chapter 4

TAG KEPT his arm firmly wrapped around Lee's waist as the two of them walked out on the porch, but the thought of their charade never once entered his thoughts. He didn't know what had happened in the house, but he was certain of one thing—she hadn't been "resting" when he'd found her sitting on the floor.

He tightened his grip on her waist and held her close against his side.

She seemed to sense his concern and turned slowly within his embrace. "I'm fine, Tag, really." Her green eyes were full of questions, but her smile never wavered.

"We'll make this quick, anyway," he promised. The woman was amazing, the way she stayed within her role even when she obviously wasn't feeling all that well. He definitely owed Betsy Mae for sending Lee in her stead.

"But, Tag?" She placed one hand on his chest, just over his heart. He wondered if she felt it flip into overtime. "We need to talk..."

"Later," he whispered. He covered her hand with his just as his grandmother called out to them.

"Well, there you are! I was beginning to wonder if you two lovebirds went and found yourselves another dark, private corner somewhere." Gramma Lenore hustled across the porch waving a gaily decorated silver cake knife. Tag ducked and Lee giggled when his grandmother made a teasing pass at him with the dull blade.

They cut the cake, Tag's arm still draped lightly around Lee's waist, his hand completely covering her smaller one as they held the knife. She smiled up at him and without even considering the implications, or his reasons, Tag leaned over and kissed her.

She kissed him back and everyone applauded. Tag blinked himself back to reality. He really had to stop kissing her once the "wedding reception" ended, but this was working even better than he'd hoped. Lee carefully fed him a piece of the cake and he returned the favor. There was a tiny bit of frosting, just on the corner of her upper lip. Tag carefully removed it with the tip of his little finger.

Lee licked the frosting off his finger with a curl of her tongue and a look of mischief in her eyes. Tag's stomach did a complete flip. He wanted to kiss her. He wanted everyone here to just go home, so he could carry her off to her room, peel that silky gown off her even silkier shoulders and make love to her until neither one of them could move.

He...he'd better remember this was all an act.

Coop handed Tag and Lee each a flute of champagne, then raised his own aloft. "Here's to the groom," he said, grinning broadly. "A young'n I recall swearing the cows'd fly down from the summer range before he'd take a bride. We're in the process of clearing the landing strip now," he added, tongue planted firmly in cheek.

He waited for the laughter to subside. "And here's to the bride, the purtiest little barrel racer this side of Durango." He clinked glasses with Tag and added, "Ride 'er, cowboy." Everyone laughed again, Lee blushed scarlet and Tag almost choked on his champagne.

He glared at Coop but the old cowboy carefully avoided eye contact. Now that he held center stage, Tag realized Coop wasn't going to give it up easily. What was he up to now?

"The boys decided you two needed a honeymoon."

Tag's head snapped around. Lee's body stiffened beside him.

"Yep. It was a surprise to me, too." Coop shrugged his shoulders and glanced apologetically at Tag. "Anyway, they cleaned up the line shack, stocked it with all kinds of tasty grub and even got your conveyance ready."

With a flourish of one gnarled hand, Coop directed their attention to the barn. Tag heard a snort, the musical clink of harness chains, and the familiar *clip clop* of Dandy's feet.

Dandy snorted again and stepped out of the shadows, led by one of Tag's men and hauling the surrey Tag's grandfather had restored for shows and parades years ago.

A big white bow practically covered the back of the leather seat and a tangle of old shoes and cans dragged in the mud behind. A banner taped to the back read "Just Married," and even Dandy had been hastily decorated with ribbons and streamers woven into his mane.

Tag took a deep breath and forced an appreciative grin. Lee giggled nervously beside him. Suddenly one of the men was shoving an overnight kit into his hands and his grandmother was handing Lee her battered little suitcase.

Lee's grip on Tag's hand practically cut off the circulation. "Tag," she hissed. "We've really got to talk!"

He patted her hand and helped her into the carriage. "Later," he said, settling her into the black leather seat. "Not here."

Then he jumped in beside her and grabbed the reins, released the brake, clicked his tongue and lightly snapped Dandy's broad haunches with the reins. "Gidyup, Dandy. C'mon boy."

Rice spattered the horse's rear end and he picked up the pace. The cans and shoes clanked and rattled along behind, and the group of well-wishers cheered.

Tag smiled and waved, wondering how he was going to get along in a one room line shack with one very small bed, and one very beautiful, sexy bride.

A bride he'd known for...he glanced at his watch...almost five whole hours.

"Let's stop here," he said, as soon as they'd rounded the barn, out of sight of the wedding guests. "I want to untie all this stuff before we head up the hill."

He pointed in the direction of a tree-studded ridge, bisected by a gravel road. "It's not really a shack." He smiled at Lee as he untied the old boots and cans. "It's a nice little cabin we use when the herd's up in the summer range. Has running water and real plumbing, in case you're worried about roughing it too much." He dragged the tangle of rope, shoes and cans over to a barrel behind the barn, then climbed back into the surrey. Lee hadn't said a word. She sat quietly in a pool of ivory silk and lace, staring pensively toward the mountains.

He snapped the reins and Dandy took off at a comfortable walk. "It's not far. The road's graveled all the way, so we shouldn't bog down anywhere. The storm's moved through. We should be having good weather for the next few days, but one night at the line shack'll satisfy everyone." He laughed quietly, then shook his head in consternation. "I had no idea the guys had anything like this planned. I hope you don't mind, but they hustled us out of there so fast I didn't have time to argue."

He clicked his tongue and Dandy picked up his step a bit. "We'll be at the cabin in a couple of hours, even at this pace. Actually, this might be a good thing. It'll give us time to work on our story, make it sound more convincing." Lee nodded silently in agreement, then sighed. Tag turned and stared at her for a minute. "Lee, are you sure you're okay?"

"I'm not really Betsy's friend." She spoke so softly Tag barely heard her whisper over the squeak of the wheels and the sigh of the breeze. She turned in the narrow seat and stared up at him, her eyes shimmering with unshed tears.

Her lower lip quivered. Tag figured he would never understand the way the female mind worked. So what if she and Betsy Mae'd had a falling out? It didn't matter a bit to him even if they hated each other. "Well, I can understand that, Lee. Betsy Mae can be a bit difficult to like, even on her good days."

"No, you don't understand." Lee grabbed his arm, her face a study in anguish. "You and me. We're not really married, Tag."

"Well, of course we're not. What made you think we were married?" He tied off the reins and let Dandy have his head, then turned to give Lee his undivided attention.

She stared blankly at him, apparently struggling for words. "A wedding, maybe?" she whispered. "You mean...?"

"You thought the wedding was real?" He swallowed back a curse. "Didn't Betsy Mae tell you it was all an act? I told you this was for my grandmother's benefit, that..."

"I know what you told me." Her voice raised, bordering on hysteria. "I don't know if Betsy Mae told me anything at all. I don't remember! You said you were only getting married so your grandmother wouldn't keep after you to find a wife. But you never, not once, said it wasn't a real marriage."

"Oh, Lee." He couldn't help himself. He dragged her onto his lap and hugged her. She'd been willing to go through with this whole charade, thinking it was a real wedding? That was certainly more than he'd ever expected! "Betsy Mae told Will you knew all the details. I just assumed..."

"Will called." She struggled in his embrace, shoved against his chest and sat back down on the seat next to him. "He said Betsy's friend, Annie Anderson, got lost in the storm and ended up at Columbine Camp. He wondered if you still needed her to come over to the Double Eagle. To marry you."

Tag stared at her as if she'd suddenly grown three heads. "Then who the hell are you?"

"I don't know," she wailed. She clasped her hands in her lap and took a deep breath. "I don't know anything at all before Coop found me walking in the rain. Suddenly I was just aware of walking down the highway, looking for the Double Eagle. I don't remember my name..."

"You said your name was Lee Stetson. You never even hesitated." His voice had a controlled, almost threatening sound to it. "I asked who you were and just as cool as you please you said, 'Lee Stetson.'"

"I got it off the jeans and the hat." She flashed him a quick smile, but the look he returned was totally unreadable.

"Jeans and hat?"

"Lee jeans, Stetson hat." He didn't sound at all as if he saw the humor in the situation. "Well, it sounded right the minute I said it, so it could be my real name. I just don't know for sure."

"You can't remember anything? Nothing at all? That doesn't make sense. How come?" He glared angrily at her, then suddenly switched his focus to a spot near her hairline. Instant understanding filled his eyes. He reached out and gently touched the dark bruise she'd tried to cover with make-up.

"You were hurt worse than you let on, weren't you? Lee, why didn't you tell me you couldn't remember? You're not sure at all how or when you got hurt, are you? Do you have any idea at all how this happened? When it happened?"

Lee silently shook her head. She knew her silence wasn't much of an answer. What was there to say?

Tag seemed to come to a decision. "You said you knew Betsy Mae. Maybe she can tell us who you are." Tag tapped his long fingers against his knee. Lee watched the rhythmic tapping, teased by a memory of long, polished nails tapping a damask table cloth.

The memory fled.

"No, dammit. That won't work. She and her blasted clown won't be back for at least a month."

"I'm not sure if I really know her, anyway," Lee whispered. "It's so weird, the image I have of her. It's like a flash of something familiar, then it disappears."

Tag took up the reins again, his eyes straight ahead. She felt the tension in his thigh where his leg pressed against hers in the narrow seat. He held the reins in a white-knuckled grip. "I don't believe this," he muttered. "I really don't believe any of this."

"I'm sorry, Tag." She had no control over the rush of words, and they tumbled out, one after the other. Condemning her completely, she knew. "Really, Tag. I am so sorry. When Coop found me I was cold and wet and miserable and confused, but he seemed to be expecting me. I figured if I just played along, it'd all come back to me. I recognized Betsy Mae's name and Columbine Camp and the Double Eagle and the minute I heard your name I knew who you were."

Tag grunted, but he kept his eyes focused straight ahead. Lee swallowed against the tightness in her throat. "I recognized you when you walked out of the house and I told myself then that since you obviously knew I was coming, I was supposed to be there. I kept waiting for my thoughts to clear up, to remember something, anything." She paused, recalling her reaction the first time she saw Tag when he stepped off the porch and into the yard.

She'd known exactly who he was. "You looked so familiar when we got to the ranch. You were the first remotely familiar face I'd seen." Her voice cracked and she cleared her throat, fighting the tears that choked her. "I figured I must know you from somewhere." She looked down at her clasped hands. "I wanted you to know who I was, because I didn't have a clue." She paused, then sighed deeply. "I still don't."

The silence stretched into long minutes, broken only by the sound of the horse's footfalls and the jangle of the harness. Lee realized she was shivering, as much from nerves as the late afternoon chill. Without a word, Tag slipped out of his jacket and draped it over her shoulders.

She muttered her thanks, then stared at Dandy's broad back. The jacket was warm from Tag's body and carried the scent of sandalwood and musk. Lee pulled it tightly across her chest, welcoming Tag's kind gesture as much as the jacket's warmth.

"The shack's just over the ridge." Tag snapped the leather reins lightly across Dandy's rump. "We'll get ourselves comfortable and figure out where we go from here, okay?"

"Okay." At least he hadn't thrown her out of the surrey. That had to be a good sign.

Within an hour they crested the ridge and rolled into a narrow valley bisected by a meandering mountain creek. A pond at one end spread lazily out into the pasture where the recent storm had knocked the tall grasses flat. Huge, dark pine trees framed the base of the hills on the far side of the valley and a tiny cabin backed up to the forest, facing east so it would catch the first rays of the morning sun.

Now, however, long shadows stretched half way across the valley and the afternoon sun rested just above the top of the highest peak. A few dark red cows with white faces raised their heads to see who was invading their quiet valley, then turned back to their grazing. Dandy whinnied and the answering call from a pair of horses poised near the edge of the trees sent a shiver along Lee's spine.

"Look there. Do you see them?" Tag pointed toward the two pale colored horses. Lee had barely a glimpse of them before they faded like ghosts into the brush. "They're wild mustangs," Tag said, the excitement in his voice evident. "These hills used to be full of wild horses, before ranchers captured most of them years ago. They're making a comeback. There's a small herd on this range, maybe a dozen or so. We don't see 'em too often, though."

"I thought the ranchers didn't want wild horses on their land because they compete with the cattle for food." Now why would she know something like that, Lee wondered. But it was true, she knew it was true!

"Most don't," Tag answered, pulling the little carriage around in front of the cabin. "Years ago, my grandfather had them hunted down and captured. He didn't want to share his range with any one or anything. We've only recently started seeing mustangs up here again. If the herd gets much bigger, I might have a problem with them, but for now we all manage to get along."

He helped Lee down from the surrey, grabbed their bags and carried them up the steps. Lee lifted her billowing skirts and followed right behind, but when Tag went into the cabin, she took a moment to gaze out at the magnificent view from the front porch. It was so peaceful up here, away from the noise of the city, the hustle and bustle of throngs of people, the clamor of traffic, the thick stink of pollution and the stress of deadlines and rewrites.

She knew all those things, knew them somewhere deep in her soul, but she was a country girl, a barrel racer, wasn't she? She tried to recall that brief flash of insight, but the resounding headache that suddenly coursed across her brow swept the memories away.

"Lee, you've got to come see what they've done." She heard Tag laughing inside the cabin. That sound was much more tempting than a memory that wouldn't stay put. Rubbing her brow, Lee turned and went inside.

Tag glanced up from the decorated basket of muffins and fruit he'd found waiting on the little kitchen table. The sight Lee made almost took his breath away. She stood just inside the door. He knew she didn't consciously pose for him. She'd merely paused so her eyes could adjust to the dim light in the cabin, but if she'd wanted to make an impression, she couldn't have done it better.

Reflected sunlight glowed behind her, casting her face in shadow but outlining her trim figure and the soft folds of her gown. They probably should have changed before making the long trip up here, but it was worth it, Tag thought, to get this glimpse of the woman he'd pretended to marry.

Damn, what a mess. Just his luck, to pluck an absolute stranger out of the storm and throw her into a charade his whole life depended on. How in the world was he going to convince her to stay in character, at least until his grandmother deeded him the Double Eagle?

She stepped further into the room and gazed around the small cabin with a look of stunned disbelief. "Oh my goodness," she whispered. Tag couldn't help but laugh.

Ribbons festooned every corner, flowers graced the wooden side board near the metal sink, a stack of split wood sat in front of the old woodstove, all ready for the fire.

There were even rose petals strewn across the thick comforter covering the double bed in the corner. Lee grimaced when she glanced in that direction and immediately turned her anxious gaze on Tag.

"Don't worry," he said, gesturing toward the bed. "I've got an extra bedroll in the closet. It won't be the first time I've slept on the floor." He couldn't help but feel a bit crestfallen at the immediate look of relief on her face. "Anyway, there's fruit and muffins in the basket, and an ice chest full of meats and cheese, cold beer and even a bottle of champagne. At least we won't starve."

"What are we going to do?"

"Do?" He took a deep breath and placed both palms flat on the table. "What we are going to do, Ms. Lee Stetson, or whoever you are, is spend the evening figuring out exactly who you are, and how you ended up on the road to the Double Eagle in the middle of the worst spring storm we've had in years. We're going to eat something, maybe have a glass of champagne, and go over every memory you've got." *Then I'm going to do my damnedest to convince you to keep on pretending to be my wife.* He flashed her a smile, the one he'd used countless times before to convince comely young women to follow his lead.

He wondered, briefly, just how far he could convince Lee to follow. The image of the rose petal strewn bed flashed through his mind. Immediately he shut down that avenue of thought.

Lee returned his smile and ducked her head. Tag was almost certain there'd been a look of relief on that beautiful face.

Now why should that concern him so much? Male ego, most likely, he hated to admit. Dismissing the thought, Tag opened the closet door and rummaged around for his bedroll.

At least he hadn't thrown her out, yet. Lee dug through her

battered suitcase and found a beautiful pair of teal blue satin lounging pajamas. Lenore must have added them to her wardrobe, because they certainly hadn't been in there earlier.

Other than stiff new jeans and a really fancy western shirt still in its plastic wrapper, the pajamas were the only option she had. Unless, of course, she wanted to put her pale blue nightgown back on. The one she'd been wearing this morning when Tag kissed her. She felt her skin go hot and cold at the memory, grabbed the pajamas and looked at Tag. "Is there a..."

"Yeah," he said, pointing to a small door at the back of the cabin. "There's a bathroom in there. It's kind of primitive, but functional and the tub's big enough for a party."

"Thanks, but I think I'll skip the party." Lee dipped her head when she walked past him, unaccountably shy all of a sudden. It had been different, this morning when he'd kissed her. Then, she'd honestly believed she was supposed to marry Tag Martin. Will's phone call had certainly upended that theory.

Tag's explanation, later, that they weren't even married, had hit even harder. She opened the door and stepped into the small bathroom dominated by the biggest claw-footed tub she'd ever seen. Lee hardly noticed the tub, so engrossed was she in trying to figure out her odd reaction when Tag had explained that their marriage was a sham.

She should have felt relief, not that terrible gut-wrenching despair. But when she'd walked into the ranch house living room holding on to Coop's arm, when she'd seen all the flowers and the people smiling and Tag standing there by the fireplace in his dark suit, Lee'd felt as if her life had finally come together.

It hadn't mattered that the man who repeated his wedding vows next to her was practically a stranger. His grip on her hand had been strong and gentle, the deep timbre of his voice had sent shivers along her spine. She'd believed every word he said, believed his promise to love, honor and cherish.

The sound of her own words, her wedding vows, had dredged up a sweet longing unlike anything she'd ever known before.

To learn it was all a farce, that he hadn't pledged a damned thing, hurt. Hurt more than it should have. They didn't even know each other, for crying out loud!

It had been as real to her as any wedding could possibly be. Tag's kiss at the end of the ceremony had sealed their promises, in Lee's heart, for all eternity.

She struggled with the tiny satin-covered buttons at her wrists, and managed the top three at the back of her dress. She even undid a couple near her waist, but stretch as she might, the others remained out of reach.

She heard Tag moving around in the main room, probably starting a fire or some other guy thing. She didn't want to ask him to unbutton her but unless she wanted to sleep in Lenore's beautiful wedding gown, she was going to need his help.

Lee opened the door a crack. Tag squatted in front of the woodstove, watching the flames catch the dry tinder. He'd removed his dress shirt, but still wore his slacks and a sleeveless undershirt. The lean muscles across his back rippled and bunched with each move he made. Lee's mouth went dry. She swallowed twice before she could get his name out.

"Tag?" He twisted around. One dark lock of hair flopped down over his eyebrow. He smiled.

That man's smile should be registered. At least labeled with one of those terse government warnings. *Warning. This smile could be dangerous to your health.* Lee smiled back. "Could you help me?" she asked. "I can't reach the buttons down the back."

"Sure."

He crossed the small room in two long strides. Lee turned, and lifted her hair up and away from the back of her dress. His fingers gently flicked the buttons open, parting the gown down her back without a bit of fumbling.

She thought she heard his breath catch in his throat but his hands were warm and steady and he completed the simple task in seconds.

He flicked the last button free. The soft fabric slipped off Lee's shoulders and fell open to the base of her spine where Lee had already released the buttons she could reach.

She grabbed the front of her gown, holding it against her breasts just as Tag clamped down on her sides to stop the fabric's downward slide.

His fingers spanned the soft flesh under her arms. She knew the exact moment when he realized he grasped her breasts. His fingers spread wide; he jerked back and stepped away. Still holding her dress, Lee whispered an embarrassed "thanks," ducked her head and slipped back into the bathroom. Her breath whooshed out in an explosive rush the moment the door shut behind her. She shivered, a belated reaction to his touch, and rubbed her bare arms.

"Oh, Lordy," she whispered. The reflection in the mirror looked back, no more familiar a face than it had been this morning, except Lee'd figured out one important thing about the woman in the mirror. Whoever she was, she really liked cowboys.

Lee giggled at the thought. Well, not necessarily all cowboys, but she was definitely interested in the one in the other room.

Get a grip, girl! What a convoluted mess. Pretending to be married to the sexiest hunk in blue jeans she'd ever seen, not to mention the fact that he looked darned good in a suit, not a clue to her real identity, no past, no solid memories, nothing.

Except a truly remarkable case of unrequited lust.

There was no use her mind's denying what her body and heart already seemed to have figured out.

She and Tag might not know each other very well, she didn't know herself at all, but...Lee sighed. Unless Tag was a whole lot stronger than she appeared to be, this marriage of convenience could prove to be most improperly convenient.

She rested her forehead against the cool mirror. *Please let me make it through tonight.*

Then she'd take it one night at a time.

"That's all, Lord. One night at a time." That depended, of course, on whether or not Tag even wanted to continue this charade. Lee wasn't the one he was supposed to have married, or not married, whichever the case might be.

She slid the wedding gown down over her hips. The shimmering satin left a sensitized trail along her thighs then pooled in a pile of ivory froth at her feet. Regretfully, Lee stepped out of it and shoved the fabric aside with her toe.

She stared at it a long moment, searching for more cohesive memories besides the quiet sense of loss she felt, then started to remove her bra. She reconsidered and left her panties on as well before slipping into the lounging pajamas.

The teal satin slithered coolly over her skin and the brilliant shade did wonders for her eyes. Briefly she wondered if Tag liked green-eyed redheads, but the minute the thought crossed her mind, she snorted in disgust.

"The man does not want to marry. Ever." She'd just have to keep reminding herself of that. A horrible thought flashed through her brain. What if she were already married?

To someone else. Someone she didn't even remember?

Oh, no. I'd know that. Wouldn't I? She glanced down at the plain gold wedding band that already felt as if it belonged on her finger. She hadn't been wearing one when she climbed into the truck with Coop. She slid Tag's ring forward to her knuckle. No white bit of untanned flesh hiding underneath. She breathed a sigh of relief. No need to borrow trouble. There was plenty waiting just outside the bathroom door. She stuck her tongue out at her image, pushed her hair back off her face, gathered the wedding gown up off the pine floor, and headed out to Tag.

COOP PICKED up the last of the beer cans while Lenore wiped off the kitchen table. Buck snored peacefully on the couch in the front room, the victim of one too many sips out of his silver flask.

Coop had been right proud of Buck, though. He'd definitely come through this morning. In fact everything had been just as perfect as it could be. So why couldn't he unwind?

Coop had been certain he'd relax once the deed was done, but the tension had been growing in him all afternoon. He wasn't quite sure why, but he had the strange feeling Lenore's proximity had something to do with it. He glanced at Lenore, bustling about the kitchen with long familiarity. It felt good, working with her like this, cleaning up the place as if they'd thrown a party together, as if they were a real couple.

Hard to believe they were both well into their seventh decade, even harder to realize he'd wanted Lenore for almost sixty of those years. Sixty years, and the yearning hadn't lessened, the wanting hadn't gone away.

He thought about Tag, about the fact he'd sworn never to marry, and hoped like heck the boy'd forgive him. The ceremony had gone off without a hitch, Tag and his new bride seemed more than compatible, and they hadn't hardly flinched when he told them about the honeymoon at the line shack.

It had sure been a shock to Coop. He'd planned on giving Tag and his bride a few days here at the ranch to get together, get to know each other in familiar surroundings, before throwing them into a situation like the one they were in tonight.

But it had been a thoughtful gesture on the hands' part, fixin' up the line shack like that. They were all pretty fond of Tag, considerin'. Coop figured a few of the wives had come up with the original idea, but still, it was a nice touch.

Of course, watching Tag and Lee kiss, first during the ceremony, then again when they cut the cake, maybe sending them off alone wasn't such a bad idea after all.

He chuckled and Lenore gave him an odd look. "It went real nice today, didn't it?" he said.

She didn't answer. She looked him up and down, a measuring stare that drew Coop as taut as a stretch of good fence wire. Then she dried her hands on a gaily embroidered towel, reached into the cupboard for Tag's bottle of good Irish whisky, grabbed two jelly jar glasses, set them on the table and pointed at one of the kitchen chairs.

Coop glanced at the chair, then back at Lenore.

"Sit," she said.

He sat.

She poured them each a measure of whisky, then raised hers silently in toast. Swallowing his questions, Coop clinked glasses with Lenore, and took a long, slow drink. It burned his throat and brought tears to his eyes, but he never took his gaze off Lenore.

"All right, Coop. Let's have it."

"It?" He swallowed, then wiped his suddenly sweaty palms down his pants legs.

"It." She smiled sweetly, but Coop knew that smile. It was an *I want to know what the hell is going on here,* smile. He'd never had it aimed at him before, but he'd seen it often enough.

Generally she was shootin' it directly at Tag.

"It," he said, then he sighed. "Just what is it you want to know, Lenore?" He cupped his hands over the glass of whisky, looked her straight in the eye, and wished he was a whole lot better at lyin' than he was.

"I want to know who that girl is, and just what you and Tag think you're trying to pull on me. I may be old, but I am not stupid. Neither are you, Cooperton Barlow Jones. You are about as stupid as a red-tailed fox." She smiled, but for some reason this time it reached her eyes. "That wedding was a set-up, Buck's no preacher and I want to know exactly why Tag pretended to marry that girl."

Coop cleared his throat and took another swallow of whisky. "Well," he said, drawing out the word. "Tag only thinks he pretended to marry that girl. Truth is, Lenore, Buck's a real preacher, empowered to perform real weddings, those two young'uns signed a real license, and them two's as married as a couple of folks can be."

He stared down at his whisky, at the old man's hands tipping the glass of amber liquid this way and that, and wondered how he'd gotten so old so fast. He remembered Lenore as a young bride like it was only yesterday, remembered the pain he'd felt when she married Big Ed. He recalled Tag's first steps, Jim and Maggie's funeral, the cold winters and hot summers, droughts and storms, all of it flown by in a heartbeat.

He smiled ruefully at Lenore, and wished she could sit there, across the table from him, every day for the rest of their lives. Sleep in his bed at night, work beside him during the day.

"Yep," he said, wondering what was going on behind that straightforward gaze of Lenore's. The woman always had been able to see right through him. That was a big part of the attraction. He grinned like a damned fool, thinking of the consequences of what he'd done today. "Them two's definitely married," he repeated. "Only problem is, Tag don't know it yet, and I'm not quite sure how to tell the boy."

Chapter 5

TAG STOOD next to the kitchen table arranging plates and silverware on woven place mats. Lee studied his strong back and broad shoulders for a moment. He appeared so engrossed in his domestic task he was unaware she'd entered the room. She watched him take a loaf of sliced bread out of the basket, then arrange a couple of platters of sliced meats and cheese and a bowl of fresh fruit in the center of the table.

He paused a moment, grabbed a bouquet of flowers off the sideboard and set them off to one side of the table, appeared to study the arrangement, then moved them closer to the center.

"It looks nice."

Tag spun around the moment she spoke. He stuck his hands in his rear pockets, like a small boy who'd been caught touching things he shouldn't.

Or a man decorating a table for a woman's appreciation.

He'd changed into a worn pair of jeans and a red flannel shirt that hung unbuttoned and open from his shoulders. His chest was magnificent, broad and muscled, smooth except for a pattern of dark hair surrounding his navel and trailing downward to disappear beneath the waistband of his jeans.

Lee caught herself mentally following the trail and shifted her gaze to the floor. His feet were bare, like hers.

Why did that feel so intimate, the fact they were both barefoot? Lee almost turned around and ran back into the bathroom. If she was already noticing such irrelevant things, it was going to be a long night. She'd be better off noticing the table, especially since he'd obviously arranged it for her benefit.

"Would you like champagne?" Tag held up the opened bottle. Two champagne flutes, one empty, the other half full, sat on the place mats. He seemed hesitant, unsure of himself. Lee hadn't pictured Tag as awkward in any situation, but she found his unpolished demeanor oddly attractive.

"I would have waited," he said, "but under the circumstances I..." He grinned at her, shaking his head from side to side, then let out a deep whoosh of breath. "I really don't know what to say. Can you imagine a bigger mess?"

"I don't know. I don't remember." Lee returned his grin. "And yes, I'd love a glass of champagne. I'd also like some of that food. I'm starving and it looks delicious." Tag pulled Lee's chair out for her, then sat in the one across the table, opposite hers. He poured champagne into the extra glass and handed it to her. Lee raised the crystal flute in a silent toast. Tag did the same.

"Are you ready to delve into your past?"

"Where do we start?" Lee asked. She stabbed a piece of sliced turkey with a serving fork and put it on her plate. An image tickled her memory. She stared at her hand holding the fork as she repeated the motion, this time arranging some cheese and fruit next to the serving of turkey.

Something about a fork? Stabbing? With a fork? That was a gruesome thought. She blinked. The image fled.

"We start at the beginning. Where else?" Tag finished his champagne and refilled the flute. When Lee held hers out, he filled it as well.

"My beginning isn't all that long ago." She stared at the pale bubbles rising to the top of the crystal flute. "In fact, for all I know, I dropped out of a spaceship around eight o'clock this morning."

"I think we can discount the spaceship."

"I guess so." Lee took a piece of sliced turkey and wrapped it around a chunk of aromatic cheese. "Mmmmm, Gorgonzola! It's one of my favorites...this all tastes wonderful." She closed her eyes and sighed with pleasure. "So much better than the place I went to last week with..."

"With?" Tag leaned forward.

Lee struggled with the memory. Like the image she'd had a moment before, she felt the teasing, tantalizing fragment of familiarity there, just at the edge of knowledge.

"Try, Lee. You can remember. You went out and ate with...?"

She knit her brows and concentrated. Nothing. At least her head didn't hurt when she tried to remember. Frustrated, she shook her head. "Nothing. There's absolutely nothing there."

"Okay, not with. You went out to eat...where? Where'd you go, Lee? Was it a restaurant in Durango? Montrose? Denver, maybe?" he prodded.

"I don't know," she wailed, slamming her palms down on the table. The dishes rattled. "It's almost there, then it's not. I have no idea who I am, I don't know what I'm doing here, I..."

"Okay. It's okay." Tag grabbed her wrists. His thumbs massaged her flesh with a tender stroke. "Calm down. Have some more champagne. Another piece of Gorgonzola." He laughed. "Food seems to jump start your memories. You remembered you like that stinky cheese. It just doesn't keep 'em going long enough. Maybe more'll come back to you if you're relaxed."

He let go of her wrists and filled her empty glass once more. She couldn't remember drinking the last glass. Maybe that was her problem. Maybe she drank so much she was having some kind of alcohol-induced blackout.

Nah. She couldn't remember much, but she knew she wasn't an alcoholic. She took another bite of sliced turkey and cheese, then a piece of chilled melon, and tried to open her mind.

Impossible. Not with Tag sitting so close, not with his shirt hanging open and all that perfect, cover-model chest on display. Even if he buttoned his shirt, she'd seen his chest. She'd know it was hiding in there, teasing her.

The same way she knew his bare feet were under the table right now, his naked toes mere inches from her naked toes. The possibilities were mind boggling.

"Let's start with what we know," Tag said, interrupting her incorrigible thoughts.

Thank goodness. She honestly couldn't recall ever getting turned on by toes before. Maybe she had a fetish?

That didn't sound right either. "Okay. I'm game," she said, sipping at her champagne. "What do we know?"

"Let's assume we know your name. When you said your name was Lee Stetson, you said it felt right. I can't imagine anyone completely forgetting their name, so, for now at least, you're Lee."

"Agreed. What do I do?"

"I'd say, from the clothes in your suitcase, you probably do something with the rodeo. Real cowboys, or girls," he amended, "don't dress that fancy unless they're in a show or a parade. That or they're working at a dude ranch and want to impress the tourists. Or, they are tourists, staying at a dude ranch."

Dude ranch? "Didn't you say Columbine Camp was a dude ranch?" Why did that ring a bell?

"I might have. Will, the one who ended up with, uh, my original bride, the guy who called? He and his sister Betsy Mae own Columbine

Camp. It's a working cattle ranch, a lot like the Double Eagle except they also cater to an exclusive clientele of wanna be cowboys. You know, mostly easterners with more money than brains who want to experience the, quote, Real West?" Tag laughed, giving Lee the distinct impression he had a pretty low opinion of easterners in general, and Will's clientele in particular.

"Betsy Mae doesn't have much to do with the business," he said, "since she's got the patience of a two year old, so Will runs the place. Will was planning to come to the wedding, but the storm must have kept him home. You'll meet him. He and Betsy Mae are the only ones, other than me'n Coop, who know about our, um, marriage."

Lee tried to imitate Coop's slow drawl. "You mean the one Coop refers to as a 'marriage of convenience?'" She giggled and held her glass out for another refill. "It's so funny to listen to him talk like that, about marriages of convenience. That's not cowboy talk."

Tag leaned forward, as if to impart a deep, dark secret, and whispered, "Don't let on I told you, but Coop reads romance novels. You know, those sexy paperbacks for women? According to Coop, marriages of convenience are a common plot device. That's what he calls it. *A plot device.* He should know. He's got hundreds of books stashed away, so I consider him an expert." Tag laughed, leaned back in his chair and stretched his legs out alongside the table. "He hides 'em in the barn, says they belong to Gramma Lenore, but we all know he buys 'em for himself."

Lee thought about old Coop, sneaking out to the barn to read his romances. She swirled the champagne in the narrow glass and covertly studied Tag's feet. They were long and narrow, with just a dusting of dark hair across the tops. It didn't seem fair. The man even had beautiful feet. Lee sighed. "He's in love with your grandmother, you know."

"Coop? In love with my grandmother?" Tag's look of astonishment gave way to uncontrollable laughter. He had an absolutely wonderful laugh. Lee propped her elbows on the table rested her chin on her folded hands and grinned, watching him.

Finally, Tag pulled a clean handkerchief out of his pocket and wiped his eyes. "I don't think so," he said, still chuckling. "Coop's never been interested in women. Doesn't have time for 'em. He's a cowboy. He's only got time for his horse...and his romance novels."

"You're dead wrong, Tag." Lee took a swallow of champagne, then met Tag's laughing gaze and stilled, abruptly mesmerized by the depths of color in his dark eyes. A woman could drown in those eyes. *She* could drown in those eyes. Especially when they focused so intently on her own. Lee wondered what he saw when he looked at her like that. Wondered what he thought.

She cleared her throat and glanced away, breaking the spell. She concentrated on Tag's feet, one propped on top of the other, visible just beneath the table. "When Coop came to get me right before the ceremony, when he stepped into the room and he and Lenore saw each other, I swear you could feel the sizzle between those two."

"They're a little old for sizzle, don't you think?" Tag swung his legs back under the table, hiding those long, narrow feet out of sight.

"No, they're not too old to sizzle," Lee declared. "I fully intend to be sizzling when I'm their age." She propped her elbows on the table and rested her chin on her folded knuckles. "It's just sad, you know. What with Gramma Lenore dying and all."

"What do ya mean, Gramma Lenore dyin'? She's not dyin', she's healthy as a horse. Why would you say that?" Tag snorted in disbelief, shook his head in denial. "That's not true."

"Oh." She looked absolutely stricken. Her eyes suddenly filled with tears, turning them into green jewels. "I thought you knew. Coop told me. He said Lenore was dying. I thought that was the reason she's been pushing you to get married, why you were rushing this whole wedding thing, so she'd know you were married before she died."

The tears were spilling from her eyes now, running freely down her cheeks. "I'm so sorry. I never would have said anything if I thought you didn't know."

"Aw, damn." Tag took a deep breath, then sighed just as deeply as the truth of Lee's words hit him. Suddenly it all made sense. He leaned over the table and rested his forehead against his hands. No wonder his grandmother'd been after him to hurry up and find a wife. She wanted to make sure he had someone when she was gone. It was her way of taking care of things.

"She's always been there for me," he said. His throat felt tight, like the muscles were tied in a knot. It was hard to get the words past. "She was there when my parents died. She made a room for me in that little house of hers in town and put up with all my hell raising in high school. She saved my hide more than once when Big Ed wanted to take me out to the woodshed for a whippin'. When I told her I couldn't live in town anymore, she put me in charge of running the Double Eagle and never once questioned my decisions." He looked up at Lee. She was sobbing outright, crying for a lady she barely knew.

"I was barely nineteen years old. Too smart for my own good, too cocky to think I needed more schoolin'. Then when I realized I needed an education to do right by the ranch, she helped me through college, even though she'd just lost her husband. Dammit, Lee. I can't believe the old bat's dying."

"Old bat? How can you talk about her like that?" Lee demanded. She grabbed her paper napkin, blew her nose and dried the tears from her eyes. "I don't believe you, Tag. She's your grandmother. Show her some respect."

"Hell, Lee. That's practically a term of respect." Tag grabbed his handkerchief and blew his nose, then wiped his eyes as discreetly as he could. Cowboys never cried. He remembered his dad telling him that when he was about eight. Big Ed had run over Tag's collie with the farm truck, then pulled out his pistol and put the badly injured animal to death.

Tag'd never liked his grandfather much after that, but he'd never let Big Ed make him cry, either. He wondered if Big Ed ever made Gramma Lenore cry? He didn't want to think about that too much. Especially not if what Lee said was true, that Coop had loved Lenore all these years.

Tag never would have guessed at such a thing.

"I used to call her the old bat when I first moved out to the ranch. I was homesick as all get out. I even missed her meddling, which was the reason I moved in the first place. She'd call me up every day and say, 'That you, Tag? It's the old bat. I'm checking up on ya.'"

"I guess I can almost see your grandmother doing that." Lee smiled and covered his hand with hers. He felt the warmth clear through him, turned his hand palm up and encircled her fingers with his. Her hands were small, dainty, soft and feminine. "She must not want you to know about her failing health," Lee said. "I never should have..."

"How could you know?" He squeezed her hand, then turned it loose. It felt too damned good to touch her, any part of her. Especially now, when he felt like his pins had been knocked out from under him. "I haven't called her that for years," he said softly, thinking of some of the things he had called his grandmother, under his breath or behind her back.

"I won't let on I know anything," he added. "Don't feel badly, Lee. It kinda puts a different spin on things, you know? I'm really glad you told me." He touched her hand again, lightly. He didn't seem to be able to help himself, not when she was sitting so close, dressed in that silky greenish-blue thing that draped and shimmered over her body. It had long sleeves and a high neck and hardly any skin showed at all, but whenever Lee moved, took a breath, even, his imagination went wild.

Material like that should probably be outlawed. Tag continued his slow caress over the back of her hand, thinking, remembering. So many memories, all jumbled together with regrets and dreams...and sensations. He took another sip of champagne, refilled his glass, then emptied the bottle into Lee's.

This probably wasn't the smartest thing, he figured. Drinking a whole bottle of champagne between the two of them, especially when the night stretched out ahead. Long, quiet, dark. A night when everyone who'd been at the wedding would be figuring they were probably doing exactly what Tag wanted to be doing right now.

He swallowed. The sound seemed to echo in the silent cabin. Lee raised her chin, looked directly into his eyes. Her lips parted. Tag thought he could crawl right in there, tasting, touching, experiencing that gut-wrenching feeling he'd felt earlier when they'd kissed.

No! Hell, he didn't even know who she was and they sure as hell weren't married. He snatched his hand away. She blinked, then seemed to return, as if she'd been lost, far, far away.

"Did you remember something?"

"No." She sighed. "Not a thing. So far, all we know about me is that my name might or might not be Lee Stetson. I'm either a rodeo queen, a dude ranch cowgirl or a dude ranch guest, or I misplaced a parade. That's not much to go on."

"I'd guess, since you seem to recognize Betsy Mae's name, that you're with the rodeo. That's her whole life, unless you count hangin' out in honky-tonks."

"Honky-tonks?" Lee frowned in confusion.

"Country western bars. How could you possibly forget what a honky-tonk is?" He thought of something that had come to him earlier, out at the ranch. "You speak Spanish, don't you? I saw you talking to Esmeralda. I know that little girl doesn't speak a word of English, but you two seemed to be conversin' just fine."

"That cute little girl with the kittens? She's adorable, a real chatterbox once she got going. I studied in Madrid for my junior year of college. The language just stuck, I guess."

Tag's mouth dropped open.

"Why are you staring at me like that? Tag?"

"I don't believe this! You can remember studying in Madrid, but you don't remember honky-tonks? Or why you were wandering down the road in a howling rainstorm without a clue where you were going? This doesn't make any sense!"

"Don't shout at me."

"I'm not shouting!" He paused, glared at her with a sheepish expression, then quietly admitted, "Okay. I was shouting. I'm sorry." He stared at her for a long, slow heartbeat. She hadn't a clue as to what was going on behind those dark, dark eyes of his. Was he going to ask her to pack her bag and catch the bus out of town? He must have noticed her momentary flash of panic.

"It's okay Lee. I'm sorry. Really." He took a deep breath and slapped both hands on the table, palms down. "We'll work this out, somehow. Your memory's bound to return, but in the meantime," he paused, looked down at his hands, across the room, anywhere but at her.

He probably thought she was a freak. "You're right," she said. "It'll come back to me. In the meantime, I'll just do what I've been doing. I'll keep pretending..." She took a deep breath. "I'll keep pretending to be your bride. That is, if you still want me?"

"Of course I do. Did you think I'd want to call it off?" He grabbed her hands, shaking his head and chuckling. "Honey, I'm in this way too deep to back out now. Especially now, if what you say about Gramma Lenore is true. She'd be devastated if the truth came out, that we're not really..."

Lee heard him swallow. The man really was terrified of commitment. He couldn't even say the *M* word! It could've been funny, except she thought it was more sad than humorous. She wondered what made him so afraid of having a real relationship with a woman. Maybe she'd ask Lenore. Or Coop. It sounded as if Coop was the only real romantic in this bunch. Except for herself. She might not know her past, but she was positive she had a romantic soul.

"Anyway," Tag continued. "I don't want my grandmother to find out we're not really married. Do you have any idea how long...?"

Lee shook her head. "No, but obviously she's confided in Coop. I'll find out what I can. Do you know who her doctor is?"

"I don't want to pry. If she wants me to know, she'll tell me. My grandmother's never been one to beat around the bush. She's as straightforward and down to earth as they come. She's got her reasons for not saying anything, so I won't either."

Lee watched the emotions flicker across Tag's face, noticed the slight clenching of his strong jaw, the bright sheen in his midnight eyes. He wasn't going to cry in front of her, but she knew he struggled with very strong emotions. It tore her apart to watch him fight his tears, especially when she knew how badly he must be hurting, how healing tears could be.

"Don't you have to unhitch Dandy?" she asked. She'd caught him confiding in his big old horse earlier today. Maybe some quality time with Dandy right about now would help.

"Already did." Abruptly Tag shoved his chair back from the table and stood up. Lee was certain she detected a look of relief on his face. "But it wouldn't hurt to check on him, make sure he's got all he needs for the night. You look exhausted. Why don't you go on to bed?"

"As soon as I clean up here," she said. "Have you got everything you need?"

He looked her over and she felt his slow appraisal like a charged caress across her skin. Then he smiled, a long, lazy smile that crinkled up the laugh lines at the corners of his eyes and popped that damned dimple back into position. "Almost," he said, grinning even more.

Her stomach pitched and her breath caught in her throat. She was absolutely certain he'd practiced that smile on every woman he'd ever come across. Every damned one of them probably reacted exactly the way she did.

That didn't make the effect any less extraordinary.

He stuck his bare feet into a well worn pair of boots by the back door, grabbed a flashlight and left her standing in the kitchen. The second the door shut behind him, Lee grabbed the back of the chair for support and exhaled all the air from her lungs. "Just get me through the night, Lord," she muttered. "One night at a time."

Activity was good, wasn't it? She quickly cleared away the remnants of their meal, tossed the empty champagne bottle in the trash, washed the dishes, and waited.

Waiting was not good. Waiting, she decided, gave her too much time to think, too many opportunities to consider the night ahead.

Lee brushed the rose petals off the bed, swept them into a pile with her hand, then tossed them in the trash. She grabbed her nightgown out of the suitcase, closed and locked the bathroom door, stripped off her lounging pajamas, slipped into her gown and crawled between the crisp sheets of the double bed, all before Tag returned.

She wouldn't let herself think of him, sleeping mere feet away across the room, wrapped in his bedroll on a hard, wooden floor. She wouldn't wonder if he slept in pajamas or underwear, or nothing at all.

She wouldn't dream about Tag Martin, or the wedding that wasn't, or the past that somehow wouldn't stay put. She wouldn't think about Tag at all, not one bit.

But he filled her thoughts, anyway, as she drifted off to sleep. The sweet scent of roses lingered.

TAG RAN THE stiff brush over Dandy's withers and along his spine, lost in the familiar ritual of grooming the old horse. He thought of the day almost twenty-eight years ago when he'd first seen the skinny little colt, trembling, bleeding from a row of deep, ragged gashes across his rump. Coop had found the day old colt not far from here. The colt, his dead mother, and the mutilated body of a mountain lion.

The big cat had been trampled to death, but not before delivering a series of lethal wounds to the valiant mare. Tag ran his fingers across Dandy's broad rump and felt the old scars from the attack. Big Ed had wanted to put the orphan down, figured it'd take too much time to feed and care for the animal.

Gramma Lenore had stood up to Tag's grandfather, something not many people dared to do. Tag figured she probably recognized two kindred spirits; the twelve year old boy and the colt, both of them orphaned and bleeding, though from different types of wounds. Whatever the case, she'd put her foot down and decided the scrawny bay colt would make the perfect 4H project for Tag.

"You've been a helluva lot more than a 4H project, haven't you boy?" Dandy nickered, a sound of pure, equine satisfaction.

Tag scratched behind his ears and the big horse lowered his head for more. "Hard to imagine a world without you in it, big fella. Almost as impossible as it seems to think of Gramma Lenore not here to drive me nuts."

If what Coop told Lee was true....

Damn, but his life was such a mess. Sometimes it seemed as if everything was absolutely perfect, but all that perfection hinged on things staying the same. Impossible. Dandy was still the proverbial healthy horse, but he'd reached the upper span of his years, Coop was practically eighty now, Gramma Lenore only a little bit younger.

The day would come when Dandy wouldn't be waiting for him out in the barn, when Coop wouldn't be concocting some outrageous new scheme and Gramma Lenore wouldn't be calling on the phone, hassling Tag about finding himself a wife.

Lee. She sure was a nice surprise. If he really wanted to find a wife...no, that wasn't going to happen. It was comforting, though, knowing she was there, waiting for him in the cabin, probably wondering what was taking him so long even though he knew damned well she'd sent him out here to be alone.

Like he needed time alone. Hell, he'd never had any trouble controlling his emotions. Emotions were for those stupid talk shows and such. Tell-all couch shows, Coop called them.

Tag swallowed and wondered why his throat felt so tight, why the big horse seemed to blur in the pale glow from the lamplight. Dandy shook his head and snorted, then rested his chin on Tag's shoulder. "You think you know so much," Tag muttered.

The horse nickered softly and rubbed his big head against Tag's cheek, as if offering what comfort he could. Tag felt a dam burst somewhere deep in his soul. He didn't even recognize it at first, the sob welling up out of his chest, the tears he hadn't cried since his parents were killed.

Then it didn't matter. The grief spilled out of him, deeply, painfully, covering a multitude of events, any number of fears he'd faced on his own. Spilled out in agonizing, wrenching sobs that tore at his throat and chest and left him shaken and empty, but strangely calm. Stronger, somehow. He didn't understand it.

No, he thought, grabbing his shirttail and using it to wipe the tears off his face. It didn't make any sense at all.

Tag absentmindedly patted Dandy's neck, turned off the light and stepped outside the barn. He stood under a sky that stretched forever, a velvet carpet strewn with countless diamonds, and thought of the good things in his life.

This ranch and all the people who worked it, Coop's loyal friendship, his grandmother's bossy but loving nature. Then Lee's image filled his heart. Try as he might, Tag couldn't get her out. He wasn't all that sure he even wanted to.

He closed the barn door behind him and headed back to the cabin. The lights inside dimmed just as he stepped up on the porch. Lee must be going to bed.

He hoped so. He didn't think he could stand crawling into his bedroll, knowing she watched him from the other side of the room. The desire to climb in beside her was much too strong.

He paused for a moment and leaned on the porch railing. Damn, what a day! For a man not all that comfortable with his emotions, he'd certainly run the gamut of them since this morning. It was such an unusual feeling, a sense of vulnerability he'd never experienced before.

The news about Gramma Lenore had sure been a shocker. It was typical, though, that she wouldn't tell him. She'd protected him all his life.

First from his mother's indifference, then from his father's drinking. Most of all she'd protected him from Big Ed's rages. Tag thought about that a minute. The only one his grandmother hadn't had to protect him from was Coop.

Talk about your dysfunctional family. *Damn.* He pulled his handkerchief out of his back pocket and blew his nose, wiped his suddenly muggy eyes and headed into the cabin. He didn't want Lee to see him upset, but he was learning that once you got started with all this emotional stuff it wasn't easy to stop.

He closed the door quietly behind him and grabbed his bedroll. Lee slept soundly, her back to the room, the blankets drawn up around her shoulders. He could see the straps from that wispy blue gown she'd worn earlier, though. The image that burned through his brain was enough to send him into the bathroom for a cold shower.

He refused to consider the sleeping arrangements back at the Double Eagle. With his grandmother firmly entrenched at the ranch, he and Lee wouldn't have any choice but to share a room.

Tag stood dead center in the big claw-footed tub, thoroughly drenched and miserable from the icy water spitting out of the overhead shower. He contemplated the next few weeks, sharing a room but not a bed with Lee Stetson.

He groaned. *Impossible.* Shivering and covered with goose bumps, Tag turned off the water and rubbed himself down with a coarse towel, then wrapped it loosely around his waist. Maybe it was time to go check the cattle in the high range. Sleeping on the ground beat cold showers hands down.

Chapter 6

"WHAT WAS the point of a phony wedding in the first place, Coop? I don't understand."

"Think about it, Lenore. Use the brains the good Lord gave you." Coop didn't think he'd ever been as angry with Lenore Martin as he was right now, at least not since the day she'd married Big Ed. Damn woman. He should have packed his horse then and moved on. He'd just never found the strength to leave her.

He'd never been able to stay mad at her for long, either. "What means more to that boy than anything in the world?" he asked softly.

Lenore blinked.

"Now think about what you've been threatening Tag with since he was just a scrawny, know-it-all kid."

Her face blanched. "The Double Eagle," she said. "Oh, Coop, what have I done? What have you done? Tag knew I never would have...."

"Well Tag sure didn't know you wouldn't have turned it over to the Foundation if he wasn't married. You've been like a burr on a dog's butt, pushin' that boy ta get married or lose this ranch. How could you, Lenore? He lost his mama and his daddy. This ranch is all he has."

"I just wanted him to be happy. He always seems so lonely out here. He's gettin' more set in his ways all the time. I wanted him to make the effort to meet some nice young woman, but I figured I was running out of time." Her blue eyes brimmed over with tears. "Coop, the deed's already in his name. I had it transferred ages ago. It's his birthday gift, but once he has the Double Eagle, my threat is completely worthless. That's why I've been pushin' him so hard. I never would've imagined him faking a marriage to fool me."

"Well, it's too late now. Like I told you, it's not fake."

"How could you do that to him?"

"It's your fault, Lenore." Coop ran his fingers through his thinning hair. "When you told me you...."

Damn, he couldn't get the words out.

He gazed at Lenore, memorizing every feature of that wonderful, cantankerous face. She glared back at him, challenging each word he said. Blast her gorgeous hide, that look gave him backbone. "When you told me you were dyin'," he said, embarrassed when he had to clear his throat, "I figgered the least I could do was grant your one wish. Remember what you made me promise? You wanted to see that boy married. Well, he's married. So get used to it."

Lenore glanced away. Unusual reaction, Coop thought, for a woman who faced everything head on. But then again, it must be difficult knowin' there was a limit on how many days you had left on this earth.

Lenore sighed, then looked squarely at Coop. "But how? How'd you get him legally married without him knowing it? That's impossible."

"I got the license from the county clerk. We go way back. Bud owes me. I helped him when he was havin' woman problems."

"You? How'd you help anyone with woman problems, old man? You can't even help yourself. Hard headed cowboy," she muttered, just under her breath.

It was loud enough for Coop to hear. "Watch what you say," he grumbled.

"Okay," she snapped. "Then what about the preacher? That brother of yours does just fine at plays and such, but..."

"Buck got ordained in one o' them mail-order churches. He did it when he was playing a preacher in some show last year. Said it would make it easier to experience the part of his character. Sent off for the registration form, paid his fee and got his papers in the mail. I jest never got around to telling Tag that Buck was a real preacher, is all."

"You scheming old man. I can't believe...."

"Quit calling me an old man, Lenore, unless you want me to call you an old woman. I'm barely six months older than you, as I recall."

"Six months in years, maybe, but we're a lifetime apart when it comes to brains. How could you do something so horrible to Tag? Does he even like the girl?" She shook her finger right under his nose, so angry lookin' he was afraid she'd explode.

Damn she was purty.

"Well, does he?"

"Hell, I don't know if Tag likes the girl," Coop shouted. "He jest met her this mornin'!"

Lenore slapped her forehead with her open palm. "I don't believe it." She glared at Coop with obvious disdain. "You and Tag deserve each other. You know that, don't you? How'd you ever talk this girl into marrying a man she doesn't know?"

"I tell ya, Lenore. She doesn't think she's really married. Tag hired her. She's a friend of Betsy Mae's. Lee thinks it's all for show, to keep you from buggin' Tag to get married. Tag didn't tell her about the Double Eagle." Coop sighed. "I guess I'll have to tell 'em both the truth. It jest seemed so perfect. Tag was throwin' himself a weddin' and you wantin' him married and all. It was supposed to be to Betsy Mae. They'd always gotten along. Then when Betsy Mae ran off and got married, she made arrangements for Lee to take her place. I jest didn't see the point of messin' with a really good plan. I thought it'd work out fine."

Lenore slowly shook her head side to side. Coop reached out and took her hands in his. Her fingers were long and narrow, the joints slightly larger than when she'd been a girl, but the skin still felt smooth and soft. He couldn't help but notice the age spots sprinkled across the backs. They looked right, like they belonged there. Like her hands belonged in his.

He'd never held Lenore's hands before, except to help her in or out of her car. It was nice, sitting here at the kitchen table, holding Lenore Martin's hands, even if she was madder'n a wet hen.

It felt even better when her fingers squeezed his back. She raised her head and smiled, a gentle smile that lit up her face. "Coop, I know you only did it because you love the boy. Lord knows, I love him more than I can say, or I wouldn't have been wanting to see him happy. I believe sometimes you have to push a bit when the ones you love get stuck in their ways."

She patted Coop's hand and her smile stretched into a grin. "You know, it just might work. I think I've got an idea," she said. "I know what we're gonna do."

"Well? Get on with it."

"We're not gonna tell 'em anything. We're going to help those two fall in love. You saw 'em together this morning. Tag could barely keep his hands off Lee and she looked at him like she'd never seen such a handsome cowboy in her life. They can't be that good of actors. I think the spark's already there. It could happen. With a little help, well, think about the possibilities, Coop. They're gonna be actin' married for my benefit anyway. I'm afraid if we don't take advantage of this situation, Tag'll never find a wife. He's too stubborn."

"He certainly comes by it honestly," Coop said. He hadn't

thought of the consequences, though. Not really. "Tag's got good reason to be afraid of marriage, Lenore. His mama and pa never stopped arguing 'cept those times when Maggie'd run off and wasn't here for Jim to fight with. Tag told me they were fighting right before the wreck that killed 'em both. Poor boy's last memory of his parents, the two of 'em arguing in front of him."

"Ed and I weren't much of an example, either."

Lenore tugged her hands free of Coop's, stood up and walked over to the sink. Coop watched her busying herself, wiping down the clean counter, refolding the folded towel, then got up and stood behind her. "Weren't you'n Ed happy, Lenore?"

"Doesn't matter. That time's past now and Ed's gone. What matters is the boy. I want to know he's happy...before I'm gone." She turned around, but she must not have realized how close Coop was to her. She practically tumbled into his embrace.

It felt perfectly natural for his arms to come up around her, even more natural for Lenore's head to rest on his shoulder.

He sighed and nuzzled his chin against her close-cropped hair. Her arms wrapped around his waist and she fit herself against him like she'd been designed for him. She smelled of good clean soap and sweet powder. He rocked her gently to and fro and felt her sigh against his chest. "Lenore, you know I'll do anything you want. You wanted Tag married, he's married. You want him and that little gal to fall in love, I'll do my best to help. But damn, woman, I hope you know what you're up to."

He reached behind him and unclasped her hands from his waist, then stepped back. "Now, I'd best be takin' my ornery brother and gettin' out to the bunk house where we belong. G'night, Lenore. Will you be okay up here at the house by yourself?"

She slanted a look at him that just about curled his toes. Then she grinned and before Coop knew what she was up to, Lenore kissed him. Not anything fancy, just a quick little peck on the lips but it felt like one of those kisses he'd read about, the kind with enough current to short circuit his parts.

Before he could catch his breath, Lenore slipped away and headed for the door. "I'll be just fine." She flashed him a big smile and damned if she didn't wiggle her butt like a school girl. "Good night to you, too, Coop," she said.

She left him standin' there with what he knew had to be the goofiest lookin' grin he'd ever had, plastered on his face.

LEE AWOKE out of a world of dark skyscrapers and a bird's eye view of Central Park, into a pool of sunlight. Instead of blaring horns she heard a steady, unfamiliar noise, a rhythmic pounding outside the window. It stopped suddenly, at the very moment she sat up in bed and stretched. The cabin's only door swung open and Tag entered carrying an armload of wood.

"Good mornin', sleepyhead. How was your night? Remember anything new?" Tag grinned at Lee, then as if he'd suddenly noticed how little she was wearing, turned quickly and dropped the pile of freshly chopped wood into a tin box beside the woodstove.

"Only that I don't like to wake up early," Lee grumbled. As furtively as possible she pulled the comforter up to cover herself. At least now she knew what all the noise had been. Tag chopping wood. She thought of those smooth muscles rippling with the swing of the ax. That was a sight she'd like to have seen.

"Early? Heck, woman, it's after seven. Day's half gone." Tag crouched in front of the stove and added a small piece of wood to the fire. "This'll burn out by the time we're ready to leave," he said, "but it'll keep the cabin warm enough for you while you're getting ready. We need to pack our things and head back. I've got a lot to do, especially if I'm going to be away most of the week." He straightened up and brushed his hands off on his pants.

"Where are we going?" Lee tightened the comforter around her shoulders. It was definitely warm in the cabin, but she felt naked sitting up in bed wearing nothing but her sheer gown.

"We aren't going anywhere. You are staying at the Double Eagle while I head up to the east range with a few of the boys to round up strays and get stuff set up for round-up. Then I'm moving over to the west valley where we're branding and separating out the culls, and if there's enough time I'll be heading over to Will's to help him do the same. With Betsy Mae gone, he'll need an extra hand."

"Oh."

The look he flashed in her direction was pure male exasperation. "Lee, don't be upset. It's better this way." Tag sat on the edge of the bed next to her and took hold of her hands. This close to her, she noticed the dark circles under his eyes, circles that hadn't been there yesterday. "You can spend some time with Gramma Lenore and I can get my work done. Maybe after a few days she'll feel like she knows you well enough, she'll head on back to town."

"You don't think we can carry it off, pretending to be married?" She thought they'd done remarkably well at the wedding.

"Oh Lee, it's not that at all." Tag chuckled softly and then he actually blushed and glanced away. "Don't you realize, with my grandmother at the Double Eagle we'll have to share a room if we're going to convince her we're married?"

"We shared a room last night. It wasn't a problem."

"Maybe not for you." This time he laughed out loud. "I don't think I can take too many nights like the one I just spent."

This time Lee knew she was the one who blushed. At least that explained the dark circles. She bit her lips and focused on the bouquet of flowers sitting on the table, visible just over Tag's shoulder. His thumbs stroked the tender skin on the inner sides of her wrists. The gentle friction sent fire exploding the length of her arms. She shivered, but made no attempt to tug her hands free.

"Besides," he said, obviously unaware of the sensual havoc his touch was causing, "if you're at the ranch without me there to bother you, you might just get your memory back. It worries me, your not knowing for certain who you are. What if someone's looking for you? Hell, Lee, for all we know, you could have a boyfriend or even a husband and kids somewhere. Just because you weren't wearing a wedding ring doesn't mean..."

Tag sighed, glanced down, looked to one side, then finally turned those beautiful dark blue eyes on Lee. He was so close, so impossibly close to her, his eyes filled her field of vision. She hadn't noticed the varied colors before, the kaleidoscope of blues, hypnotic, mesmerizing, so completely and wonderfully compelling.

"It's too tempting," Tag said, and though he smiled, it was a rueful, self-deprecating smile, "knowing you're so close, wearing a gown that's better'n any invitation I ever saw. I don't have any right to want to touch you, but all I thought about last night was this..." Still trapping her hands lightly in his grasp, he leaned over and kissed her on the cheek. "And this..." His lips found the birthmark at the corner of her mouth. "And this..."

His mouth covered hers completely. He released her hands and ran his fingers teasingly the length of her arms and along the column of her throat. He cupped her jaw lightly in his big hands, controlling the kiss, deepening the impact on her senses. Then, whispering her name, he embraced her, drawing her gently but firmly against him.

His lips traced the corners of her mouth, drawing a frantic

whimper from somewhere deep inside of her. Opening to his gentle assault, Lee lost herself in the rhythmic pounding of her heart, the rush of blood to her center.

She floated with his kiss, parting her lips and tasting him. Her thoughts flowed aimlessly, disjointed, as if fragments of her were kissing Tag, while other fragments, other parts were...where? Somewhere, some almost familiar place, a beautiful restaurant. Across the table, not Tag but someone else, someone with blond hair and pale blue eyes, a man...a man! She tore her lips free of Tag's possessive kiss.

"I remember," she said, taking a deep breath and slipping out of his embrace. She scooted back against the wall. "Not everything, not a lot, not even very much, but there's a man..."

"What kind of man? Who is he?" Gasping for air as if he'd just run a mile, Tag scrambled back and stood up, distancing himself from her as if she were covered in thorns.

Lee blinked, startled by the possessive edge to his voice. She tried to recall the image. It faded, just beyond perception. "I don't know," she wailed. "I get this vague mental picture of a man wearing a suit, sitting across a table from me. I know that I know him, but I don't think he's my husband...maybe a boyfriend?" She struggled with the quickly fading image. "He's got blond hair and blue eyes, if that helps any?"

"I'm not the one trying to remember." Tag's sarcasm wasn't lost on her. Neither was the fact he was backing across the cabin floor, distancing himself even farther from her.

So much for that mind-boggling kiss. Lee sighed.

It really was better this way, at least until they knew for certain. But surely she'd remember another man if he'd kissed her the way Tag did. When she closed her eyes and tried to recall him, nothing happened. When she closed her eyes and thought of Tag...wow!

Another thought intruded. This time when Tag kissed her, it hadn't been for Gramma Lenore's benefit. He'd wanted to kiss her, said he'd thought all night about kissing her. He'd practically admitted he hadn't slept at all with Lee in the same room.

Interesting.

She'd worry about it later.

"Why would I dream of New York?" She might as well throw it all at him at once. "Skyscrapers and horns blaring. A place I think might be Central Park?"

Tag halted in mid-escape, took his battered cowboy hat off, stared inside it like he might be looking for answers, then put it back on his head. "I don't know, Lee. I honestly don't know." He studied her a minute longer, a totally indecipherable expression on his face, then without another word turned on his heel and went outside.

Lee wrapped the comforter around herself and headed for the bathroom, the image of a handsome, blonde man tickling her memories. Maybe a soak in that great big tub would help jog her thoughts. Then again, maybe she'd just relax in there for awhile and think about Tag's kisses.

What if the stranger in her dreams was her husband? Tag had mentioned children, but she was positive she wasn't a mother. Maybe he was her boyfriend. What if he was her fiancé? She glanced down at her left hand. No, if she were engaged, she'd have a diamond, she was certain of it. Now, the only thing on her hand was Tag's wedding ring.

Where had he gotten a wedding ring? She hadn't even wondered. She hadn't wondered about a lot of things, Lee realized, suddenly concerned with her lack of concern. She needed to get back on track, to figure out where she was going from here. Little things, like what was going to happen when she did remember. Or what would happen if she didn't? What would it be like to stay out at the Double Eagle, with Tag somewhere off in the hills, chasing cows around the fields?

Mumbling to herself, Lee opened the bathroom door and glanced over her shoulder just as Tag stepped back inside the cabin. He stood in the doorway, watching, smiling wistfully in her direction. The look on his face tied her stomach in knots and stopped her breath in her throat. "Did you forget something?" she asked.

"No." He shook his head, paused as if he might have something he wanted to say to her, then took a deep breath. "No, I didn't forget anything." He watched her a moment longer, then spun around and went back outside.

What did he want from her? There'd been such a look of yearning on his face, a look he'd shuttered the moment Lee turned and saw him.

Maybe it wasn't such a bad idea for Tag to head for the hills. At least until he figured out what it was he really wanted and she figured out who the guy with the pale blue eyes might be.

And why a cowgirl should dream about Central Park.

TAG FOUND more old clothes in the cabin for Lee to wear home, a soft pair of faded blue jeans with holes in both knees that looked a lot more comfortable than the stiff, new ones she'd packed, and a heavy flannel shirt that would keep her warm. In deference to the chilly morning, she'd slipped a pair of cotton socks over her bare feet, but there weren't any shoes or boots that fit her. The wedding dress was carefully stored in the boot at the back of the surrey, Dandy had been brushed and curried until his coat gleamed, all his silly bows were gone and the clear, blue sky promised a perfect day ahead.

Tag flipped the reins lightly across Dandy's broad rump and the surrey lurched forward. Lee settled comfortably into the leather seat next to Tag and watched the countryside unfold as they followed the narrow road back to the Double Eagle.

The silence between them was easy and untroubled, restful even. Lee's thoughts wandered, unbound and unfettered by the glorious mountains, thick stands of aspen and dabs of wildflower color against green meadows, all perfectly placed to please the eye. Amnesia wasn't all bad, she decided. This was like seeing Colorado for the very first time and it was magnificent.

They had crested the final ridge and dropped down into the valley and the Double Eagle before Tag spoke up. "Betsy Mae went to a horse show in Madison Square Garden last November."

"What?" Lee'd been a million miles away, racing bareback across the ground on a beautiful golden mare, Tag behind her, his arms firmly wrapped around her waist, his powerful thighs pressed to hers as they gripped the horse...just Lee and Tag, the two of them breathless, together....

"Madison Square Garden," Tag repeated. "Betsy Mae was there for a big horse show. A bunch of the gals on the circuit did a barrel racing exhibition at Madison Square Garden. Anyway, they stayed over and toured New York and had a really great time. Maybe you were there, too. Maybe that's why you remember skyscrapers and all that stuff. I know it made a big impression on Betsy Mae. She couldn't get enough of all the bright lights."

Regretfully, Lee dumped the sexy fantasy. She tried to picture New York, the way it would look to a Colorado cowgirl. "Maybe," she said, but she knew she didn't sound very convincing.

"It's the only explanation, Lee." He slapped his hat on his knee in exasperation. "What's the first thing, the very first thing you remember, yesterday morning. When Coop found you, what had you been thinking?"

"I was thinking," she paused, then laughed aloud with the images she could remember. "I was thinking I was getting too old to race barrels. I was cold and wet and more miserable than I can remember, my head hurt something awful, but I remember thinking I'd been dumped on my butt before and gotten back up to ride." She grabbed Tag's hand. He squeezed hers back. "I was feeling really confused, but I know I was trying to get to either the Double Eagle or Columbine Camp."

"Well, that makes sense if you're a friend of Betsy Mae's. She would have talked about both places because she spends nearly as much time at the Double Eagle as she does at home." He grinned at Lee. This might work. He felt another step closer to learning her identity. Once he knew who she was, knew for certain there wasn't a husband or significant other waiting in the wings, well, there wasn't any reason they couldn't explore the possibilities of this marriage of theirs...on a temporary basis, of course.

Definitely temporary. He was one cowboy who wasn't giving up his freedom. He had to admit, though, there was something about Lee, something that made him want to touch her, to run his fingers through her hair, kiss her.

Hell, he didn't even have to kiss her. Sitting this close, aware of the subtle scent of soap and shampoo and Lee. He took a deep breath. She filled something he hadn't known was empty.

She fit beside him and he'd only known her for a day. Tag shook his head in a vain attempt to clear his thoughts. Whatever was empty had damned well better stay that way. No matter how well she fit next to him, he certainly wasn't going to let himself get used to it.

Maybe it was time to rethink exploring possibilities.

It sure would help if he knew who she was...and who might come looking for her. He didn't like the idea of her remembering some blond dude in a suit, that was for sure.

He was not jealous, merely aware of the problems a strange man showing up at the Double Eagle would cause, especially if Gramma Lenore happened to be there.

Everything was so damned confused.

He was gonna kill Coop, blast his ideas.

"Why?" Lee's hand slipped out of Tag's.

"Why what?" Tag snapped his thoughts back into the conversation, plopped his Stetson back on his head and clicked the reins lightly across Dandy's rump.

"Why does Betsy Mae spend as much time at the Double Eagle as she does at Columbine Camp? Does she work for you?"

"Well, uh, not exactly. She's a, um, friend, you know. A real good friend." He cleared his throat and grinned thinly at Lee. This really wasn't a conversational direction he wanted to be taking, at least not now, not the way Lee was glaring at him.

"How good a friend?"

Amazing, how those green eyes that flashed such warmth and passion when she and Tag kissed could look so...glacial. "Well, Lee." Tag focused on the space between Dandy's ears. "Betsy Mae and me, we've known each other since we were kids. Her brother Will and I are best friends. Me'n Betsy Mae, we grew up together, played with each other, spent, uh, time together...get my drift?"

"Oh, I get your drift, all right." She scooted as far away from Tag as the narrow bench seat would allow. "You originally planned this whole charade with Betsy Mae. If she were your bride and Gramma Lenore was staying at the ranch, you two'd be sharing a room and there wouldn't be a problem, right?"

Tag looked away.

"Am I right?" she demanded. And wondered why it mattered. Why all of a sudden the thought of Tag Martin sharing a room, sharing anything with Betsy Mae Twigg, or any woman, should infuriate her so.

But it did. It infuriated her a lot.

"Well that's just a bit different, don't you think?"

"You don't have to sound so testy," she replied. She studied the gold band on her left hand.

"I've known Betsy Mae all my life," Tag said. "You I met yesterday. Not only don't I know who you are, *you* don't even know who your are."

"Well, I'm figuring it out." She was, actually. Things were coming back. Kind of. Lee met Tag glare for glare, then counted the points out on her fingers. "So far we know my name is Lee Stetson, I probably ride rodeo with Betsy Mae, I've been to New York City and I've studied in Spain. That's a good start."

"It's not enough."

"It's not enough for what?"

"For sharing a room, dammit," he shouted. "For sex, Lee. You know, S, E, X? That thing people do when they sleep together?"

"You think that's what this is about? You think I want to sleep with you? Why of all the..." But that was exactly what this was about. *How embarrassing...*she'd let that fantasy, the two of them racing across the meadows, their bodies so close together...she'd let the stupid fantasy rule her brain and her tongue.

"Well, what else do you expect me to think, arguing with me over sharing a room?"

He didn't have to sound so condescending.

Lee backpedaled. "Well..." Frantically she searched for an argument, any argument, that might make sense. It came to her in a flash of inspiration. She straightened her spine and sent him an icy glare. "I certainly don't intend to sleep with you. I'm only thinking of Gramma Lenore. That's the whole reason we're even playing out this stupid charade, isn't it? Originally it was to get your grandmother off your back, now it's to convince her you're happily married and she can quit worrying about you. Am I right?"

Tag exhaled one, long, frustrated sounding breath. He pulled up on the reins and the surrey came to an abrupt halt. He stared at Lee for a minute, but for the life of her she couldn't figure out what he was thinking.

Then he tugged on the reins, turning Dandy's head so that the horse headed left, down a fork in the trail.

"Where are we going?" Lee asked. "This isn't the way to the Double Eagle."

"No, it's not," Tag said, staring straight ahead. "It's the way to Columbine Camp. Betsy Mae is off on her honeymoon for the next few weeks, but Will knows a lot of her friends. Maybe he knows you. If we can clear up just who the hell you are, it might make both of us feel more comfortable."

More comfortable for what? Lee wondered, knowing full well she had a pretty good idea.

Then another thought hit. *What if Will doesn't know?* Lee twisted her hands nervously in her lap. *What if he's never even heard of me before? Then what?*

COLUMBINE CAMP looked like Hollywood's version of a western ranch. Green pastures dotted with well-fed cattle and sleek, graceful horses, the sprawling log ranch house with a covered porch running all the way around and a huge red barn set off to one side filled the entire end of the narrow valley.

The only difference as far as Lee could tell was the series of neat little cabins tucked in under a grove of aspen trees and the expensive cars parked in front of each cabin.

She didn't think the average cowhand drove a BMW, a Lexus, a Mercedes sports utility vehicle, or a Jaguar convertible.

Tag stopped Dandy in front of the ranch house, set the brake and helped Lee down. He grabbed her wrist and unceremoniously dragged her up the steps in her stocking feet, knocked once on the front door and stepped inside the main house before anyone could possibly have a chance to answer.

They were met by a tall redhead dressed in worn Wranglers and a blue checkered cowboy shirt. She glanced briefly at Lee, then spent a much longer time scrutinizing Tag before sticking out her hand.

"You've gotta be Tag Martin. I'm almost sorry I got lost."

"Lost?" Tag frowned as he shook hands with her.

"If I hadn't gotten lost, I might'a kind'a married you, but I'd never have met Will Twigg. Annie Anderson," she added, nodding to Lee.

Suddenly it clicked. Betsy's friend. The hired bride. *The other hired bride.* Lee gritted her teeth against an unexpected surge of, *no, it couldn't be, could it be...jealousy?* She frowned, then caught herself and returned Annie's smile.

"Nice to meet you, Annie. Is Will here?" Tag glanced toward a closed door with an office sign over the top.

"He is, but he's left orders not to be disturbed. One of his guests didn't show. Some hoity-toity New York author...Michael Carrison? You know Betsy Mae's handwriting." Annie shook her head. "Well, Betsy Mae took the reservation a couple of weeks ago, didn't remember to get a credit card or phone number or anything. Not only did the guy not show up, he didn't even have the decency to call in a cancellation. Will's trying to fill the slot, calling on some of his regulars. I expect he'll be on the phone a while." Annie looked at Lee again and frowned. "Don't I know you from somewhere? You look awfully familiar."

Lee shoved her surprisingly possessive thoughts into the background, startled by Annie's comment. If this woman could help solve her identity..."I'm a friend of Betsy Mae's," Lee said. "Don't you race barrels, too?" She grabbed Tag's hand and gave it a quick squeeze.

"Not nearly as well or as often as Betsy Mae. That woman's a maniac!" Annie laughed, a deep, gleeful sound that tugged a reluctant smile out of Lee. "But I do go to watch her and I'm sure that's where

I've seen you before. What's your name, honey?"

"Lee. I'm Lee Stetson." She watched the striking redhead's face. Nothing. No sign of recognition at all. *Damn!*

"It's a pleasure to meet you, Lee." Annie held out her hand and Lee took it. "Even though I'm absolutely positive we've met before, somewhere. So..." She grinned at Tag. "You two tied the knot yesterday, huh? Will said you didn't need me anymore. Now I see why. When the real thing comes along, who wants pretend? Congratulations."

Tag's quick squeeze of her hand stifled any comment Lee might have been planning to make. He was right, though. The fewer people who knew the truth, the better off they were.

But Annie had met her before! Finally, a person who associated Lee with rodeo. A beautiful woman who didn't seem to mind that she'd lost a chance to "marry" Tag.

A woman whose hands were every bit as callused as Tag's. Lee rubbed her thumb over her own smooth palm. There had to be an explanation, something simple, for her lack of calluses.

She'd worry about that little point later. At least she knew something. Lee was a cowgirl. Annie had recognized her...kind of. It wasn't much, but it was a start.

"Have Will give me a call when he gets a free minute, will you?" Tag said. "It's been a pleasure meeting you, Annie. I hope we'll be seeing more of you."

"Oh, you will Tag, Lee. Most definitely. Will Twigg's not getting rid of Annie Anderson nearly as easy as he thinks." She laughed again, a bold infectious sound, and winked at Lee.

Lee's original opinion of Annie made a quick one eighty...now that she realized exactly which man Annie had set her sights on. Tag tugged at Lee's hand, pulling her toward the door.

She stifled a giggle. Tag was certainly in a hurry to get away from the tall redhead. *What would he think if he could read my mind?* Lee wondered. *What if he knew what I was feeling?*

The feelings of possessiveness she couldn't dismiss. The sense of rightness about the man stomping along beside her.

Annie was still chuckling when Lee and Tag stepped off the porch and climbed into the surrey.

"What do you think she meant by that?" Tag muttered, clucking his tongue and snapping the reins lightly over Dandy's rear.

"Meant by what?" Lee asked innocently. "Oh, you mean that

we'd be seeing a lot of her?"

"That, and that bit about Will not getting rid of her too easy. What'd she mean by that?"

Tag couldn't possibly be that dense, could he? Lee giggled. "That's Annie's way of saying Will's met his match. She likes him, she wants him, she'll get him."

"Well, he'll have some say in the matter, don't you think?" Lee thought Tag sounded decidedly cranky.

"Not necessarily," she said, goading him.

"Will and I both swore we'd never marry. She can try all she wants, but she won't snag Will Twig."

"Was Betsy Mae in on this oath of yours?" Lee asked.

"Well, yeah, but..."

"And didn't Betsy Mae just this week marry?"

"She's a woman. Can't trust a woman to keep a promise."

"I see." She did, actually. She really did see. But for a hard living gal, one with rodeo in her blood, Lee just didn't have it in her to give up.

No, not on a cowboy as sexy, ornery, cute and sweet as Taggart Martin. It was going to take some work, but Lee was convinced he'd be worth the ride.

She snuggled just a bit closer to him.

He drew away, stared straight ahead and ignored her.

Lee grinned. Somehow, she knew she'd always loved a challenge.

Chapter 7

IT WAS even worse than Tag had feared. Coop and Grandma Lenore were waiting on the front porch when he and Lee pulled into the yard. At the precise moment Tag noticed the casual, familiar manner in which Coop's arm rested over Lenore's shoulders, the old cowboy straightened up and stepped to one side, then raised his hand in greeting.

Tag glanced at Lee. The smug look on her face practically screamed *I told you so.*

He flicked the reins roughly against Dandy's rump. Instead of moving forward, the old horse came to an abrupt halt, turned his head and glared at Tag.

"You, too, you damned nag?" Hell, even his horse had turned on him. "Gidyup," Tag mumbled, with a lighter tap of the reins. With a regal toss of his big head, Dandy stared straight ahead.

Tag gritted his teeth. "Please, Dandy?" Lee's quiet chuckle grated like fine sandpaper over his nerves when Dandy twitched his ears and smoothly stepped forward, pulled the surrey around in a neat circle and stopped in front of the porch.

"Didn't expect you two home so soon," Coop said. He rocked back on his heels and grinned at Tag. "Thought you'd take advantage of the time off." Coop tipped his hat to Lee, then ambled down off the porch to help her out of the surrey.

"Too much work to do. You know I can't get away this time of year." Grumbling under his breath, Tag set the brake before climbing down, then grabbed their suitcases out of the boot. He'd wrapped Lee's wedding gown in a clean blanket and she was right there beside him to carry it into the house. Tag handed the large bundle to her, carefully avoiding any contact with her hands, her eyes. Essentially avoiding Lee, he realized.

Her quiet "thank you" raced across his flesh like a caress, then she turned away and sprinted up the stairs. He tried not to think about leaving her alone tonight, sleeping in that big empty bed while he tried to find comfort in a cold bedroll under the stars.

His grandmother'd been uncharacteristically silent. Tag didn't want to think about that. He didn't want to think about anything that had to do with Gramma Lenore dying.

Nor did he want to think about what might be going on between her and Coop. No, he wouldn't touch that one with a ten foot pole, either.

It was giving him a headache, trying to remember all the things he didn't want to think about. He needed a new plan. Anything had to be better than the way this one was going.

There was so much that could go wrong.

Like....

"I need to go call Will." Tag spun around and handed Lee's suitcase to Coop, then tucked his overnight case under his own arm. "You help Lee get settled, will you Gramma? I've got some business to take care of." Before anyone could respond, Tag headed into the house. He needed to talk to Will before his buddy said something to Coop about Annie. The fewer people who knew about Lee and her lack of memory the better off he'd feel. That included Coop, the man who'd set this fiasco in motion.

Tag dialed the number. He stared absentmindedly at his reflection in the window, counting off the tone each time Will's phone rang, thinking about Lee, worrying about his grandmother. When had life become so complicated?

Will answered the phone. As Tag launched into his creative explanation for Lee's presence at the Double Eagle, the answer suddenly came to him.

Things had gotten complicated the minute he'd veered from the truth. When the lies started piling up, his life had begun crumbling down around him.

It was with a deep sense of guilt he accepted Will's surprised congratulations. Now, not only was Tag lying to his grandmother, he'd added Coop and his best friend to the list. He hung up the phone and quietly left the room. How was he ever going to be able to keep his stories straight? How was he going to keep Coop and Will apart, before the two of them swapped tales of "Betsy Mae's friend"...and Coop discovered she wasn't the woman sharing his room? Somehow, he had to get away, back up to the summer range and the dawn to dusk work that had always been his salvation.

Most of all, he had to get away from Lee. He thought of her, sitting so proudly beside him in Big Ed's old surrey, regal as a queen in a faded flannel shirt and the old blue jeans Tag hadn't worn since high school. He'd chewed tobacco then, at least until his grandmother found out, but the faded circle on the back pocket where he'd carried his can of chew during those few months of teen-aged rebellion remained.

There was something awfully sexy about that perfect little worn circle stretched tightly across Lee's rounded derriere. Something that tugged at his gut when Tag saw her shapely legs filling out his old blue jeans, the way the buttons on his plaid work shirt pulled across her firm breasts. It had taken all the control he had not to reach out and touch her, especially knowing she most likely wouldn't have pushed him away.

Even with all the questions, Lee seemed more than willing to accept the attraction between them, the tempting fascination simmering not so far beneath the surface. Tag had to keep reminding himself how dangerous that temptation truly was.

He really did need to get away from her, no doubt about it. The empty spot she'd started to fill was beginning to itch. No way in hell was he going to let her scratch it.

"WELL, LEE, what do you think?" Gramma Lenore opened the door to Tag's parents' old room with a flourish.

Lee couldn't believe the difference. A coat of fresh ivory colored paint, new curtains in a soft, moss green and a matching bedspread had totally changed the look of the bedroom.

"How could you possibly...? It's lovely," she said. "Absolutely lovely."

"Coop helped me." Lenore stepped into the room ahead of Lee and swept the curtains aside. The flower box outside the window spilled out fresh impatiens in a cascade of pink and coral and white. "I had the curtains and bedspread stored away. Bought 'em years ago but never had a reason to use them. Do you like it?"

"Of course. But you didn't have to go to all this trouble." Lee placed her suitcase on the floor in front of the big oak dresser and leaned one hip against the edge. Tag was right. It wasn't going to be easy lying to Lenore. Not when this marriage obviously meant so much to her.

"It wasn't any trouble at all. Besides, I kind of enjoyed working with Coop. We've been friends for years," Lenore added.

Lee wasn't surprised to see the older woman blush a deep crimson. "Friends?" she asked. "Are you sure that's all?"

"That's all it could be," Lenore said. The look she gave Lee was steady, yet filled with remorse. "I was a married woman."

"You've been a widow for a long time, Lenore." Lee pushed away from the dresser and gently confronted Tag's grandmother. "I'd have to be blind not to see the way he looks at you. Anyone would."

"So?" Lenore drew herself erect.

"So, what are you gonna do about it?" Lee smiled.

Lenore's shuttered expression told Lee absolutely nothing. Then, as if the question had never been asked, Lenore smiled and gestured toward the freshly polished oak dresser. "I've emptied the drawers for you and Tag." She glanced at Lee's tiny suitcase. "There should be more than enough room for your things."

Recognizing a dismissal when she heard one, Lee began unpacking her clothes. She opened the first drawer on the right side of the dresser. It was filled with neatly folded white undershirts and plaid flannel boxer shorts.

Lenore, or possibly Coop, had already moved Tag's clothing into the room. Lee was certain she'd never shared dresser space with a man's underwear before. Biting her lips against the sudden blast of intimacy, she slammed the drawer shut and tugged open the empty one next to it.

She carefully arranged her few items, aware of Lenore's curious gaze boring into her spine. Questions hovered in the air between them, questions without ready answers. Lee sighed and turned around, her arms folded across her chest. Someone had to take the first step. "Why's Tag been so set against marriage all these years?" she asked, thinking, *question number one.*

"He married you, didn't he?" Lenore responded as if she were throwing down a gauntlet. "Maybe he just had to fall in love with the right woman."

"There's more to it than that," Lee countered. "I love Tag and I want to be a good wife to him." There. She'd said it. Suddenly, deep in her gut Lee knew she meant every word. She swallowed, cleared her throat and continued. "Somehow I get the feeling he married me more because the time was right than because he really wants or needs a wife. Why would he feel that way?" She was fishing, she knew she was, especially since she knew the marriage was a sham, but for some reason she felt compelled, no, driven, to know more about Tag.

It was even more important than learning more about herself.

Lenore glanced away, her thoughts impossible to read behind a look of infinite sadness. "I blame myself, you know." She trailed her fingers across the new bedspread. "I stayed with a man I didn't love. I watched my son struggle through a loveless marriage when I knew a single word of support from me would have given him the courage to move on. Jim and Maggie were so wrong for each other. He was a cowboy from the very beginning, she was a big city girl running from her troubles. The only good thing those two ever accomplished in their lives was the baby boy who grew up to marry you."

Lenore's soft laughter lacked any sense of humor. "Somehow, Tag got the best parts of both his parents. The only thing he got from me was his blasted stubborn streak...and a serious fear of commitment to anything other than the Double Eagle."

The smile she turned on Lee was filled with sorrow, but with hope as well. "The only consistent things in that boy's life have been Coop and this ranch. You've got the chance to break the legacy Tag's grown up with. He needs a good woman who'll love him so much he quits running. It's not going to be easy. You know that, don't you?"

"The important things never are, are they?" Lee returned Lenore's sad smile. "Our situation, mine and Tag's, is a bit," she paused, then shrugged her shoulders, "different. That's about the only way I can describe it. Our relationship is different. But I don't plan to give up on him. I don't think he realizes that yet."

"Kind of an odd conversation to be holding the day after a wedding, don't you think?" Lenore stepped closer to Lee and wrapped an arm around her waist for a quick hug.

"It's an odd conversation to hold any time," Lee countered. "It's the best I can do." She returned Lenore's hug. "Now, what are we gonna do about that old cowboy who's got his eye on you?"

"The same thing you're gonna do about that young cowboy lookin' at you, Mrs. Martin. We're gonna rope 'em, haul 'em in and tie 'em down." Lenore stepped back and held out her hand.

Lee took it, surprised at the strength in the older woman's grip. "Agreed," she said, shaking Lenore's hand.

At that moment, Coop burst through the door. The women literally jumped apart. Lee got the giggles and Lenore covered her mouth with both hands.

Coop swung his grizzled head back and forth, staring at first one, then the other. Lee tried to choke back another burst of giggles. Coop frowned. "Ya gotta stop him," he said, obviously talking to Lenore, but keeping his eye on Lee. "He's takin' off, dammit. The boy's head'n for the hills."

"What are you talking about, Coop?" Lenore wrapped her fingers around his forearm. Coop halted his tirade, his gaze fixed on Lenore's hand.

"Tag already explained everything," Lee said. "He told me he was headed up to the east range to look for strays, then over to the west valley to get things set up for the round-up. Even though the actual round-up isn't supposed to start for a few days, he wants to make sure everything ready to go. I'm supposed to wait here."

Lenore swung around to address Lee. "You're not really going to let him go off on his own, not the day after your weddin', are you girl?"

Lee blinked twice. Understanding slowly blossomed. She had a choice. She just hadn't realized it before.

"No," she drawled. "No, I don't think I am." She turned to Coop. "Is there a horse I can take?"

Coop scratched his chin, then grinned at Lee. "Yep. Dandy's plum wore out, but Daisy's in the back corral. Just had her shod yesterday and she'll be ready to go. She's a cute little sorrel, a bit sprightly and still in training, but a barrel racer like you shouldn't have a problem. You've ridden with just a hackamore before, ain'tcha? She's got a real tender mouth, so we don't use a bit on her."

"Uhm, I..." What in the world was a hackamore? Some kind of saddle? What did a tender mouth have to do with it?

"Pack your things," Lenore ordered. "I'll help Coop get Daisy ready." She glanced down at Lee's stocking covered feet. "You got boots?"

"Yes," Lee sighed. Her blisters hadn't heeled yet, but Tag was leaving without her...or at least he thought he was. She grinned, thinking of his reaction when she rode up beside him on a horse, all packed and ready to go.

"I'll get my things together." She turned to grab the few items of clothing she'd stuffed into the empty drawer. Lenore and Coop headed for the door. "Wait a minute," Lee called. "How long are we going to be gone?"

"Round up usually lasts a couple a'weeks," Coop said. "Since you're going up early, you'll need at least two pairs of jeans."

"You mean I have to wear the same jeans for a whole week?" The door slammed as Coop and Lenore headed for the barn. If either one of them heard her question, they chose not to answer. *Two weeks.* Somehow, Lee didn't think she ever wore anything more than once before laundering it.

She tugged the dresser drawer open and eyed the meager contents. "I don't have nearly enough underwear," she muttered. No way was she limiting herself to two pairs of panties! She didn't question her motives for following Tag. She didn't want to think about taking off on a strange horse through unfamiliar territory. She did, however, feel a quiet sense of nostalgia for a suitcase, lost somewhere, filled with absolutely exquisite, sexy, lacy underwear.

A clear picture of expensive luggage popped into her mind. Luggage filled with sophisticated styles and lingerie from Victoria's Secret. Luggage lost in a swirling river of chocolate.

The image faded almost as quickly as it appeared.

Shaking her head, Lee opened the drawer next to hers and grabbed a handful of Tag's boxer shorts. She was tough. She was a cowgirl, wasn't she? She'd make do with flannel boxers. Besides, maybe they'd give her seat a little extra padding.

Lee tugged on a thick pair of Tag's socks and shoved her tender feet into her pointy-toed cowboy boots. She grabbed her entire wardrobe and rammed everything, along with her make-up kit, back into her beat-up little suitcase. There was a heavy coat, probably an old one of Maggie's, hanging in the closet. Lee grabbed that as well, shoved her crumpled Stetson on her head and closed the bedroom door behind her.

She wouldn't think about it. Not about her motivation for following Tag, nor her sudden desire to run screaming back into the house in a blind panic. No, she'd take this one step at a time, one hour at a time.

She could do this. She could get up on that horse and ride. She could sleep out in a bedroll, help with the branding, maybe prove once and for all she was exactly who she thought she was.

A barrel racer. A cowgirl. A very confused woman falling head over heels in love with the sexiest cowboy alive.

TAG CHECKED the bedroll tied to the back of Chief's saddle and tightened the straps on the bulging saddlebags. He really should go tell Lee he was leaving, even though what he really wanted to do was just get on the big gelding and ride out.

Sneaking away from your own ranch isn't your style, cowboy.

No, as much as he liked the idea of leaving without any further contact with anyone, Tag knew he couldn't do it. He'd explained his reasons to Lee. She seemed to understand, even though she obviously wasn't as bothered by the attraction that flashed between them as he was.

He'd almost reconsidered until he'd seen that gleam in her eye when she talked about Annie Anderson and Will. She was just like every other woman out there, a predator. Only in Lee's instance, she was a predator with a hidden past.

He just wished she wasn't such a gorgeous predator.

He also wished he didn't feel so guilty about abandoning Lee to his grandmother, but there was no way he could share a room with her here at the Double Eagle. One night in the shack had been more than enough, thank you.

He'd never spent a longer, more miserable night in his life.

Tag leaned his head against the roan's warm flank. He had way too much to do to be worrying about a pretend bride in a make believe marriage. Maybe once Lee's memory returned, when Gramma Lenore finally gave up and headed back to town...maybe then he could establish some safe ground rules, then he and Lee could spend some quality time together.

A loud snort and the jangle of harness startled Tag out of his reverie. He spun around just in time to see a very pale looking Lee ride out of the barn on Daisy, the sorrel filly Coop had been working with.

Daisy lifted her feet in quick, nervous steps, the whites showed around her deep brown eyes and she snorted and pranced like a horse ready to explode.

Lee tugged ineptly at the split reins attached to the hackamore headstall, sawing away like the greenest tenderfoot at the filly's soft nose. Thank goodness Coop hadn't put a bit in her mouth, or there'd be hell to pay!

"Whoa," Tag said, reaching up and gently patting Daisy's shoulder. "Take it easy, Lee. You know better than to tear at her like that. You're gonna undo all Coop's training."

Daisy immediately calmed down with Tag's soft words. Lee, on the other hand, looked ready to shatter. Tag patted her leg. The muscles beneath the worn denim were taut with more than Lee's grip on the horse. If Tag hadn't known better, he would have thought she was scared to death.

Then he noticed the bedroll tied to the back of the saddle and the fully loaded saddlebags. Maybe she had a good reason to be scared...of him. "Just where the hell do you think you're going?" he asked. It was an effort not to shout.

Lee looked over his shoulder, down at the ground, then closely studied her fingers clamped around the split leather reins. "Um, Gramma Lenore said I have to go with you."

"Oh, she did, did she?" Tag gritted his teeth. "And I suppose you put up a terrible fight, said you weren't going, that no one could make you, right?"

"You don't have to be so sarcastic," Lee hissed. She glanced back over her shoulder, as if looking for Coop or Gramma Lenore. "It's not that I want to go," she whispered, "but your grandmother insisted if you were headed up to the east valley and then wherever else, I had to go with you. She suggested it didn't look as if we were very married, you taking off so suddenly after the wedding. I didn't know what else to do."

Daisy impatiently shook her head and Lee's leg muscles under Tag's hand flinched. "Relax," he said, stroking the length of her thigh. Her muscles loosened up under his touch, but her leg was naturally firm and well-rounded, the denim stretched tautly across her thighs. Lord, but it felt so good to touch her.

Damn. He slipped his hand to one side and rested his palm against the smooth leather saddle. Everything about Lee felt good to the touch. Too good. "Why are you so tense?" he asked, directing his thoughts away from the feel of Lee under his hand.

"Daisy's a great little horse. She's young, but Coop's been working with her. She's part Arab, part quarter horse, has a terrific gait. Compared to racing barrels, riding this little gal should feel like sitting in a rocking chair. Just treat her easy, don't yang back on the reins like you were doing a minute ago. You know better'n that."

"Tag?" Lee's voice cracked. For a minute, Tag thought she sounded like she might cry. "I don't think I do know better."

"What do mean? Of course you do." He stared up at her, waiting for the punch line. Her face was pale, her hands white knuckled where she grasped the reins. It suddenly dawned on him she wasn't kidding.

"I must have forgotten how to ride. It's like I've never been on a horse in my life. Luckily Coop had her all saddled and I managed to get on without any problem, but none of this feels familiar. I was so sure I'd remember horses," she wailed.

"Ssshhh!" Tag glanced at the barn, but there was no sign of either Coop or Gramma Lenore. He took a deep breath, knowing full well he was making a very big mistake. "Okay," he said. "Here's what we'll do. I'm going to tell Coop we're leaving. You just give Daisy her head. She'll follow Chief. I bet after a few minutes it'll all come back to you. If not, we've got time for a little riding lesson once we get away from the ranch. Okay?"

"Tag?"

"What, Lee?"

"How do I give Daisy her head? Isn't it already attached?"

Not now, Lord. Please? This wasn't happening, not really...was it? Tag took a deep breath, let the air out and silently counted to ten in Spanish. "That means you don't try to control which way she turns her head. You just leave the reins loose along her neck and she'll follow Chief. Be careful. Coop's got her trained to neck rein. You remember that, don't you?"

He should only be so lucky.

"No." She sounded like a very discouraged twelve year old.

"It means when you want her to turn, you gently tug the reins in the direction you want her to go. You want to go left, you increase the pressure on the left rein and rest the right rein alongside her neck. She'll follow her nose, whichever way you direct it. Can you remember that?"

"You don't have to sound so condescending," Lee said. "I'm sure it'll all come back to me."

Tag stared at her for a moment, noting the confusion in her troubled green eyes, the slight pout to her full lower lip. Then he shook his head, absentmindedly patted Lee's leg and quickly turned away to find Coop.

The last thing he wanted to do was feel sorry for her. Not when she was doing everything possible to make his life miserable. He couldn't believe it, a barrel racer forgetting how to ride a horse.

He'd thought it was something like riding a bike. Once learned, never forgotten. Well, it was obvious Lee had forgotten more than most women ever learned. It was so easy for Tag to imagine her sweeping the length of an arena on a lightning fast quarter horse, her slim body stretched over the saddle horn along her mount's muscled neck, the reins clasped in one gloved hand, the other holding her hat down tightly on her flying auburn mane.

Lee moved with the natural grace inherent in most horsewomen, a strength of movement, a precision of motion that had attracted Tag from the beginning. Her lack of familiarity with horses was hard to believe, but her fear appeared to be the genuine thing. Amnesia was certainly funny stuff.

Hard to believe she could remember studying in Spain when she couldn't recall how to ride a horse. It made no sense at all.

Tag bit the inside of his cheek to keep from grinning when he caught Lee's quiet, almost pleading words to the horse. "Good girl, Daisy," she said. "We're going to be really good friends, aren't we? Really, really good friends."

Tag glanced back at her as he stepped into the barn. Lee gave him a defiant look in return. He flashed her a grin, then called out for Coop.

Maybe it wouldn't be so bad up in the east valley. They'd be camping out and the nights were so cold they'd probably have to sleep in their clothes. There wasn't much trouble they could get in to, both of them wrapped in heavy jeans and flannel shirts.

It would be a lot warmer if we shared a bedroll. No, absolutely not. He wasn't about to fall into that trap. Tag dusted his hat off against his leg and groaned. If only Lee had agreed to stay behind!

"You ready to go?" Coop ducked out from under the stall he'd been mucking out and wiped his hands on his filthy jeans. "Sorry about the girl," he said. "I figured you were trying to get away from her, but you know Lenore."

"Yeah. Well, tell her we're leaving. By the way, if you run into Will, I told him Lee and I were really married. I let him think it was love at first sight. In fact, I didn't even mention she was Betsy's friend. I just let him think I'd suddenly met the girl of my dreams." Tag snorted in disbelief. "Do you believe he actually swallowed that? Just as well. I figured the fewer people who know this marriage is a scam, the better off we'll be."

Tag suddenly realized Coop was looking everywhere but at him. He hadn't really considered the impact of all this lying on his old friend, even though the whole thing had been Coop's idea from the beginning. Tag took a deep breath, closed his eyes against the weight of his problems, then shook off the growing sense of unease he'd felt since the first moment Lee walked into his life.

"Relax, Coop. It'll be fine," he said. Coop grunted and reached for the pitchfork, so that Tag was talking to his back. "I doubt we'll be gone more than a couple, maybe three nights this trip out, but I want to check on strays, and if we've got time, go over to the summer range in the west valley and see to the placement of the temporary chutes. You got that calf table repaired?"

"It was a busted spring on the gate. It's fixed." Coop stuck the pitchfork in a bale of hay and turned around. "I'll get the equipment loaded up and ready to go. You want to plan on Monday for the summer range? I can have the crew and the rest of the gear up there before ten if the weather holds."

"Sound's good. We'll be back by then. I can help you move the stuff. See ya in two or three days." Tag turned to leave.

"Take good care of my gal."

"Excuse me?" Where'd the old goat get off talking about Lee like that? "What gal?"

"Why Daisy, of course. Treat her gentle. She's never known a thing but kindness all her life. Some of those racers, well they're tough on their animals. Not that I'm sayin' Lee would...I jest don't..."

"You don't have to worry a thing about Lee or Daisy. I think the two of 'em are going to get along just fine. At least I hope they do," he muttered under his breath. "Tell Gramma we had to leave. I want to set up camp before sundown." Tag shoved his hat back on his head. "By the way, Coop. That's my grandmother you had your arm wrapped around. Don't forget it, okay?"

Coop blushed a deep scarlet. Tag tried his damnedest not to laugh, but he couldn't help himself. He was still chuckling when he left the barn.

Served the old coot right, after all the teasing Tag had had to put up with. It'd serve him even better if Coop ended up married to a woman as stubborn as Gramma Lenore, especially after all his years of single superiority.

Coop and Gramma Lenore married? Tag would have to think on that one for awhile.

Then he remembered his grandmother's illness. Remembered she probably wouldn't be around to irritate and aggravate him for much longer.

Tag decided he didn't want to think about it after all. He put his left foot in the stirrup on Chief's saddle and swung easily up on the big roan's back. With a flick of the reins, Chief headed out the main road from the ranch. Lee's little filly followed docilely behind.

Tag slowed his mount to a walk and Lee rode up beside him. She still looked scared half to death, but she was copying every move he made, watching how he sat the horse, how he held the reins. Her quiet concentration made him feel terribly self-conscious, but he kind of liked knowing she was studying him.

"Do we need to do this?" Lee asked as the two of them passed through the first gate and headed out the east trail. "I know the whole point of your leaving was to get away from me. I'm sorry I messed up your plans."

"It's okay." Tag smiled at her and Lee seemed to relax a little. "This may work out even better. I really do have to check on things up there and it'll give us a chance to get a little more comfortable around one another. How's Daisy feel?" he asked, suddenly changing the subject.

"Like a horse, I guess. How's she supposed to feel?"

"I don't understand it a bit, Lee. You remember studying in Spain, walks in Central Park and eating out in a fancy restaurant, but you can't remember doing something you've probably done most of your life. I can't believe you'd forget how to ride a horse. It doesn't make any sense at all."

"It does if you've never ridden a real horse before."

He almost missed her whispered comment. He actually kind of wished he had. "What do you mean by that?"

"I'm not sure, Tag. But as much as I want to believe I am who I think I am, I have a feeling I'm not." She gave him a sickly grin. "This is too new to be something I've done before. The way it feels to sit in the saddle, the leather reins in my hands. Haven't you noticed? I don't have any calluses on my hands. Annie Anderson has calluses. I'm sure Betsy Mae does, too."

The image of Lee's soft, perfectly manicured hands filled Tag's mind with a growing sense of horror. He stared at her, wanting to deny every word she said.

"I keep thinking Daisy's nothing like the painted ponies on the carousel." Lee looked so forlorn, Tag was afraid she might cry. She bit her upper lip and said in a beseeching whisper, "If I can remember a carousel ride in a park when I was a little girl, shouldn't I remember riding a real horse if I'm a professional barrel racer?"

He didn't want to think about it. Absolutely, positively did not want to know the answer to that one. He closed his eyes in mute denial, but he had to ask. "Then who are you, Lee? Just who the hell are you?"

The tip of her tongue darted out nervously, wetting lips that already appeared to be chapping in the dry Colorado air. "I don't know Tag. The only thing I'm sure of is that I recognized you the first time I saw you and I know I've seen the Double Eagle before." Her brittle laugh was filled with apprehension. "Oh yeah, and we didn't really get married yesterday. I know that."

"That's it?"

"Sorry."

"Your name isn't really Lee?"

"I don't know. It still sounds familiar. I'm just not certain."

"You've never raced barrels?"

"Don't think so."

"But how?"

"How?"

"How come you thought that's what you did? How come you know Betsy Mae? How come you went along with marrying me? It doesn't make a lick of sense, Lee...if that's even your real name," he mumbled.

"We've been over this before," she said, sounding about as exasperated as he felt. "I don't know. I just figured you'd like to be kept current. You know, as to what I do and don't recall." She flashed him an appealing grin like this was the newest game in town.

Tag didn't quite see the humor in the situation. He thought of something else she'd recalled, earlier. A blond man with pale blue eyes.

He felt like throwing up. The horses maintained their steady pace, climbing now along the trail leading to the east valley. It would be so nice to be a horse, totally oblivious to anything other than the weight on your back, the hard packed earth under your feet, the fresh grass to munch on at trail's end. Tag took three deep breaths, counted silently to ten in Spanish, repeated the process in French, then ran through his numbers once more, in Portuguese.

He only went to Portuguese in really tense situations.

This one seemed to qualify.

"It'll be okay, Tag. Really. I'll do my best not to blow it, I promise. Besides, even if Gramma Lenore figures out we're not really married, what's the worse thing that can happen?" Lee reached over and patted his hand. "She'll merely go back to looking for a bride for you, right? Look at it this way, it'll give her something to do. Take her mind off...things."

Tag slowly turned his head to stare at Lee. She didn't have a clue. To her, this entire operation had begun as a set-up to keep his grandmother from matchmaking. He'd forgotten. Forgotten completely that Lee didn't know about the deed to the ranch, or the Foundation for the Preservation of Wild Horses, or the damned threat his grandmother'd been holding over him most of his life.

No wonder she wasn't nervous about the mess they were in. He took another deep breath, tried to count. Couldn't. Not even in English.

Lee rode silently beside him, looking relaxed, not nearly as afraid. She was obviously enjoying the ride. Daisy's ears pointed forward as she picked her way carefully along the trail, no longer nervous with the new rider on her back.

Lee might never have ridden a horse before, but so far she was taking to it like a duck to water.

Tag forced himself to relax as well. Maybe this would all work out. Maybe his birthday would come and go, his grandmother would transfer the deed and everything would happen as planned.

And maybe cows would fly. Tag glanced at Lee. She smiled back. Her green eyes sparkled with the adventure of the moment. She licked her lips and straightened the disreputable Stetson covering her thick auburn hair. Sunlight turned the thick waves over her shoulders to a cascade of bronze and gold.

Tag could barely breathe for the beauty of her.

Damn, it was going to be another really long night.

Chapter 8

"SHE WENT with him? He didn't mind?" Lenore stepped around the side of the stall, but remained in the shadows.

Coop had known she was there the whole time he and Tag were talking. Hell, he knew whenever Lenore was close by. He always had. Sometimes it felt like he had radar where Lenore was concerned. "Yep," he said, wiping his filthy hands along his pants leg. "They're off, just for a couple-three days this trip. They'll be back before round-up, which'll give 'em another two weeks together, though I don't know what good it's gonna do. He is one confused young man."

"Well, that's not surprising." Suddenly Lenore was right there, standing in front of Coop with both hands on her hips, her chin jutted out like she was ready to take on the world. "Especially with you settin' an example. I'm convinced all men are confused. It doesn't seem to matter if they're young or old."

"Now what'd I do?" He stepped back and almost tripped over the pitchfork.

"It's what you don't do, Coop." Now she merely looked exasperated.

"Huh?" He took off his Stetson and scratched his head. Then he remembered what was all over his hands and wished he hadn't. It was bad enough to be standing this close to Lenore in a barn that smelled to high heaven from the stalls he'd been mucking out. He shoved his hat back on his head and wiped his hands on the seat of his pants.

"Have you ever thought about kissing me, Coop?"

Only every day of most of my life, he wanted to say. Maybe he would have if Lenore hadn't suddenly looked like she wanted to cry. "Yeah," he said, tripping over even that simple response. "I've thought about it."

Damn, that wasn't how it sounded in the books he read. When the guy wanted to kiss the girl, he said the most wonderful things, words that would convince any woman she was the most beautiful female on the face of the earth.

Except he couldn't recall any woman as beautiful as Lenore. Coop took a deep breath, swallowed, wished he could say the things he read, say what was in his heart. Lenore just stood there and watched him, her eyes swimming in tears while it was all he could do to swallow a lump the size of Texas and try to remember to breathe.

She practically looked right through him for what felt like forever, then sighed and lowered her eyes. Before Coop could stop her, Lenore turned around and headed back to the house.

He stood there a moment longer, reeking of manure and sweat, wondering if Lenore had any idea at all how much he loved her. Any idea of how little he had to offer.

He wanted to follow her across the yard, run over to her and tell her she'd been the only woman for him his entire adult life. What stopped him now had always stopped him.

He had nothing to offer. Nothing but a heart that had always loved her. What was that to a woman of means, a woman who owned a huge cattle ranch and a beautiful house in town, a woman who'd been married to one of the wealthiest, most powerful men in the county?

An old cowboy's heart wasn't much. It wasn't near enough. Coop heard the door slam. He felt it clear to his toes, broadcasting Lenore's anger and disappointment loud and clear.

It came to him then, suddenly, that he'd hurt her. She wasn't asking him if he'd thought about kissing her because she was curious. Hell, she was inviting him to kiss her.

Like the jackass he was, he'd stumbled over his words until she must have thought he didn't care.

He'd hurt the woman he loved more than life itself, a woman who didn't have a lot of living left to her. If kissing a worn out old cowboy would give her even a moment of happiness, the least he could do was get over his pride and follow his heart.

But he wasn't going to kiss Lenore out here in the barn, smelling of manure and worse. No, Coop decided. He had a couple of days before Tag got home. A couple of days to court the woman of his dreams the way a woman was meant to be courted.

Whistling, Coop shut the gate on the stall and headed for the bunkhouse. It wasn't even near quittin' time, but a shower and a clean change of clothes sounded like a good place to start. He might not have a lot to offer, but that danged woman was going to get the best he had. And dammit all, it was gonna be clean.

LEE WAS SO caught up in the green, aspen covered hills and the lush meadows of yellow and gold she almost forgot to be terrified. Almost.

She stroked Daisy's warm neck and listened to the creak of the leather saddle, the steady tramp of the horses' hooves on the beaten trail, and knew she'd never done anything like this in her life. It was an experience she'd only read about.

Tag obviously didn't want to talk about it.

In fact, Tag hadn't talked about much of anything for the past hour, but the silence hadn't been uncomfortable. Everything today was new and exciting. Lee wasn't about to let Tag's lack of conversation ruin it for her.

She grinned, settled her tender bottom more comfortably on the saddle and studied the broad shoulders of the man on the horse in front of her.

Tag rode as if he were an extension of the big strawberry roan. He'd explained, quite abruptly in Lee's opinion, what a strawberry roan quarter horse was and why he called Chief a gelding and Daisy a sorrel filly. When she'd asked for those simple explanations, Tag had actually gotten a little wide-eyed. Lee finally decided that was the point where he'd begun to believe her...that she'd never ridden a horse before.

That she wasn't who he wanted her to be.

Until then, he'd proved himself to be a master of denial. So typically male, she thought. *If I don't discuss it, it didn't happen or it doesn't exist.* Tag wanted everything all wrapped up in a nice neat package. It was a much more acceptable package when she'd been a down on her luck barrel racer looking for a job.

Tag obviously had no idea how to handle a woman with muddled memories of New York City and Central Park, a confusing past that might include a European education and a strange man with pale blue eyes. Lee understood his discomfort. She wasn't all that certain, herself, what direction her life should take.

The only thing she felt moderately certain of was her attraction to the sexy cowboy astride the big strawberry roan quarter horse. That, and the fact that same cowboy was doing his best to deny the attraction he felt for her.

Suddenly Tag's hand came up in a signal to halt and he drew back on Chief's reins. Lee's mare moved alongside and stopped without any direction from Lee. "What's the matter?"

"Do you hear that?"

The only thing she heard was the soft sigh of wind through the trees punctuated by the raucous cries of a flock of nearby ravens. Then Lee caught another sound, a soft grunting and the crackling and snapping of disturbed brush.

"It's not a bear, is it? Please, Tag. Tell me it's not a bear." The grunting grew louder, followed by a snort and the sound of heavy breathing. Lee grabbed Tag's arm. "Tag?"

"No, I don't think it's a bear. You stay here. I want to check this out." He reached down and peeled Lee's fingers off his wrist, carefully removing them one by one.

She glanced up at his face. His grin spread ear to ear, the buffoon! She yanked her hand out of his and sat stiffly astride Daisy. Tag dismounted and handed Chief's reins to her.

"Hang on to him," he said.

I can do this, she thought. Then she realized Tag was pulling a rifle out of a scabbard attached to his saddle. "What do you need that thing for?"

"Just want to be on the safe side," he said. "Just in case it is a bear." He winked, then held his finger to his lips and immediately disappeared into the thick brush alongside the trail.

Daisy's ears twitched and she snorted, shaking her head impatiently. Chief copied the little filly and almost pulled the reins out of Lee's hands. She thought about dismounting and giving her sore backside a rest, but the thought of being on foot and alone in the Colorado wilds nixed that idea.

Especially if there was a bear nearby. Lee shuddered and clung more tightly to Daisy's saddlehorn and Chief's reins.

The ravens' cries suddenly ceased. The silence was as unnerving as the sense of isolation creeping across Lee's shoulder blades. Where was Tag? She knew he'd only been gone a couple of minutes, but it felt like hours.

Chief snorted and tugged at the reins. Daisy shifted her stance, cocked her hip and almost unsettled Lee in the process. Lee gripped the horse's sides with her knees and Daisy took it as a signal to move forward. Lee tugged back on the reins with her free hand and Daisy turned to her right, following the pull on the hackamore.

Lee raised her left hand with Chief's reins clenched tightly in her fingers, holding them over her head to keep them untangled as Daisy completed a slow spin to the right. Lee felt herself slipping, leaning, sliding gently to one side. Contact with the ground was becoming a distinct possibility.

"What the hell are you doing?" Tag stood at the edge of the trail with a look of utter confusion on his face, the rifle balanced easily across his chest.

"What do you think I'm doing? Dancing a ballet, you idiot! Take your horse. I can't stop Daisy without using both hands. She keeps going in circles."

Tag stepped forward and gently grabbed Daisy's nose, effectively halting her slow spin. The look he gave Lee was priceless. "I think she's had enough dancing lessons for one day," he said. "Besides, I need your help. Get down and we'll tie these two so they won't go anywhere."

"What's the matter?" Lee dismounted carefully, groaning when her legs practically buckled beneath her. They'd only been riding for a couple of hours, but her knees wobbled and the muscles in her thighs and calves quivered with exhaustion.

"There's a mare down, a wild mustang in labor. She's old and I don't know if she's going to make it. She's so weak, she let me up close to her. I want to pull the foal, but I'll need you to hold her head."

"What? You want me to hang on to a wild horse?"

"She's in pain, Lee. A lot of pain. We can't leave her."

"Oh. Okay." Lee searched her faulty memory banks. Nowhere did she recall delivering babies of any kind.

Tag pushed his way through the thick scrub, holding the branches back for Lee. In just a few minutes they stepped out into a small meadow, completely surrounded by buck brush and scrub oak. The soft grasses had been torn and ripped to the bare earth by the mare's labors.

She lay on her side, her once black coat spattered with mud and grass, its sheen dulled from hunger and advancing years. Her hip bones jutted, painfully framing her distended belly. Saliva and foam flecked her neck and chest. White circles surrounded her terror filled eyes, but she only grunted when Tag knelt beside her.

Lee heard him crooning softly to the old horse. Amazingly, the stricken animal responded. Her eyelids lowered and a shudder passed through the pain-wracked body. Tag stroked her forelock, all the while speaking in a sing-song voice, soothing the mare, familiarizing her with his touch.

"Come closer...slowly," he instructed Lee.

She did as he asked and knelt down beside the horse. The animal snorted and tried to raise her head, but Tag took Lee's hand in his and stroked the mare's sweaty neck. Within moments the horse had calmed.

"I'm going to check for the foal," Tag said. "Keep stroking her, sing to her, anything you can think of to calm her down. Can you do that?" He turned Lee's chin with just the tips of his fingers, until she was looking directly at him, then he smiled. "Yeah, you can do it," he said, grinning at her. "Remember, do a good job. I'm going to be down by the end that kicks."

Before Lee realized what he was up to, Tag kissed her on the nose and scooted on his hands and knees to the back end of the mare. The old horse grunted, then groaned and the big muscles along her side rippled with her efforts.

Tag moved her tail aside then grinned at Lee. "Got two feet," he said. "Keep her as calm as possible. I'm going to try and get a grip on this little guy."

Lee focused all her concentration on the mare, on the horse's labored breathing, her Herculean efforts to deliver her young. The animal's eyes had closed completely now, her breathing grew shallow, even the painful groans and grunts subsided.

The mare's suffering was barely visible through Lee's sudden and uncontrollable tears. How long had this valiant animal suffered? What if she and Tag hadn't come along at precisely the moment they had? "C'mon, Mama." She kept her voice low and soothing, mimicking Tag's gentle tones even as she wept. She had no idea where the words came from, but suddenly Lee knew she could pour her heart out to the laboring mare.

"You can do this," she crooned. "Such a good, strong mama. We're gonna help you have your baby, but you've got a little bit more to do. Then you can rest. I promise you. Then you can rest." Sobbing brokenly, whispering words of comfort in a soothing, sing-song voice, Lee rhythmically stroked the mare's throat and cheek, praying for an end to the animal's pain.

Suddenly the mare raised her head and cried out, a long, low whinny that escalated into a scream of agony. "Got it," Tag yelled, falling back in a rush of fluid, holding a blood-soaked, ebony mass in his hands.

The mare's head dropped, falling heavily into Lee's lap. She felt the animal shudder and gasp. Lee sensed as much as heard the mare's final silence.

"Help me, Lee. Quick."

Weeping uncontrollably, Lee moved the heavy head aside and rushed to Tag. He'd removed his flannel shirt and was massaging the lifeless looking foal, pressing against the tiny animal's chest, willing it to live. Lee could barely see through her tears, but she took the shirt from Tag's hands and copied his actions.

Tag wiped the mucous and blood away from the foal's mouth, then blew air into its nostrils. He repeated the process once, twice, a third time.

Lee watched silently, her frantic movements along the bony little body slowing as she saw defeat cloud Tag's eyes.

Then she noticed a tiny bubble form in one shiny black nostril. "Tag," she whispered. "Look."

The bubble broke.

The tiny chest heaved.

One leg straightened out, then another. The foal shook his head, tried to raise up, then snorted, blowing more nose bubbles, before it flopped, exhausted, back into Tag's lap.

Tag raised his head and grinned at Lee. His face was streaked with tears. He wiped them away with the swipe of a bloodied forearm, leaving a dark smear across his face.

Lee thought she'd never seen anything more dear in her entire life. "You did it," she said, running her fingers along the foal's damp neck. "You saved his life."

Tag briefly closed his eyes, then cleared his throat and ran his bloodstained hand along the mare's bony flank. "We lost the mother, though. She's an old mare. I recognize her, that star on her forehead and the three white socks. She's from the herd that roams through here every spring." His voice broke. He took a deep breath and steadied himself. "She must be at least twenty. For a wild mustang, that's old. I wish we could have saved her."

"You did what you could, Tag. What the mother would have wanted." Lee wrapped her fingers around his corded forearm and squeezed lightly to make her point. "It's human nature, animal too, I imagine, to want life for your child. You said she'd lived a long time. Be thankful you were here when she needed you."

Tag glanced down at the fingers wrapped around his arm, then covered Lee's hand with his own. "Yeah," he muttered, clearing his throat.

"What about this little guy?" Lee asked. She let go of Tag's arm and stroked the newborn. "What can we feed him?"

"I've got some powdered cow's milk replacer at the line shack in the east valley. We keep it on hand for orphaned calves. If we can get the foal there in one piece, we can feed him formula until we get him down to the Double Eagle."

"What about his mama?" The mare seemed to have shrunk since giving birth, her tired body nothing more than skin and bones.

"We'll leave her here."

At Lee's stricken look, Tag explained. "It's all part of the cycle, Lee. If we hadn't come along, both mother and baby would have died. Within a few days, scavengers would have taken care of both bodies. This way they'll only get the one, but it's nature's way. C'mon. We need to get some warm milk into this little guy."

"Okay. You're right. It just seems so callous to leave her like this, after she worked so hard to have her baby." Lee smiled sadly at Tag, her eyes sparkling like green emeralds through her tears. "It doesn't seem fair," she added, biting her lips and looking away.

"I guess this is where I'm supposed to say life's not fair, right?" Tag stood up and lifted the foal in his arms. "Well, I'm not gonna say it, so quit waiting to hear it. If life weren't fair, this little guy would've died with his mama."

"You're right." Lee stood up and ran her hand along the colt's flank. "Is he heavy?"

"No, and that's good because we've got a ways to go before we get to the line shack. You'll have to lead Chief for me. I don't want to try holding on to this bag of bones and my horse at the same time."

As if it understood Tag, the colt's long legs stiffened and stuck out like broomsticks. It struggled a moment, then snorted and rested quietly against Tag's chest.

Lee led the way through the brush, holding branches aside to protect both Tag and the newborn. Dusty streaks marred her cheeks and blood and dirt covered her hands. She'd done everything Tag had asked since they'd left the ranch without complaining.

She might not remember riding a horse but she wasn't afraid to try something new. She had a good heart and a soul filled with compassion.

Deep in his heart, Tag knew he couldn't have saved the baby if he'd been alone. He'd needed Lee beside him, if only for that brief moment. She'd been a partner to him, the kind of partner he'd only imagined.

For the first time in his life, Tag found himself really wondering what it would be like, to know that such a woman would stand by him for the rest of his life.

Would be there, loving him, needing him the way he needed her, mothering their children, holding the family together. Tag glanced at the warm dark body nestled in his arms and imagined his own child there. A daughter or a son.

He couldn't remember his father ever holding him. He had no memories of his mother, other than the pain of watching her leave, the disappointment when she didn't call, the emptiness he'd felt when she died.

"I'll lead both horses, instead of trying to ride, okay?" Lee's gentle question snapped Tag out of his memories. He blinked, adjusted the colt in his arms and nodded in agreement.

Lee seemed to understand his silence. "Do you want some water?" she asked, pouring some out of the canteen onto her kerchief and using the damp rag to wipe the blood off her hands.

"I'm fine," Tag muttered. "We'd better get moving. We need to get some nourishment into this little guy. I'll wait to clean up at the shack."

"First, let me..." Lee rinsed the cloth with clear water. Before Tag had a chance to react, she was gently sponging the side of his face, cleaning the muck and blood away as if she were wiping breakfast crumbs off her child's face. "There," she said, stepping back and smiling. "That's better."

"Thanks, Ma," he drawled. "You're not gonna be one of those moms who spits on a tissue and cleans her kid's dirty face with it, are you?"

"I don't know." Lee rinsed the kerchief off and tied it back around her neck. Her look was pensive. "Guess I never thought about what kind of mom I'd be. Why? Did your mother do that?"

"No," Tag mumbled. "Let's go."

Lee grabbed the reins for both horses and followed Tag along the winding path. They climbed over a low knoll and the trail leveled out, following the ridge line for about a mile before dropping down into a narrow valley.

Lee spotted what had to be the line shack, a small log structure tucked up close against the trees. "Is that it?" she asked. Her boots pinched her toes and her legs were beginning to wobble. She could only imagine how Tag must feel, carrying the awkward weight of the foal as he hiked over the uneven surface.

Tag merely grunted, adjusted the youngster in his arms and continued down the rocky trail. Daisy and Chief snorted, obviously eager to pick up the pace. Lee hung tightly to the leather reins and hoped the horses wouldn't decide to pass her.

Here, where the route led down into the valley, there was a fairly good drop on the right. In some areas, the hillside had fallen away and trees had taken root below the trail. The brushy tops swayed in the light breeze, level with the hikers.

The leafy treetops caught Lee's attention and she paused for a moment, staring. What was it about the sensation of looking down into branches that seemed familiar? Chief impatiently tossed his head, almost tugging the reins out of Lee's grasp.

Whatever memory had teased her thoughts, fled with the abrupt movement. "C'mon, horses," she muttered, tightening the leather straps in her fist and rushing to catch up with Tag. He'd already made it to the bottom of the hill and was carefully working his way across the boggy valley floor.

Lee was soaked to the knees by the time she reached the cabin. Tag had placed the foal on a dry pile of burlap bags in a warm sunny spot out of the wind and was rummaging around in a wooden storage cabinet on the porch. "Just stick Daisy and Chief in the corral," he said, nodding in the direction of a small fenced pen behind the cabin. "There's a spring-fed trough in there. They'll be fine 'til I can unsaddle 'em."

"Do you need any help?" Lee opened the gate and led the horses inside. She held the reins carefully, aware of the tender beginnings of blisters on her palms.

"Yeah. There's an old army blanket just inside the cabin door. Oh, and bring me one of the canteens. They've been in the sun long enough, the water should be fairly warm."

Lee grabbed the canteen off of Chief's saddle, then carefully slipped the bridals over both horses' heads, the way she'd seen Tag do it earlier. She hung the gear on a post outside the corral, carefully latched the gate and handed the canteen to Tag. The pile of neatly folded blankets was just inside the door of the cabin. Lee grabbed the one on top and laid it on the porch next to the colt, then squatted down next to Tag.

"Thanks," Tag mumbled. He measured a bland looking powder into what looked like an oversized baby bottle with a long rubber nipple, added the warm water from the canteen and shook the bottle to mix it. Lee absently stroked the foal's soft neck. The black coat had dried to the texture of warm velvet and the animal's tiny hooves glistened like ebony.

"Shouldn't he be more alert?" she asked. The baby seemed so

listless, not anything like the newborn horses she remembered from old Disney movies. Those babies were up and nursing within minutes after birth.

"This little guy had a rough start and he hasn't had a thing to eat," Tag said. Then he grinned at Lee and added, "yet."

Tag dribbled a small amount of the formula around the baby's mouth, then gently worked the soft nipple between the rubbery black lips. "C'mon little guy," he muttered. "It may not taste quite like mama's, but you don't know the difference. C'mon, you can do it." The colt tried to suckle, choked, sneezed, blinked, then glared at Tag when the cowboy removed the bottle.

But his head came up and he rolled over onto his chest, folding his spindly legs beneath him. Lee carefully supported the tiny body and Tag offered him the nipple once more.

This time the colt got it right. He suckled greedily at the bottle, took too much and choked again. Tag backed away with the bottle and stood up.

The baby struggled, rising up on his forelegs in search of the elusive nipple. Lee stood too, just in time to help steady the colt's bony back end as he thrust his hips into the air, then wobbled upright on four skinny legs.

Lee didn't know whether to cheer or cry. Instead, she grinned at Tag through a blur of tears. He smiled back, his eyes overly bright and sparkling with relief. Tag held the bottle while the colt got the hang of things. Within minutes, the tiny black whisk-broom of a tail was wagging back and forth in time with the loud slurping noises coming from the other end.

The baby emptied the bottle, looked around for more and snorted. Tag brushed back the bristly forelock between the colt's stiff black ears, exposing a perfect white star, the only mark the animal carried.

"I was going to ask you if you wanted to name him, but it seems almost too obvious," Tag said. "What do you think?"

"I think Star probably needs a nap," Lee said, covering the burlap bags with the warm blanket just as the colt's skinny legs folded and collapsed underneath him.

"Good timing." Tag knelt down and stroked the soft neck, then pulled an edge of the blanket up to cover the baby's flanks. "I guess I'll take care of the others. Can you keep an eye on this little guy?"

"You're kidding, right? I can hardly take my eyes off him." Lee covered Tag's hand with her own. "I've never had an experience like this, ever. You seem to take it all in stride, but I feel as if I've witnessed something so special today..."

"Birth...and death, are always special." Tag turned away and stared in the direction of the lowering sun. "You were more than a witness, you know. I appreciate your help, Lee. You didn't panic. You did everything I asked. This little guy might not have made it if you hadn't been there. I'm..."

He turned back toward Lee. His expression was unreadable, angry, if anything, his dark eyebrows bunched together in a slight frown. "I'm glad you came," he said. "Thank you."

Before Lee could respond, Tag abruptly stood up and headed for the corral. For a guy who said he was glad she had come along, he certainly didn't act very happy to have her around. Lee shivered, more a nervous reaction than anything else. What had she done to make him so angry?

One more thing to wonder about. She folded her legs and sat quietly next to the sleeping foal. Too many questions, she thought. Too many questions and never enough answers.

TAG SLIPPED the saddle and blanket off of Chief's broad back, then repeated the procedure with Daisy. Both horses snorted, but where Daisy merely shook her dainty frame, Chief spun around and went down in the soft grass, rolling completely over to rub his back. He snorted again, waved his long legs in the air, then rolled back over, lurched to his feet and shook like an oversized dog.

Tag grabbed the curry comb and brush out of the tool box near the gate and started on Daisy. He'd always loved working on the horses after a long ride. It was a quiet chore, one that gave him time to think, time to work out the problems of the day.

Why, though, with all the problems facing him right now, could he think of nothing but Lee? He'd meant every word of what he said to her, even though it scared the hell out of him to admit to any woman he'd actually needed her help.

But she had helped. She'd been there for him, was still there for him, patient, helpful, smiling. Even though Tag knew she was confused. He knew this little jaunt today had convinced both of them that they didn't have a clue to her real identity.

Riding a horse had to be like riding a bike. Something you never forgot, no matter what. Lee Stetson obviously hadn't ever ridden a horse in her life. She'd never witnessed the birth of a foal, never seen the beautiful Colorado mountains.

Who the hell was she?

For all Tag knew, Lee Stetson had a husband somewhere. And as naturally good and gentle as she was with the foal, she might even have children.

Tag didn't think he could handle that. Another man...maybe. All he had to do was look at a guy as a competitor for his lady's hand.

Children were another matter altogether. Tag couldn't possibly do anything that would break up a home where children were involved. He'd grown up in a broken home.

It wasn't a good way to raise a child.

He swept the brush down Daisy's long back, watching the late afternoon sunlight play across the mare's sorrel hide. The deep reddish coat was almost the same color as Lee's hair, maybe a little lighter than his lady's rich, auburn tones.

His lady. Now when had he started thinking of Lee as his lady? He'd have to stop that nonsense, right now. The whole point of this charade was to save him from marriage. The last thing he needed was to start thinking of some little gal as his lady.

Tag patted Daisy on the rump and whistled to Chief. The big roan was patiently waiting his turn, but he nipped at the little mare as she trotted by.

"Reminding her who's boss, 'eh big guy?" Tag brushed and curried the horse then put the equipment back in the storage box. Long shadows stretched across the meadow and the air already had a nip to it. Time he started thinking about building a fire, setting up camp.

"Tag?"

He spun around. Lee stood on the other side of the fence, next to the saddles.

"Sorry. I didn't mean to startle you," she said. "I wanted my saddlebags. It's getting dark and..."

"I was just bringing them in." He vaulted the fence, surprised when Lee backed off, away from him. He frowned. "Is everything okay?"

She drew her dark brows together as she watched him, wary, like a filly about to bolt. "Yes. Why?" she asked.

"No reason." Tag slung the saddle bags over his shoulder, grabbed the insulated pack filled with food and led the way to the cabin. Star was awake, barely. His nose rested on one shiny hoof and his eyes were half closed. Lee had grabbed another blanket and covered him so that only his head and neck and tiny front feet were visible.

"I'll get a fire going and we'll move him inside," Tag said. "The shack's pretty primitive, but keeps the heat in and the critters out."

"Critters? What kind of critters?" Suddenly Lee was much closer, the wary look replaced with one of outright concern.

"Oh, the usual," Tag said. He dropped the saddlebags on the floor and scrounged through the wood box for some old newspaper and kindling.

"Tag?"

"Possums, skunks, raccoons..." He let the sentence dangle.

"And...?"

Tag bit his cheek to keep from grinning. "Bobcats," he said. "Mountain lions...bears..."

"Why did I know you were going to say that?" Lee folded her arms across her chest and shivered. The cabin hardly looked strong enough to keep out a rabbit, much less a hungry bear. It was small, maybe ten by twelve feet square, with storage boxes and a small woodstove, no running water and light from one small window.

She'd found a kerosene lantern, but wasn't quite sure how to light it and the bathroom facilities left much to be desired. She'd discovered the "one holer" behind the cabin. The only thing good she could say about it was that the inside appeared to be free of spiders and there'd been a roll of tissue handy.

Not quite the vacation she'd imagined.

Vacation? Now where did that come from? If only she could remember!

"Maybe because you want to think the worst of me," Tag said.

The fragment of memory fled. Lee sighed. "What?" she asked.

"You said you expected me to say that," Tag repeated. "I think it's because you want to think the worst of me."

Lee shook her head in denial. "That's not it at all."

"Are you okay?" Tag brushed the dust off his hands and stood up. The small fire he'd built was already warming the cabin.

"I'm fine," Lee said. "For a minute there, I thought I remembered..."

"What?"

She laughed. "I don't remember."

"C'mon, then. Let's get Star settled inside and figure out something for dinner." He headed for the door.

"Tag?"

He turned around.

"I'm sorry, really. I wish I knew who I was. I'm sorry I got you into this mess."

Tag shoved his hat back on his head, then took it off and stared at the crown. When he raised his head, the look on his face was one of tender regret. "Lee," he said, "the only mess I'm in is one of my own making. Nothing here is your fault. If anyone should do any blaming, it's you. Coop and I literally dragged you off the road and tossed you into our own stupid scheme. I never intended..."

"I know," she said, wishing things were different, wishing she knew. "Get Star. I'll see what's packed for dinner."

Tag studied her a moment longer, then shoved his hat back on his head and went outside.

Lee held her breath. There'd been such a look of longing in his eyes it made her stomach clench. He wanted her. He didn't know a thing for certain about her, but he wanted her.

Lord only knew, she wanted him just as much. More maybe.

But wanting and having were two different things altogether. How could she possibly give herself to Tag, until she knew her identity?

How could she admit the feelings growing stronger by the moment until she was certain she was free?

Lee stretched her arms over her head, reached down and tried to touch her toes, gave up on that fruitless maneuver and yawned. Exhaustion filled her, heart and soul, but she knew she could only blame part of it on the day's ride.

Sighing, she reached for the insulated food bag Gramma Lenore had packed for Tag, slid the pouches and containers of sliced meats and salads out on the table and sighed again. The sigh evolved into a yawn. She stared blankly at the food.

Dinner she could handle. Her attraction to Tag was something else altogether.

His footsteps sounded just outside the door.

Lee's heart pounded an erratic welcome.

It was going to be a very long night.

Chapter 9

GROANING, LEE stretched and rolled over, then blinked awake in surprise. Daylight filtered through the cabin's one small window. She'd slept the whole night through! If she'd had any doubts, the pressure points on her hip and shoulder would attest to the fact she'd barely moved all night long.

She was well aware she'd just had another new experience. No one, under any circumstances, could forget a night sleeping in a bedroll on a cold, hard, wooden floor.

Sleeping alone, while the sexiest cowboy alive slept in a similar bedroll not three feet away. She'd thought last night would be awkward, both of them so overly aware of one another, so attuned, each to the others' presence, but as it turned out Lee'd been so exhausted after her long day she'd been in her bedroll, asleep shortly after dinner.

She imagined Tag hadn't stayed awake much longer. Lee shoved her hair out of her eyes and studied the motionless pile of blankets next to hers. Had he already gotten up?

Tag's bedroll suddenly shifted and turned and a well-muscled arm slipped out from under the covers as Tag rolled over on his side. Lee swallowed, painfully aware of his proximity, of his bare shoulder, the tousled mop of dark hair flattened on one side, the sleepy, midnight eyes beginning to focus on her face, the slow, lazy smile that turned her heart to mush.

She couldn't possibly have known him for a mere two nights and days, not and have these feelings, this desire, raging through her. She had to have known him before, wanted him at some time in what, she now tentatively referred to, as *life before.*

Before what?

"Mornin'." Tag rubbed his hand over his jaw, then propped himself up on one elbow. The blanket fell away, baring his torso. "You sleep okay?"

Lee watched as he ran his long fingers across his chest in an absentminded gesture, then reached up and shoved the unruly dark hair back from his forehead. The rugged shadow of two day's growth of beard covered his jaw...he hadn't taken time to shave yesterday, either. The effect on Lee's libido was, to say the least, interesting.

In spite of her blisters, she clenched her hands into tight fists. The urge to run her fingers through Tag's hair was almost more than she could stand. The thought of that whiskered chin abrading her breasts and belly sent her heart rate into overdrive. She took a deep swallow and tried to remember his question.

"Yeah," she said. "I can't believe I slept all night. I thought Star would wake us up at some point."

"I got up and fed him around three," Tag said. He sat up and stretched. The blankets slipped down to pool around his hips. As far as Lee could tell, he wasn't wearing a thing.

Not even a pair of those plaid boxer shorts he seemed to like.

Tag twisted to his left, then his right. The lean muscles across his back and shoulders swelled and rippled. When he bent forward to grab his toes through the blankets and stretch, Lee focused on the long line of flesh he exposed from shoulder to thigh.

His upper body was tanned to a deep bronze, a stark contrast to the fair skin at his waistline. A smattering of dark hair began on his thigh just below his hip and disappeared beneath the heavy blanket. Tag bent himself almost double, effortlessly working out the kinks. His muscles rippled and bunched.

There was no doubt in her mind...the man had a perfect body. Lee bit her lips. This time her swallow resembled a gulp, plainly audible in the small cabin. Tag peeked at her from under his outstretched arm and winked.

Damn him! And he'd been such a gentleman last night! Lee stood up with the blanket wrapped firmly around her body from throat to toes. "I'm going to use the facilities," she muttered. "Please have some clothes on when I return."

"Yes ma'am," Tag replied. Lee thought he looked as if he were trying to chew a hole in his cheek.

At least he didn't start laughing until she closed the door behind her, but it didn't help much. She could still hear him as she walked barefoot down the icy trail.

An hour later Lee settled her tender bottom on Daisy's saddle while Tag adjusted the colt as comfortably as he could in front of him on Chief. The sun was barely peeking over the tree covered ridge when they started the slow trip back to the Double Eagle.

As stiff and sore as Lee felt, she almost didn't mind the fact Tag had decided not to bring her back up for the round-up.

Almost. She hadn't questioned his decision. From the bleak look in his eyes when he'd told her she'd be staying at the Double Eagle with Gramma Lenore, she figured it hadn't been an easy decision for him.

Nor was it one she was willing to countermand. Not this time. He'd said Coop was too valuable during round-up to stay behind. Someone needed to be at the ranch to help care for Star and keep an eye on Gramma Lenore.

Lee knew that was just an excuse. If Tag's libido was as overtaxed as hers, and with him feeling as strongly about not getting seriously involved with anyone as Lee felt about knowing her past before she could, it was the only sensible thing.

But did she really want to be sensible? Especially around a cowboy as good looking, as tough and tender, as Tag Martin?

Lee watched as he shifted Star in his grasp, balancing the skinny little colt more comfortably. Tag's strong arms made the juggling act look effortless.

She really had to quit thinking about those arms...and everything else connected to the man's body. If only she could reconcile her disjointed memories of a past with the graphic images of the present!

"Is it hard to foster a colt?" she asked, forcibly shifting her thought processes. Tag had mentioned an old brood mare of Coop's he hoped would accept the orphan. He'd explained how the mare had nursed a neighbor's orphaned mule without complaint.

"Sometimes, but this old gal is so gentle, I think it'll work. She's got a filly due to wean, so she's still got milk. Star'll be a lot healthier with the real thing." Tag shifted in his saddle to look back at Lee. "We keep feeding him calf milk replacer, he'll grow up and think he's a cow."

"Really?" It didn't sound right, but what did she know?

Tag's disgusted snort told her she didn't know much. "I keep forgetting you can't remember what you never knew in the first place. Anything else come back to you?"

"No," she said. "Nothing at all." But it would, she promised herself. It had to.

LEE DISMOUNTED first and reached for the tiny colt. He was much heavier than he looked, but she was able to lower him gently to the ground when Tag put him in her arms.

"Go tell Gramma Lenore we're back early," Tag said, swinging his leg over the saddle and sliding off Chief's back. "I'll find Coop. He's gonna have to help me with Star."

Tag picked up the spindly-legged colt and headed for the bunkhouse, followed by a pack of mismatched mutts, all barking and yapping greetings. Lee grabbed the reins for both the horses and led them into a small fenced enclosure. She removed their headstalls, loosened the cinches on the saddles and turned Chief and Daisy loose in the holding corral. Carefully latching the gate behind her, she headed for the house.

For once, Tag hadn't had to give her instructions. Lee couldn't hold back the grin that spread across her face—she'd actually managed to do the right thing on her own. Well, she'd come here to learn about horses and cowboys, hadn't she? Obviously, she was learning.

Her grin faded. She came to a complete halt in the middle of the driveway. Where did that come from? For what reason could she possibly want to learn about cowboys?

Why couldn't she remember? She stared at the shiny new roof on the barn, an oddly familiar image, and waited a moment for inspiration, a memory, even a hint of a memory, about cowboys.

Nothing.

Still pondering her odd flashes of recognition, Lee continued on to the house and stepped into the cheery kitchen.

Where she caught Coop and Lenore, sharing breakfast in their bathrobes.

Once again, Lee stopped in her tracks. Tag, charging through the door behind her, practically knocked her over.

"Coop's not in his room," he said. "No one's seen him since yesterday afternoon. We've gotta..."

"Mornin' Lee, Tag." Lenore's smile looked slightly strained.

Coop's greeting sounded belligerent and a bit more to the point. "You weren't due home until tomorrow," he said, half rising from his chair. "You said you'd be at the line shack for two nights."

"Well, it's a good thing I decided to come home, old man. What are you doing in here with my grandmother?"

"Tag?" Lee grabbed his wrist and squeezed a warning.

Tag stiffened beside her.

"He's doing what he should have done years ago," Lenore said. She stood up and moved behind Coop, then gently shoved him back into his chair with a firm grip on his shoulders. "More important, what we're doing is none of your business, Taggart Martin. We're both adults. And since we're doing what we're doing in my house, I would suggest you watch your tone of voice."

"It always comes down to that, doesn't it?" Tag's bitter reply startled Lee. He yanked his arm free of her grasp. "The Double Eagle might be your ranch, Grandmother, but until you fire me, I'm the manager. Coop works for me and he's needed in the foaling barn."

Tag spun around and slammed out of the kitchen. Lee watched his angry retreat, then turned to Lenore for answers. The older woman appeared to have aged years in a matter of moments.

Then Coop reached up and covered her hand with his. Lenore smiled, leaned over and kissed the top of his balding head.

"He'll get over it, sweetheart. He always does," Coop growled. "Now, missy, what's the problem in the foaling barn? We haven't got anyone due."

Lee cleared her throat. "Um, Tag and I rescued a baby horse yesterday." She immediately corrected herself. "A, um, foal, I mean. A boy, er, a colt. I think Tag wants to try putting him with one of your mares."

"Well, in that case, the boy needs me. I better go get some clothes on." He stood up, kissed Lenore with enough intensity to make Lee blush, tipped an imaginary hat and headed back to the bedroom.

Lee almost giggled at the besotted look on Lenore's face.

"My goodness." Lenore fanned herself with widespread fingers. "That old cowboy can kiss."

TAG WANTED to kick something, or at least put his fist through a wall. Instead, he counted to ten in Spanish, then in French and again in Portuguese. He was working his way through the numbers in German when Coop marched into the barn.

"Don't you ever, ever talk to your grandmother in that tone of voice again, young man, or I swear I'll beat the living tar outta ya."

"Excuse me," Tag muttered. "Did I miss something here? You're in there, fornicating with my grandmother..."

"Watch your mouth. What your grandmother and I do is none of your business. We're both adults, if you hadn't noticed."

"How long has this been going on? Answer me that." Tag glared down at the old cowboy, his fists clenched, aware of a rage boiling through him totally out of proportion to the circumstances.

"Not long enough," Coop said. "Not nearly long enough." He

smiled sadly at Tag, a look of bittersweet joy so heartrending Tag's anger escaped in a breath.

"I've loved your grandmother for as long as I can remember," Coop said. "Like a damn fool, I've wasted more years than you've lived. I'm not gonna waste another minute. Now, I think you owe that fine lady an apology, don't you?"

"Coop, I'm sorry. I just...everything's changing, you know?" Tag ran his hand over his eyes and took a deep breath. "Sometimes I feel like it's all running out of control." He gestured, pointlessly, aimlessly, trying to find the words.

Why did he always have so damned much trouble finding the right words? "I know about Gramma, Coop. Lee told me. Do you know how long...?

Coop seemed to crumple a bit as he leaned against the neatly stacked bales of hay. His blue eyes misted, whether from age or emotion Tag couldn't tell. Coop brushed his hand across his forehead, dislodging his battered Stetson with the motion, then grabbed a clean handkerchief out of his pocket and blew his nose. "I'm glad you know. She made me promise not to tell you, but that's not news she should keep from kin. I don't know any details, son, only that she's dyin'. Doesn't seem fair to ask her more than she wants to tell, ya know?"

"I know, Coop. Don't let her know I found out. Let her have her way in this."

"Hell, boy, she's gonna have her way no matter what. She al'as has." Coop blew his nose again, then straightened his hat. "One good thing, in a way. Knowing her days are numbered, well, it gave me the courage to say some things, do some things I should have done years ago."

"What's that?"

Coop flashed a cocky grin at Tag and stuffed his handkerchief back in his pocket. "I told your grandmother I love her, told her I always have and I will till her dyin' day. Then I spent the night in her bed. That woman..."

"Don't go there, Coop. Please?"

Coop pushed himself away from the piled bales. "I'm a bit mature for you to be givin' me orders about where I spend my nights, boy."

"No, no, no, no, no," Tag pleaded. Lord, his skin felt hot. He hadn't blushed in years! "When I said 'don't go there,' I meant don't tell me...please? You're right. You and Gramma Lenore are both mature, responsible adults...but I don't want the details, okay?" The image of his grandmother and Coop, well...no, he didn't want to think about it.

Coop's understanding chuckle cleared the air, enough so that Tag suddenly remembered why he'd come home in the first place.

He carefully blanked his mind of everything else. Some day, maybe, he'd be able to tell Lee about this conversation. She was bound to see the humor in it. "C'mon," he said, heading across the barn. "I've got a hungry little colt over here in the pen. I thought maybe we could foster him with Goldie, if you don't mind."

"Changin' the subject ain't gonna make it go away, son." Coop's gentle touch on his wrist brought Tag to a sudden halt.

"I know, Coop." Tag slipped his arm over the old cowboy's shoulder. "Lee told me there was something between you and Gramma. I didn't believe her. Guess I shoulda listened, huh?"

"You know how it is with women, son."

"No, Coop. I don't think I do." Tag laughed and led Coop over to the stall where he'd left Star. The little colt was on his feet, searching for the bottle. "I know horses and I know cows, but there's a lot about women I guess I need to learn."

"Well, at least you know ya gotta learn it. That's a start." Coop ignored the colt and stared at Tag. Suddenly he grinned and punched Tag lightly on the shoulder. "All this talk about women. Could there be something more than a business deal happenin' between you and your bride?"

"Don't go there either, old man," Tag said, shaking his head in denial. "I've got enough to worry about without you confusing the issue any more than it already is. C'mon, I want you to take a look at this little guy and tell me what you think."

Coop coughed as if to clear his throat, then opened the gate and stepped into the pen. He ran his hands lightly over the colt's flanks and chest. "He's a beaut. I think Goldie'll take to him just fine. Any mare that'll nurse one o' them ugly baby mules shouldn't mind another little horse."

"Don't tell Goldie you think her little mule baby was ugly. She'd never forgive you." Coop laughed and Tag breathed a deep sigh of relief. For now, anyway, some of his world was back to normal.

LENORE, DRESSED and ready for the day as if nothing out of the ordinary had occurred, waited in the kitchen with a cup of hot tea and a platter of cookies when Lee, wrapped in the faded blue terry cloth robe, returned from her shower.

Lee took a bite out of one of the cookies, savoring the buttery almond flavor. She wondered if she'd eaten these before, if someone else had ever waited for her with a tray of cookies.

She didn't think her mother liked to bake, but she couldn't be sure. She couldn't be sure of anything.

Except the fact that Lenore Martin had finally found true love with Coop. "I wasn't surprised to see you and Coop together this morning," she said. "But I think you shocked Tag's socks off."

"He'll come around," Lenore said. "Taggart is stubborn and hard headed as they come, but he's always been a good and loving grandson. Besides, he loves Coop as if that old geezer was his father. He'll come around," she repeated.

"He loves you both," Lee said. She covered Lenore's hand with her own. "He said Coop was more a father to him than his real one and you more a mother."

"He had a rough start, but he's a good boy." Lenore slipped her hand free of Lee's and grabbed a tissue out of her pocket. "I am so glad he's found you, Lee. Tag's lived a lonely life, but with you as his bride...well."

"Do you think he loves me?" Now where did that come from?

"Of course he does, dear. He married you, didn't he?"

Lee gulped. She'd forgotten again...not her past this time, but her present. It was so easy to believe Tag felt something for her, something more than whatever it was they supposedly had!

"He just seems so, well, preoccupied," she prevaricated. The whole point of this charade was to make Lenore think the marriage was real. She'd have to watch herself.

"It's that time of year," Lenore said, as if Lee knew what she meant. When Lee didn't respond, Lenore explained impatiently. "He should be up in the summer range with his crew right now, rounding up the herd, doctoring whatever needs to be doctored, vaccinating, castrating, dehorning..." Lenore's hands fluttered. "Well you know, doing everything you do during spring round-up. It's a busy time of year, Lee. That's why I was so shocked you two chose now to get married."

"It was time for us, I guess," Lee answered inanely.

"Which reminds me," Lenore said. "Why did you come back so soon? You were supposed to be up there getting everything ready for the crew. You can't possibly have finished."

"Go on out to the barn," Lee said, rising to her feet. "Let Tag show you why we had to come home. And," she added, "why I'm not going back up with him."

"You're not?" Lenore stood as well and patted Lee's hand. "The air just sizzles when you and that boy are near each other," she said, winking slyly at Lee. "If you've got any doubt about his feelings for you, then maybe you need to take a more active role in this marriage. He can't make you stay here at the ranch. Don't waste the sizzle, sweetie. Take if from one who knows."

Lee watched the door swing shut behind Lenore. She'd felt the sizzle between Lenore and Coop that very first day. Sizzle that had obviously lasted for close to sixty years.

Did she and Tag really have that? How would she know? Lee headed down the hallway to her room, contemplating the power of sizzle. Wondering if she had it with someone else. She and Tag had something, but whatever it was, spending time alone together could only make this whole complicated mess more convoluted and confusing than ever.

The phone in the living room detoured her. She grabbed the receiver on the second ring. "Double Eagle Ranch, Lee speaking," she said.

The voice on the other end was vaguely familiar. Suddenly she recognized Will Twigg, Tag's neighbor. They'd never met, but he'd dropped a sizable bombshell on her the day of the wedding.

It felt as if he might be dropping another. She wrote his message for Coop and Tag out on the notepad next to the phone. As Lee wrote, she realized her fingers were shaking. Why should news of the discovery of a partially submerged car in the river unsettle her so?

More important, who was Rhonda?

Maybe it would come to her along with the rest of her memories one of these days. She tucked the message in her pocket, grabbed a magazine off the coffee table and headed for her room. Tag had said he wouldn't head back up the hill until late this afternoon. With any luck and a good, boring story, Lee figured she could at least get an hour's nap before she figured out whether she was going to do the sensible thing and stay behind, or pack her bags and go for the sizzle.

"REMINDS ME of the day Coop showed up with Dandy." Lenore stroked the colt's velvety black nose with one hand and scratched under the mare's pale gold chin with the other. "I'm so glad Goldie accepted him...there's no little boy here anymore who needs a 4-H project. 'Course, now that little boy's got himself a wife, maybe..." She grinned at Tag, her blue eyes full of mischief.

"Give us time, Gramma." Damn if he wasn't blushing again, but the sudden image of Lee, round with his child...Tag caught Coop's eye. It looked like time for another change in plans. "If it weren't that Lee's planning to go with me on the round-up, I'd turn Star's care over to her," Tag said. "As it is, I wondered if you and Coop wouldn't mind keeping an eye on things?"

"Why, I'll be up the hill with you, boy. Have to get the men going at dawn, what with all we've got to do."

"I was kind of hoping you'd let Ramón handle the job," Tag said, referring to one of the more responsible, but younger cowhands. "I hate to leave Gramma here by herself."

"Why, Tag that's ridiculous," Lenore sputtered. "I'm perfectly capable of taking care of myself. Besides, Lee already told me you wanted her to stay here."

Tag glanced at Coop and caught the grateful look of understanding the older man returned. He hoped Coop realized the reason behind his sudden shift in priorities. "I changed my mind, Gramma. I'm a newlywed, remember. I want my bride with me, not here with you filling her head full of lies about me."

Coop smiled and wrapped his arms loosely around Lenore. "The boy's right, woman. He should have his wife at his side. Besides, a sweet, fragile little thing like yourself, why you need a real man around to keep you safe." He kissed her on the cheek. She blushed a deep shade of pink.

How could he have ever missed the love between these two? Tag removed his hat and held it loosely in front of him. He studied the brim a moment, then looked directly into his grandmother's eyes. "I'm sorry Gramma. I shouldn't have said what I did this morning. I was out of line and I want to apologize. I can't think of any two people I'd like to see together more than you and this old bum...it's just," he grinned broadly. "Gramma, I thought you had better taste!"

They were still laughing when Lee entered the barn. Tag felt her presence before he actually saw her, another phenomenon he figured he'd adjust to sooner or later. She wore his father's faded blue terry-cloth bathrobe again. He'd never thought of that particular piece of clothing as sexy, not in his wildest dreams.

Until Lee Stetson wrapped it around her slender frame. She

paused in the doorway, her stance restless and uneasy. "Hi, Hon," he said, as surprised at the ease with which the endearment slipped out as Lee seemed to be to hear it. "Come see how Star's taking to the real thing."

He stepped to one side to give Lee a better look at the little colt and dropped his arm comfortably around her shoulders. She tensed, then relaxed against him.

Star suckled greedily from the placid palomino mare, his whisk broom of a tail snapping back and forth like a flag in a brisk breeze.

"They don't seem to have any problem at all," Lee said. "Guess we won't have to worry about him thinking he's a calf." Tag felt her arm slip around his waist and squeeze. "I took a call from Will Twigg. He said there's a car submerged in the river, just above the fork..." She looked questioningly at Tag. "I assume you know what fork he means?"

"Yeah," Tag said. "Whose car?"

"He didn't say. Just that he wondered if you could bring Rhonda?" There was an obvious question in her voice...and maybe a hint of jealousy?

"If Rhonda's not busy, she'll be happy to oblige. She's a real obliging girl, our Rhonda." He was almost afraid to look at Lee's face, but he couldn't help himself.

Yep, she looked jealous. Now why should that make him feel so good?

"Quit teasin' your bride, Tag," Coop said. He turned to Lee. "Rhonda's the tractor. Tag named her after some dumb song...you know, 'help me Rhonda, help, help me Rhonda?' Never could make sense of it."

Coop clapped his hat against his leg then stuck it back on his head. "I'll call Will and tell him I'll bring her over. Since I'm not going to be needed elsewhere." He winked at Lenore.

"Oh, you'll be needed, old man," she said. Lenore's wink was aimed at Lee. "I better get in and start packing some grub for you two. I also need to keep an eye on a certain old cowboy."

Tag watched his grandmother walk to the house. There was a new bounce to her step, a swish to her hips he'd never noticed before. Is that what love does? he wondered.

One thing for sure, when Lee said those two had sizzle, she hadn't been kidding. Tag thought he still sensed the sparks that flew between his grandmother and Coop.

Or was that something happening between himself and the woman leaning against his side? "What's wrong?" he asked, tipping her chin up so he could see her eyes.

Damn, he could drown in those eyes, those deep green pools that let a man look right into her soul. If they didn't look so forlorn right now, he'd kiss each one, then her lips, maybe trace that tender skin along the column of her throat, maybe....

She stiffened against him, then stepped away. "First of all, it sounds like you've changed plans again without telling me. I wish you'd stop doing that. I don't think it's a good idea for me to go on the round-up with you."

"Now, Lee. We can talk about that..."

"Tag, I've never been here before. I've never seen you before. I know now why you and the Double Eagle looked so familiar to me."

"What made you come up with all that?" He didn't want to patronize her, but they'd already figured she didn't have a clue about barrel racing, though as quick as she took to ranch life, Tag had wondered if she might be involved in the business end of raising cattle.

"What made me come up with all that," Lee wrapped her arms protectively around her middle, "was the issue of Western_Horseman I found in a stack of magazines on the coffee table. I must have read that story about you and the Double Eagle. Every memory I have of you and this ranch, every visual image I see, they're all in that magazine. Even Betsy Mae's pictures, smiling at the camera, barrel racing on her horse...Tag, don't you understand? The few memories I was certain of, they're all from some dumb magazine article! Even the first memories I recall, about getting dumped on my butt but getting up to ride again? They're a direct quote from Betsy Mae!"

"What's it matter?" Tag gave into the impulse. He pulled Lee back into his arms and kissed her lips. Softly, just a taste right now. He was pleased as punch when she unfolded her arms from around her own waist, encircled his and kissed him back.

"You probably read that magazine right before you got that bump on your noggin and lost your memory. That just reinforces the fact, in my mind, that maybe you're somehow involved in the cattle industry or ranching. Why else would you have been reading Western Horseman? What else would you be doing up here in cattle country? Think about it, Lee. We know your memories are all mixed up, but they'll come back. And I don't honestly see you being a different person than you are now. You'll just know more about your past. Trust me on this."

"But don't you understand?" Lee stepped back, once again pulling herself out of his embrace. "Every time I think I know something about myself is true, I find out it isn't! I thought I was a barrel racer...obviously I'm not. I thought I was at least a cowgirl, but we know that's not true either. The one thing I could hold on to was the fact I knew you from somewhere even if you didn't remember me, the ranch looked familiar, there was something here I could count on."

Tears streamed down her cheeks. Tag cupped her chin in his palms and brushed the moisture away with his thumbs. "You know you can count on me, Lee. I won't hurt you."

"But can you count on me? I don't know who I am, Tag. I get fragments of knowledge, the stuff of dreams and disjointed musings, but nothing real. Then to find out my memories are the result of photos in a magazine...Tag, it's just too much."

Tag took her hands in his. She grimaced as if in pain and he turned them over. Torn blisters from the leather reins marred both palms. She'd never complained...not a word. He lifted both her hands to his lips and kissed them.

"I'm so sorry sweetheart. Why didn't you say something? You need some bandages on these and a pair of gloves." He folded Lee back into his arms, tucking her head just under his chin. Her hair smelled clean and lemony and her body fit just perfectly against his. He imagined they'd fit perfectly doing a lot of things and he stirred, immediately aroused by the images exploding in his brain.

Lee sniffed. Tag nuzzled her soft hair and grinned. She hadn't a clue as to what he was thinking, thank goodness, she was so caught up worrying about that dumb magazine article.

Well, he'd give her something else to think about. "About the round-up," he said, tilting Lee's chin up with his fingers. "I got to thinking how Gramma may not have all that much time left and here she and Coop have just discovered how they feel about each other. Well, it just doesn't seem fair to separate them right now. We're both adults. We know our relationship is a temporary thing. We're not looking at a future together, but that's by choice. Gramma and Coop don't have any choice, not with her dyin' and all..."

Tears streamed once more down Lee's cheeks. She must be as moved by Coop and Gramma Lenore's ill-fated love as he was. "I knew you'd understand," Tag whispered. He kissed away the salty tears while gently, soothingly, rubbing the tension out of Lee's shoulders. She sighed against him, a sound Tag took for agreement. At least something was going his way.

MAYBE ALL cowboys are insensitive jerks, Lee thought. Was that what she'd come to Colorado to learn? She knew, deep in her heart, this state wasn't her home. Unlike Tag, she wasn't all that quick to assume she knew anything at all about cattle or ranching or the Great American West.

She did know she must be some kind of idiot. Why else would she be falling in love with a man she'd only known for three days, a man who didn't have a clue what was going on in a woman's mind...or heart? What other reason could there be?

Sure, he was strong and handsome, he loved his ranch and his animals, he was, mostly, good to his grandmother and he obviously thought the world of his crusty old foreman. He'd kissed Lee's blisters as if he truly cared how much they hurt.

Tag's arms tightened around her. Automatically her heart responded and she pressed her tear-dampened face against his warm, muscular chest. Only an idiot would allow herself to be lulled into comfort in this man's arms.

After all, he'd admitted from the beginning he never intended to marry. It shouldn't hurt so much, hearing him repeat the fact their relationship was a temporary thing, that they had no future. Lee knew some of the reasons Tag feared commitment. Maybe, once she learned all the reasons, her own feelings would make sense.

"I need to go talk to Coop before he heads over to help Will," Tag said. "You get your things packed, see if you can borrow some gloves from Gramma to protect your hands. Meet me out here..." He glanced at his wristwatch. "About four. That'll get us out of here by five and up the hill before dark. Okay?"

Sighing, weary and sore in every muscle and sinew, Lee nodded against Tag's chest in agreement. She slipped out of his embrace and headed back to the house for her things. What was the point of arguing? He wouldn't listen anyway.

He'd said to plan on being gone for about two weeks. She tried to imagine what could happen over the next two weeks, considering the myriad directions her life had gone in a mere three days.

Two weeks with Tag and a whole crew of cowboys. Cowboys who thought the two of them were married...which meant they'd have to act married.

Suddenly Lee's mood shifted and she grinned to herself, considering the possibilities. Tag did have a lot of good points, she had to admit. At least this would give her the chance to get to know him better, in his natural environment.

And, just maybe, it would give Tag a chance to get past his fear of commitment, a chance to consider a few other options in his life. Maybe, once he spent some quality time with Lee, he'd decide he couldn't survive without a certain befuddled redhead.

It was the befuddled part that had her concerned. The vague memories of life in New York, of a handsome blond man with pale blue eyes. If only she knew how he fit into her past.

She touched her lips with the tips of her fingers, remembering Tag's kiss. She knew she'd never been kissed like that in her entire life, knew she could never accept anything less than the passion she felt with Tag. Which made it fairly easy to dismiss the threat of the blond stranger.

Lee felt as if she'd stepped right into the plot of a western romance. Her life had never been so exciting, she'd never felt so alive. Now she was going on a round-up. It might even be fun.

Of course it would be fun. A round-up couldn't be all that difficult, could it?

Chapter 10

JUST BEFORE four in the afternoon, Lee stood outside the corral and watched while Tag struggled to saddle a restless horse. The animal skittered and shied away, threw its head back and snorted. Tag moved slowly around the enormous white beast, his motions calm and unhurried, stroking and soothing the animal until it finally stilled and watched him with wide, anxious eyes.

Lee let out a huge breath, unaware until then she'd been holding it. "You're not going to ride that thing, are you?" she asked.

Tag turned to her and grinned. "Of course I am. He's just a bit frisky, is all. What do ya think?" He stroked the horse's long white mane with obvious pride. "I've only had him a couple of weeks, but he's settled down just fine."

"He looks dangerous." Lee backed away from the fence as Tag led the horse closer. "And hungry."

"Horses aren't carnivores, Hon. They eat oats and hay, not beautiful women." Tag readjusted the worn leather saddle on the animal's broad back, acting as if the fact he'd just called her Hon and said he thought she was beautiful meant nothing.

Maybe it didn't mean a thing, to Tag at least. "I'm all packed," Lee said, exhaling a frustrated breath. She stretched her arms over her head and wondered if her body would ever be the same. "Do you realize I've only known you for three days and we've been up and down that mountain every single one of them?"

Tag straightened up and stared at her. "And your point is?"

"Never mind." Obviously she still had a lot to learn about cowboys. "When are we leaving?"

"Soon as I get this fella ready." The big white horse looked resigned to his fate. He cocked one hip and lowered his eyelids until he appeared half asleep.

Lee knew appearances could be deceiving. She figured he was just waiting to strike. "He's a lot bigger than Chief, isn't he?" She tried to sound as if she really cared. This monster wasn't nearly as cute as Star or as lovable as Dandy.

"He's a stud," Tag said, as if that explained everything. "He hasn't been gelded like Chief, so he's developed a thicker neck and broader chest. He's half quarter horse, half Arab, just like Daisy."

"How can he be half a quarter horse?" Lee asked. This horse didn't look like half of anything. He looked more like a whole lot of trouble.

"Quarter horse is a breed, just like Arabians. He's got speed and cow sense from his dam, endurance and heart from his Arab sire. He should be perfect for working cattle in the terrain we've got." Tag grinned, obviously warming to his subject. "He's something new Coop and I decided to try. Most folks around here stick with full-blooded quarter horses, but we both liked a quarter/Arab cross of Will's so much, we decided to try a little horse breeding on our own. We'll put this big fella with Daisy when she's a bit older, see what kind of offspring we get."

"Oh." Lee mentally compared the size of the big white stud with the dainty little mare and shuddered. Then she compared Tag's lean strength and broad shoulders to her own relatively petite frame and a delightful shiver raced along her spine. She studied the white stallion with a new perspective.

He snorted and shook his head as if he knew exactly in what direction her mind was straying. Lee gulped and stepped back from the fence. Tag readjusted the cinch on the saddle and Lee turned her attention to the yard, aware of an increase in activity about her, a sense of expectation. A group of cowhands struggled to load equipment into the back of a flatbed truck and a couple of men herded a small band of horses into one of the corrals.

The sound of a heavy engine starting echoed from the depths of the barn. The roar increased as Coop drove a huge tractor out through the wide double doors. Tag waved to the old man, who tipped his hat before driving down the main road toward the front gate. Lee watched him disappear in a cloud of blue smoke, then leaned down to smooth the worn leather chaps Lenore had insisted she wear.

She adjusted her leather gloves over the fresh bandages on her palms, tilted her hat to keep the sun out of her eyes and turned her attention back to Tag. He was watching her with an odd little half smile on his face.

Just enough of a smile to pop that damned dimple out on his cheek. "What?" Lee asked, wishing he wouldn't look at her like that. It did such strange things to her stomach. "Did I do something stupid again?"

"Never," Tag said. He reached over the top rail of the corral and tilted her chin so that he could see her eyes more clearly. He didn't think he'd ever seen eyes quite that shade of green before. She didn't wear a lick of make-up, not even lipstick, but her lashes were thick and dark, her lips so soft and kissable it was all he could do to stop at just touching her.

Damn she had him confused. His grandmother and Coop weren't helping the situation, either. Especially Coop. He never should have listened to Coop, but he couldn't get the old cowboy's words of advice out of his head. Tag had just wanted to go over some projects here at the ranch before he and Lee left, but his foreman had other ideas. One thing for sure...that old man read way too many romance novels.

Tag splayed his fingers along the edge of Lee's jaw. "It's gettin' late so we need to head out," he said. "Do you think you can hang on to the lead rope and ride Dandy at the same time, or are your hands too sore?"

She blinked, then backed out of his grasp. "Gramma Lenore bandaged my hands and gave me a pair of her gloves. If you tell me what a lead rope is, I guess I can handle it."

"We're gonna pack all our gear for the next couple of weeks on Daisy and Chief. We'll set up a base camp, so once we unload the gear we'll each have two horses. That way we can switch animals when they get tired."

"What about if we get tired? Who's gonna switch with us?"

Tag laughed. She didn't really expect an answer to a dumb question like that, did she?

LEE FELT LIKE her left arm was about ready to detach itself from her shoulder and her palms stung like crazy. She'd been hanging on to the lead rope, hauling the heavily packed Daisy and Chief along behind Dandy for the better part of two hours.

Her butt and lower back hurt too. The insides of her knees were rubbed raw and if it hadn't been for Dandy's placid temperament and easy gait she'd have fallen off long ago.

Tag shouldn't have been having any better time than she was, fighting a constant battle of wills with the flashing white stallion as it pranced and side-stepped every inch of the rocky trail. When Tag told her the horse's name was Nitro, Lee hadn't been the least surprised.

No, he should have been tired and exhausted as well, but instead he appeared to be having the time of his life. The only one in the group who seemed as tired and sore as Lee was the skinny black and white mongrel with one floppy ear that had joined them sometime earlier.

"Are we almost there yet?" Lee asked, giving the mutt trotting alongside her a hopeful look.

"You sound like a little kid in the back seat," Tag said. He shifted around in his saddle. Lee could have hauled off and belted him one. He looked as rested and unruffled as if he'd just begun this endless trip.

Lee knew she looked like hell and smelled like horse. "I'm not a child, Tag. I'm a very tired, hungry, filthy, dirty, adult woman." She carefully enunciated every word. "I meant it when I asked you, are we almost there yet?"

"Yup." He grinned, then hauled back on the reins when Nitro took offense at a rock in the trail, snorted and jumped sideways.

Tag resettled himself with an ease that impressed Lee in spite of her foul mood. "Just through those trees. I thought we'd spend the night at the cabin where we stayed night before last, since it'll be our last chance at running water and indoor plumbing for awhile. The summer range isn't all that far."

Lee urged Dandy forward and tugged the lead rope. The dog grinned up at her, its long pink tongue lolling from his mouth. A bath. That huge, claw-footed tub, filled to the brim with hot water. A real, honest-to-goodness bath. The words filled Lee's mind like a mantra. She figured she could handle just about anything, as long as there was a bath waiting on the other side.

LEE DIDN'T even offer to help unpack the horses. She crawled out of the saddle, grabbed the stirrup for support when her knees buckled, then finally made her wobbly way into the cabin.

She had her chaps off and her shirt unbuttoned before she reached the bathroom. She tossed in some bubble bath while the tub was filling, wondering briefly why cowboys needed bubbles, then slipped into the hot, soothing water.

Lord, what a day. Sleeping on a hard wooden floor, a long ride down the mountain, another long ride up the mountain, and all of that time spent in the company of the sexiest macho jerk she'd ever met.

Why was she so hopelessly attracted to a man who made her crazy? A man willing to carry out a sham marriage to fool an old lady, a man so insensitive he didn't even realize the bride he'd hired was falling in love with him.

Damn. It probably wasn't the smartest move, coming up here with Tag, no matter how important it was to give Lenore and Coop time alone together, no matter how much Lee wanted to be with the man. Didn't Ann Landers constantly caution women about the impossibility of changing a man? The last thing Lee needed was time alone with Tag. It was a recipe for disaster.

Disaster and heartache with a capital H. Lee sighed and dipped her head under the water, then leaned back against the curved end of the tub. She felt the aches and pains of the day easing out of her sore muscles. Even her hands didn't hurt as much. She peeled the dirty bandages off her palms and didn't realize she had company until she glanced up in search of a waste basket.

The black and white mutt sat beside the tub, his chin resting on the chipped porcelain, his mouth open in a doggy grin. The bathroom door was wide open.

He must have pushed it open with that pointy nose of his.

Lee was just rising from the tub to shut the door when Tag walked into the bathroom.

"Oops," he said, backing out. "I didn't realize you were in here. You shoulda shut the door."

Lee slid down in the water until it reached her chin. She tried to place the washcloth and bubbles as strategically as possible. "I did shut the door," she muttered. "Your dumb dog must have opened it."

Tag poked his head back around the corner, grinning. Lee glared at him. "I see you've met Bob the Dog," he said. "I thought I saw him tagging along."

"Bob? That's his name?" She reached one hand out of the water and tentatively stroked the dog's head.

"Bob the Dog's his name," Tag said. He walked boldly into the bathroom and sat down on the lid of the commode. Bob the Dog immediately shifted his loyal gaze to the cowboy and moved closer to have his ears scratched.

Lee sunk a little deeper in the tub and prayed for the bubbles to last.

"Coop wanted Ramón to bob his tail, like he's done with the other ranch dogs. Ramón just didn't have the heart to do it, so he intentionally misunderstood the directions and started calling him Bob the Dog. It stuck, right along with the tail."

As if he knew the punch line of the story, Bob the Dog waved his beautiful long black tail with the white tip. Lee giggled. "He has a very nice tail," she said, but she was looking at Tag.

Who was staring right back at her. The heat in his eyes raised the temperature in the tiny bathroom another ten degrees. "Yes, he does," Tag answered in a husky whisper. "That tub sure looks inviting."

Lee had to agree. "It sure feels good, after that long ride."

"It's probably the biggest bathtub anywhere on the Double Eagle," Tag added.

"You told me, the first night we came up here, it was big enough for a party." Lee slipped to one side to show him just how much room there was.

"I guess I did, didn't I?" He tipped his hat back, as if studying the size of the tub for the first time. "Party of two?"

His voice sounded hopeful. Lee knew hers had a desperate edge to it. She was playing with fire, going against every argument she'd given herself against doing exactly what she knew was going to happen.

The two of them were going to make love. Right here in this big old bathtub with the steam rising off the water and a stupid flop-eared dog as witness.

She shivered, even though the water was definitely warm enough. Why couldn't she remember all the reasons not to get any more involved with this man?

Hadn't she just been going over them, one right after the other? Suddenly her mind blanked. Not only couldn't she remember her past, she was having a terrible time with the past five minutes.

"A bath sure would feel good," Tag said. "After a long day in the saddle, there's nothing better than a long, hot bath." He stood up, his gaze still locked with Lee's, and began to unbutton his shirt. Lee thought about asking him to leave before this went any further, but for some reason her mouth refused to work, her lips wouldn't form the words and the only sound she made was a nervous swallow.

His blue chambray shirt came off, then the cotton undershirt as well. Lee'd seen his chest before. It had the same effect on her libido this time.

Only Tag wasn't stopping at his shirt. He sat back down on the commode and removed his boots and socks, then stood up and unfastened the heavy silver belt buckle. Lee swallowed again and nervously licked her lips.

Tag peeled the worn jeans and plaid boxers down his long legs, but Lee's gaze stopped at the juncture of his thighs. Everything she'd read about cowboys must be true, she thought, almost hysterically. No wonder they made such popular heroes in romances.

Bob the Dog whined, as if sensing the tension filling the room. Tag shooed the reluctant beast out the door, latched it securely behind him, and with one quick step eased himself into the big tub opposite Lee.

The water sloshed over the edge, then the bubbles settled back into place. Lee drew her knees up to her chest, almost preternaturally aware of Tag's long legs stretched out on either side of her. He nonchalantly grabbed a washcloth and began to soap his chest and arms, as casually as if the two of them bathed together on a regular basis. She couldn't take her eyes off the slow, sensual movements of the cloth in Tag's elegant, long-fingered grasp as he slowly dragged it across his chest.

The hair on his calves tickled Lee's hips and she drew her feet back as close to her body as she could. She wasn't quite ready to touch him intimately, especially not with her toes.

Lee looked up, risking eye contact, and giggled. Tag shot her a quizzical glance. She bit her lips together, then lost it.

He frowned and paused, washcloth in one hand, soap in the other. "What?" he asked.

"Do you always bathe with your hat on?" she asked, struggling to control the quiver in her voice.

Tag blushed a deep shade of red and shut his eyes. He tugged the Stetson off his head and tossed it across the room in disgust. It landed in the sink. "Guess I blew the image, huh?"

"You were working on an image?"

"You know, persuasive cowboy, bubble bath, cool, suave approach. Coop had a little talk with me before we came up here." At least Tag had the sense to look embarrassed.

"You're taking lessons from Coop? He must be eighty years old!" Lee didn't even try not to laugh this time. The idea of Tag listening attentively while the old cowboy told him how to finesse a woman was just too much.

"Yeah, well he got the girl, didn't he?" Tag laughed along with her.

"Good Lord, Tag. It took him sixty years. Have you got that much time?"

He stared at her for the longest stretch. Stared until Lee knew she counted each beat of her heart, each breath she took. She and Tag both blinked at precisely the same moment.

"Whatever it takes," he said, reaching for Lee. He tugged gently on her hand and she floated to him in the warm water, finally coming to rest with her back against his chest, his arms comfortably wrapped around her waist.

"I thought you didn't want to get involved," she said, doing her best to ignore Tag's blatant erection against her backside. "Isn't that what this whole fake marriage is about? A temporary relationship to keep your grandmother happy?" She tilted her chin so she could see his face.

He looked as confused as she felt.

"It started out that way," he said. "Maybe it still is that way. I don't know, Lee. Damn." He rubbed her shoulders. "I enjoy being with you...a lot. I want you all the time. It's just, I..."

"Your grandmother told me about your parents," Lee said, interrupting before he said even more to hurt her. "Gramma Lenore said their marriage wasn't very happy."

"My father was a country boy, my mother belonged in the city. She hated it here but Dad would have died if he'd done what she wanted and left the Double Eagle. Instead he stayed and drank himself stupid every night to forget her, but she came back just often enough to remind him of what he couldn't have. Their marriage was a nightmare that never should have happened," Tag said. "So was my grandmother and grandfather's. I grew up hearing my parents argue whenever they were together and listening to my grandfather say terrible, hurtful things to my grandmother. I've never seen a marriage that didn't bring both people misery."

"My parents were happy," Lee said.

"How do you know?" Tag's hands tightened on her shoulders. "You said you can't remember your own name. How can you remember your parents being happy?"

Lee turned around so that she knelt in front of him. The water barely covered her breasts. "I don't know much, but I know that. Tell me, if you've got so many questions about us, if you're so afraid of getting involved with me, why did you take off your clothes and get into this tub? It certainly wasn't because you wanted me to scrub your back now, was it?"

Tag's blue eyes sparkled. "That's not all that bad an idea, Lee. If I just sort of turn around..."

Lee laughed and grabbed the washcloth out of his hand. "I know

I'm willing to take a chance on you, you stubborn lug. Are you willing to take a chance on me? I don't know my past, Tag. I certainly don't know what the future holds, but..."

His lips covered hers. Lee realized she didn't give a damn about the past or the future, not when the present tasted so wonderful, not when it was presented with a mouth that fitted so perfectly with her own.

At some point in her hidden past Lee surmised she must have at least read about making love in an over-sized claw-footed tub. She knew she'd never done this before, never personally experienced the dream-like sense of floating weightless while skilled hands skimmed over her slick body, while lips and teeth and tongue pleasured her until the ecstasy bordered on pain.

She cried out as Tag positioned her over his body, then settled her down upon him so that he entered her with a slow and steady thrust. Slow enough and steady enough to give her time to adjust and accommodate his heat and size.

Rocking gently, Lee rode him, loathe to splash more water on the floor. Within seconds Tag took control, holding her hips in his strong grasp, raising and lowering her against him in an ever-increasing tempo.

Her entire world centered on Tag, on that point where their bodies meshed until she felt herself tightening, the spiraling heat growing, burning, dragging the air from her lungs, the thoughts from her mind until she shattered, falling into a hundred thousand separate pieces of a woman who had once been whole.

Tag called out. Lee heard her name like a groan of pain as he emptied himself into her. She fell against his chest, limp and shivering. He still pulsed within her and Lee clenched her thighs more tightly around his hips.

Holding him. Keeping him close.

Afraid if she let him go, he'd be gone forever.

HE'D EXPECTED awkwardness. There'd been none, at least on Lee's part. She hadn't asked for promises of love, only that he take a chance. Hell, he'd taken more than a chance. Tag couldn't believe how dumb he'd been, making love without protection.

Over and over again, and he'd never even considered the consequences. That's what his parents had done, why he'd come along just four months after a wedding that never should have happened. Lee stirred beside him on the narrow bed, her eyes still shut, a contented little half smile on her lips.

They'd finished bathing each other, eventually, then cleaned the water from the bathroom floor, eventually, and finally tumbled into bed to make love again.

Now bright moonlight filtered through the open window, Lee blinked and gazed up at him from her spot cuddled under his arm and Tag couldn't believe he wanted her again.

Sudden screams pierced the silence, punctuated by Bob the Dog's frantic barking. Tag bolted out of bed and grabbed the rifle he'd left by the front door. "It's the mustangs," he said. "Don't worry. They're just curious about the new kids in the valley. This'll run 'em off."

Startled awake, Lee did the only thing she could think of...she followed Tag out the door. He aimed the rifle into the air and fired. A loud blast shattered the night, followed by the thunder of pounding hooves and the sound of tearing brush. The silence that ensued was as unnerving as the screams had been. Bob the Dog trotted up the steps to sit by Lee's side and nudged her bare leg with his cold nose.

Sounds of the four horses shifting restlessly in the small barn echoed through the wooden walls. "I'm going to go check on the animals," Tag said. "The mustangs won't be back for awhile. They were probably just curious about Nitro. Nothing gets their attention like another stud in the area...or a mare." He grinned, giving Lee a look hot enough to melt wax, then pointed to something behind her. "Grab that flashlight by the front door, will you?"

Lee stepped back into the cabin and fumbled around the small table in the dark until her fingers landed on the cool metal flashlight. She switched the beam on, catching Tag in its brilliant shaft of light. He stood a few feet away from the porch, the rifle over his shoulder, his bare skin gleaming in the light. Lee thought of a Greek statue, the perfect definition of lean muscle, cords and sinews.

"Don't you think you should put some pants on?" she asked.

"No one here but us, sweetheart." Tag grinned and held his free hand out. Lee handed him the flashlight but he grabbed her wrist instead. "Come with me," he said. Hesitantly, Lee allowed him to lead her out to the barn. She wasn't used to walking around stark naked in the moonlight, especially when there could be all kinds of wild things nearby.

Somehow, though, knowing Tag was leading the way with a rifle over his shoulder made this little jaunt feel more like an exciting adventure. She waited by the barn door, close to where he'd left the gun while Tag settled Nitro, Daisy and Chief with an extra taste of grain and a few quiet words.

He fed Dandy, as well, then clipped a lead rope to the big horse's halter and led him out of the stall. "Turn off the light," he instructed Lee. She flipped the switch, plunging the barn into darkness.

Slowly, as her eyes grew accustomed to the light, she realized she could see more than she'd expected. Moonlight filled the small valley, throwing the surrounding trees and hillsides into dark relief, bathing the open areas with an ethereal glow that made the wildflowers glisten and sparkled off the tiny creeks and ponds.

"It's beautiful," she whispered.

Dandy grunted and Lee glanced at the big horse. Tag sat astride like a naked warrior ready for battle, his long legs gripping Dandy's middle, one arm stretched down to grab Lee.

She tried, but couldn't suppress a nervous giggle. "You don't actually expect me to ride a horse naked, do you? Lady Godiva I'm not. My hair's too short. Besides, it's nighttime. It's dark out, you idiot!"

Tag grinned at her, his teeth glinting in the pale light. Obviously that was exactly what he expected.

"What about the wild horses? Won't they come back?"

"C'mon, Lee. They're not coming back, not tonight, anyway. Think of this as a new experience." He scooted way back on Dandy's rump and gestured with his free hand. "It's too pretty to stay inside. I thought we'd just ride out into the meadow where we can see the stars."

"You can't see the stars. It's too bright out."

"You just said it was too dark. Make up your mind." He wiggled his fingers just under her nose.

"Oh, what the...it'll never work." Lee grabbed his wrist. Before she knew what happened Tag was shifting her into position in front of him on Dandy's bare back.

This was definitely a new experience. Lee gripped the horse's broad shoulders with her knees and tried to position her tender crotch on the animal's bony withers. Tag held her firmly around the waist, his chest plastered along the length of her back, and urged Dandy forward.

There was something to be said for the rocking motion of the animal's slow walk, the sensation of all that muscle and sinew moving between her legs. Lee tangled her fingers in Dandy's mane and hung on for dear life.

Snippets of conversation entered her mind, an argument she'd had about...about..."Tag," she asked, leaning away enough that she could turn and watch his face. "Have you ever made love on horseback before?"

His grin looked almost feral in the moonlight. "Nope," he said. "Why? Got some idea cookin' in that forgetful brain of yours?"

"I vaguely recall somebody telling me it's impossible, but I was just wondering..."

"I take it you're looking for proof," he said. "Kind of like a scientific experiment, right?"

"I guess you might call it that." Dandy continued his slow, measured walk out into the pasture. His stiff hair abraded Lee's tender knees and thighs, but the sensation wasn't completely awful. Neither was Tag's obvious interest in the subject, interest that was making itself known quite solidly behind her.

Tag draped the lead rope over Dandy's neck and rubbed his hands slowly along Lee's sides, reaching clear to her knees with his gentle strokes. "Turn around," he whispered, spanning her waist with his big hands. "Let's find out how impossible it is."

She raised one leg over Dandy's neck, tucked the other one up and turned, with Tag's help until she straddled his thighs, facing him. Dandy continued his steady pace even as Tag scooted back on the horse's broad rump to give the two of them more room.

Giggling, Lee lifted herself up just enough to come down firmly planted, with a little help from Tag, on his erection. Dandy paused, turned and gave the two of them such a disgusted stare that they both dissolved into laughter.

"C'mon now," Tag pleaded. "Don't make me laugh. We're doing this in the name of science, Lee. It's important we get it right."

"Oh, I think we're getting it right," Lee said. If the tiny shudders and shivers building at her center were any proof, they were way past right. She clung to Tag's shoulders as Dandy picked up the pace, headed for something only of interest to a horse on a moonlit night. Bob the Dog, trotting alongside, barked and nipped at Dandy's heels.

Dandy broke into a trot.

Without warning it struck, a climax so powerful, so perfectly timed between Lee and Tag that the aftermath left them boneless. Lee collapsed against Tag's chest, giggling, sighing, then shrieking in outrage when they both slipped off of Dandy's broad back into the mucky wet grass alongside a narrow creek.

Thank goodness she'd landed on top of Tag. She sprawled across him, her body jouncing with his muffled laughter. "I trust you're not injured," she said, trying so hard to keep her voice serious, but failing miserably.

"Oh God, woman. You're trying to kill me." He wrapped his muddy arms around her. Lee shrieked again when the wet muck plastered her sides.

"It was all in the name of science, Mr. Martin. Good scientists take risks." She sat up, grabbed a handful of mud and grass and threw it at his chest.

Tag didn't fight back. He merely wrapped his arms around her and rolled both of them into the creek. The icy water took her breath away. At least most of the mud went with it.

They stood up, shivering, still giggling, both streaked with mud. "Well, now you can tell whoever said you can't make love on a horse, they don't know what they're talking about," Tag said. His teeth chattered over the words.

"We're gonna end up with hypothermia if we don't get back to the cabin and dry off," he added. Lee's teeth chattered so much she could only nod her head in agreement. Hard to believe just moments ago she'd felt hot enough to light coals.

Tag whistled for Dandy and the horse trotted back to the edge of the creek. He grabbed a handful of Dandy's mane and mounted first, then held a hand out to Lee. This time she got on behind Tag so she could wrap her arms around his waist.

He clicked his tongue and Dandy headed back across the meadow. Lee turned to watch the moon, now close to setting over the ridge of trees. The image shimmered, shifted, altered in her mind. Instead of towering pines she saw the silhouette of tall buildings and the flash of neon lights.

She muffled a startled gasp. When she blinked, she saw only moon-washed mountain peaks, but the memory remained, clear and bright. Lee didn't know if it was the power of a good orgasm or the shock of that cold water, but something was bringing her past to light.

She was a city girl. Lee knew that much. She was a city girl straight out of a New York high rise and Tag was a country boy, lifetime resident of Grover's Mill, Colorado. And she knew, without question, Tag would never risk the pain he'd watched his father endure. The last thing Tag wanted was a city girl.

Why couldn't she have remembered sooner? Lee sighed and rested her cheek forlornly against Tag's strong back as the memories rushed into her mind. Just her luck, to go and fall in love with a cowboy.

Would it have made a difference, she wondered, if she'd known who she was before?

Tag turned around and smiled at her, that loopy, lop-sided smile that popped the dimple out in his left cheek and she knew, without a doubt, it wouldn't have made any difference at all.

Chapter 11

THIS TIME when they bathed, Lee was so exhausted she hardly noticed Tag's gentle ministrations. He filled the big tub, crawled into the steamy water with her and carefully washed the mud and muck from her body with a soft cloth. He helped her rinse the twigs and grit out of her matted hair, then toweled her dry like a sleepy child.

They stumbled into the narrow bed together. There was no question of sleeping apart, not after the past few hours they'd spent. Tag pulled Lee into his secure embrace and promptly fell asleep.

Lee wasn't so lucky. Exhausted, both mentally and physically, she couldn't keep her thoughts from whirling and spinning. How could she possibly reconcile Lee Stetson, a character in a book she'd written but hadn't sold, with the Lee Stetson she'd become at the Double Eagle?

With the woman, Michelle Garrison, she knew herself to be?

How was she ever going to admit the truth to Tag? Once he knew his fake bride was none other than Michelle Garrison, one of Coop's multi-published romance authors, he'd be furious. Tag would never believe she hadn't known her past. It was too far-fetched even for Michelle. He'd assume she'd been using him to research a story.

Which, Michelle had to admit, wasn't all that far from the truth. It was the reason she'd originally come to Colorado. She just hadn't planned on any of it, not the storm or the accident or the amnesia...or falling in love with the sexy cowboy hero of her imagination.

The whole thing defied belief. Why, if she were to send in a proposal plotted like the past few weeks of her life, Mark would laugh in her face.

Suddenly Michelle sat up. Tag grunted and rolled over. "Oh no," she moaned, covering her eyes with her hands. Not only had she gone and fallen in love with a cowboy, she'd had unprotected sex. Lots of really spectacular unprotected sex.

It was all too much. The fake marriage of convenience. The sexy cowboy. Making love in a claw-footed tub and again on the back of a horse. There was even a lop-eared dog, a stunning white stallion and a mysterious woman with amnesia. Her entire life was evolving from one bad cliché into another.

The only thing missing was the secret baby...the perfect ending, she thought ruefully, to her own ill-fated romance. She pressed her abdomen with both palms and stared wide-eyed into the darkness. She'd have to tell Tag the truth. When she did, he was going to hate her. If, by chance, she was pregnant, he'd think she'd set out to trap him, the way his mother had trapped his father forty years ago.

Even if she wasn't pregnant, she knew he wouldn't want any thing more to do with her, city born and bred that she was. She winced, accepting the truth. Even though she'd be destroying any chance the two of them might have had of ever being together, she had to tell him. Shuddering at the thought, Michelle lay back down beside Tag. She would definitely tell him.

Later.

After the round-up was over and they were back on familiar ground. After she'd had two weeks with the sexiest cowboy alive. In the meantime, Lee Stetson would keep her mouth shut, do her job, and enjoy every moment she could with Tag Martin. She had, after all, agreed to stay with him as long as he needed her.

Rationalizing, Michelle discovered, did not lead to a restful night.

It was a long, long time before she drifted off to sleep.

"LENORE, WE'VE got a problem." Coop slammed the kitchen door behind him and stalked into the kitchen. He threw a tattered romance novel down on the table.

Lenore looked up from the pot she was stirring on the stove and smiled at Coop. My, when he was fired up like this he looked thirty years younger and way too sexy for his own good.

He made her feel thirty years younger, too. She couldn't remember ever having this much fun. Not in her entire life.

"Take your hat off, dear. Lunch is almost ready."

Coop snorted impatiently but did as he was told. He pulled out a chair and sat, nervously running his fingers through his sparse hair. "Remember that car I helped Will and the sheriff haul out of the river? The little rental job?"

"Of course. How could I forget. It just happened day before yesterday. The same day Tag and Lee went up the hill." She shook her head and turned to dish up a couple of bowls of soup.

"Well, we know who rented it." Coop paused, as if for dramatic effect. "Before I tell you, though, there's something else you should know." Lenore set a bowl of soup and a basket of rolls in front of him. She'd learned there was only one way Coop would ever tell a story...his way.

"Lee Stetson is not who she claims to be." Coop frowned. "Tag and I both thought she was Betsy Mae's friend. She's not. Turns out Betsy Mae's friend has been staying at Columbine Camp with Will. They're an item," he said. "I think Will Twigg's met his match with Annie Anderson."

"So who did Tag marry?" Lenore sat across the table from Coop. "Where did Lee come from?"

"Lee Stetson came from that little rental car we pulled out of the river. Only she isn't Lee Stetson, she's Michelle Garrison and she was headed for Columbine Camp as a guest. It took Will a bit to make the connection because he couldn't read Betsy Mae's handwriting and she's the one took the reservation. I recognized the name as soon as I heard it." Coop flipped open the back page of the romance and slid it across the table to Lenore. "You'll understand why I figured we had a problem the minute I dug this out of my stash o' books in the barn."

Lee Stetson, hair perfectly styled, make-up faultless, silk scarf artfully draped, smiled back at her. "Michelle Garrison? Oh my." Lenore looked at Coop. "I used to love her books. The last couple, though..."

"Forget the books. I didn't say a word to Will yet. I wanted to show this to you first, but we have to tell Tag. I don't know what kind of double cross this woman's pulling on the boy, but she's up to no good. He still thinks she's someone Betsy Mae sent to him."

"Now Coop." Lenore covered his hand with hers. "We don't know she's pulling anything. If her car went into the river she could have been injured. She did act confused. You said you found her walking alongside the road with her little suitcase. Maybe..."

"That's a little too convenient, don't you think? She's scammin' the boy, Lenore. I'm sure of it. We've got to go up to the summer range and warn him."

"Now, just a minute. Hold on." Lenore quickly read the paragraph below the author's picture. "According to this, she's single, lives alone in an apartment overlooking Central Park. Spends all her time either writing or traveling to research her stories."

"Research? You don't think she's using Tag for research, do you? That's disgusting." Coop's mouth dropped open. "This is terrible, Lenore. Tag sent a note down with one of the boys requesting, uh, well..." He blushed and looked away.

"Requesting what? What did he want?"

"Ah, ruh, uh, ruh..." Coop looked like he was about to choke. "He asked for a box o'rubbers," he said, turning an even darker shade of scarlet.

Lenore laughed. "Well at least he's being careful." She traced Michelle's picture with the tip of her finger. The girl was much prettier in real life, without all that make-up and the fancy hair style. "This is not necessarily a bad thing, Coop. I told you those two were settin' off sparks." She laughed again. In fact, it might even be better than she'd hoped.

Tag didn't love lightly, she knew that much about her grandson. In fact, as far as she knew, he'd never really loved at all. At least not until he married his imitation bride. Lenore was certain she'd sensed a powerful attraction between Tag and Lee, or Michelle, or whoever she was.

Did it even matter, as long as they fell in love?

"You're right, Coop," she said. "There's something going on, but I don't think it's anything bad, just the stuff that happens naturally between two healthy young people attracted to one another. Nothin' bad at all...other than you all conspiring to convince me they were really married, which Tag and the woman still think I believe, even though you told me they really are married which neither one of them knows yet."

Lenore glared at Coop. She hadn't really considered all the implications of the lies before. "It's confusing," she said, suddenly angry with all the fraud and deception. "I don't like being lied to."

"I didn't lie to you for long. I told you the truth."

"Only because I guessed it, but that's not the point. Look, this says she lives alone, so there's probably no one looking for her. Let's give those two until the end of round-up. It might be enough time to convince them they have something going. We'll find out soon enough if she's up to no good."

"What about Tag?" Coop demanded. "I don't want him gettin' hurt. I just hate to think of that woman lying to him."

"I wouldn't feel too badly about it," Lenore said dryly. "They're both still lyin' to me. Now eat your soup. It's gettin' cold." Lenore realized her hands were shaking. What right did she have fussing over someone lying to her? Whatever was Coop going to say when he realized she'd told him the biggest lie of all?

Sighing, Lenore pushed her bowl away. Suddenly she didn't have much of an appetite after all.

ALMOST TWO weeks into the round-up Michelle decided she was actually having fun. Once she got the hang of working the calf table, a wonderful tilting contraption that held the calf secure to make branding and dehorning more convenient, got over the nauseating smell of burnt hair and blood and quit throwing up every time one of the cowboys castrated a poor little bull calf, she realized she was thoroughly enjoying the excitement and thrills.

Of course, the pay-off came at the end of the day when she and Tag would ride the few miles to the little cabin with its great big bathtub. After the first night they'd both realized it was worth the extra miles for the luxury of a warm bath and a soft bed.

They didn't make love every night. Sometimes they were both so tired they curled up in each other's arms and slept the night through. When they did come together, as far as Michelle was concerned, it was wonderful. Tag was wonderful. And prepared.

She wasn't certain where the condoms had come from, but hopefully they weren't using them for nothing. It was too soon to know if she and Tag were too late.

Michelle was still Lee Stetson as far as everyone, including Tag, was concerned. She'd almost come to terms with her deception. She'd decided there was no point in revealing her identity until after round-up. Tag had enough on his mind without informing him he was making love to a multi-published romance author from New York City.

Over the course of a couple of days, Michelle was certain all her memories had finally returned. Her only concern was her editor, Mark Connor. He must be worried sick by now. She'd been gone for almost three weeks.

Well, she decided as she fastened the latch on the calf table, checked to make sure the little critter was firmly secured and gave it a spin, it served him right. He was the one who'd sent her out here in the first place.

Learn about cowboys, he'd said. Maybe you'll be able to write a real western. She'd done everything Mark had wanted and then some. She could ride a horse, she was learning to rope calves, she'd worked her very first round-up...she'd fallen head over heels in love with her very own cowboy hero.

And, she'd made love on the back of a horse, proving once and for all that editors didn't know everything.

Michelle glanced up at Ramón's shouted instructions. She'd been so lost in thought she hadn't realized he'd finished with the calf and wanted her to release the little guy. She flipped the table back, unlatched it and the calf scampered away—minus his horns and a couple of other valuable parts of his anatomy. Bob the Dog barked and nipped at the calf's heels, heading him toward his bawling mother.

"I need a break, Ramón," she said. A young cowhand stepped in to take her place.

"Señora," he acknowledged.

Michelle nodded to him and headed for the shade of a huge cottonwood tree. She could see Tag, resplendent on Nitro, working to separate a calf from its mother. The horse was performing beautifully, the man on his back was pure poetry.

She still couldn't believe she'd fallen in love with a cowboy. It had been so natural when she'd been Lee Stetson. Michelle Garrison was still a bit in shock over the whole thing.

The round-up was almost over. Once they headed back to the Double Eagle, Michelle knew she'd have to tell Tag the truth. Sooner or later someone was going to identify her and the story would be out.

In fact, she was surprised Coop hadn't recognized her at the very beginning, as much as he read romance novels. Of course, she probably hadn't looked much like the glamour shot on the book jacket when he found her wandering down the highway in the rain.

Maybe he didn't read Michelle Garrison romances. That was probably closer to the truth. Michelle smiled at the thought. In her other life, before Colorado and before Tag, an idea like that would have devastated her. Now, though, Michelle realized it didn't bother her a bit. Her life was too full for a little thing like readership to affect her.

Her heart overflowed with love for Tag Martin, her mind balked at the fear of losing him.

She didn't have time to worry about who did or didn't read her books.

She pulled her gloves off and washed her hands. She'd filed her nails all the way down to neat little squares and the blisters were long gone, replaced by thick ridges of callus that protected her hands from the demanding work almost as much as the leather gloves.

Bob the Dog shoved at her hand with his wet nose. Michelle's eyes misted over. She'd even fallen in love with the dumb dog. And she'd experienced three of the most intense weeks of her life. Michelle knew she'd never worked so hard, accomplished so much, or loved so fiercely.

She couldn't tell Tag how she felt. She couldn't bring herself to say the words that rested like stone in her heart until she was strong enough to be truthful. She didn't know how he felt about her. She only knew that she loved him more than she'd ever thought it possible to love anyone. She loved him, and when she told him the truth he'd never want to see her again.

Sighing, she took a long, cool drink of water, whistled for Bob the Dog to follow and headed back to work.

TAG WATCHED as Lee slipped her gloves back on her hands and headed back to the branding with Bob the Dog hot on her heels. She'd worked her cute little tail off, day and night for the past two weeks. A cute little tail wearing his plaid boxer shorts. Some days that image kept him so riled up he could hardly wait until night...when she gave him a taste of heaven he'd never imagined possible.

To think this had all started out as a scam to trick his grandmother. He wondered how Lenore was doing, how her health was. He hadn't heard much from Coop and Lenore since moving to the upper ranges. Just the occasional note about ranch business when Coop sent supplies to the men. There'd been a happy face sticker on the condoms he'd requested.

Tag wondered if Lenore and Coop were still in love.

Tag had love on his mind a lot, lately.

Damn, he hadn't wanted this to happen, but he was almost certain he was falling in love. If only Lee knew her past. It hung over him like the Sword of Damocles, not knowin' if there might be a man somewhere, lookin' for her.

Tag didn't think he'd be able to stand it, wondering if some strange dude might drive up to the Double Eagle one day and ask what Tag was doing with his wife.

Oh Lord. The Double Eagle. Tag tugged back on the reins in dismay. Nitro snorted, reared and pawed the air. Tag barely noticed. Lee didn't know. He'd never told her the truth. She still thought the reason Tag had wanted to hire a bride was to get his grandmother to stop her matchmaking.

Lee had no idea he'd been lying to her from the get go. As sweet and honest as Lee had been with him, telling him up front she didn't have a clue about her past even though he knew she was afraid he'd run her out...hell, if she ever learned the real reason...Tag shuddered, imagining Lee's reaction when she finally learned the truth.

No way in hell could Lee Stetson love a man who'd used her to scam a little old lady, a dying little old lady, out of her ranch. It hardly mattered that, once he'd found out about Lenore's health, winning the Double Eagle hadn't been nearly as important as making his grandmother happy. No, Tag was absolutely certain Lee wouldn't want any part of a relationship that had begun with a lie as selfish as his.

He also knew that, somehow, he'd have to tell her the truth. He wasn't a man who could live with lies...he'd learned that the moment he and Coop had put this stupid plan into action.

Nitro dodged to the right, momentarily jolting Tag out of his misery. Tag gave Nitro his head and the big stallion expertly cut between a skittish little white faced calf and its bawling mother, neatly separating the youngster and moving him toward Lee and the calf table. The stud had proven to be an even better cow pony than Tag had dreamed. He patted the animal's muscular neck. At least something was working right in his mixed up life. It was all going to go wrong the minute he had that talk with Lee.

MICHELLE TIGHTENED the cinch on Chief's saddle and led him away from the small corral. Tag was giving final instructions to the half-dozen cowhands who would be staying up at the summer range to break down the temporary corrals and pack up the equipment for the next round-up.

A gust of wind almost whipped the Stetson from her head as Michelle mounted the big horse. She jammed the battered hat down tightly over her eyes as she settled into the saddle. Chief skittered to one side and she expertly controlled his movements with just enough pressure of her knees and a mere tug on the reins. The big horse calmed immediately, shook his head and settled into what Michelle had dubbed his waiting mode.

She'd explained to Tag, early in the first week, that when Chief cocked one hip and shuffled his front feet, he wasn't really relaxing, he was actually getting ready for take-off. He hadn't dumped her yet, but a girl couldn't be too careful about a lot of things. Michelle patted Chief's neck and sighed.

She still couldn't believe she understood this damned horse. She couldn't believe the round-up was almost over. The first few days in the summer range had been so overwhelming she'd thought she'd never survive. Not merely the physical labor and excruciating exhaustion of working the cattle, but the psychological toll of learning her true identity and keeping it secret, of coming to terms with the fact she loved a man who had sworn never to allow himself to fall in love.

She only wished she could be so strong. Tag was the strongest, most honorable man she'd ever known. He'd been up front with her all along, explaining the reason for the sham marriage, the reasons he never planned to marry. Once their relationship had become physical, something she'd wanted every bit as much as Tag, he'd protected her without complaint or comment.

Honest to a fault, respected by his men, loved by one terribly flawed women. Michelle wondered how she'd been able to face herself in the mirror each morning.

Actually, she did know. She'd been able to face herself because she was too damned selfish to ruin a good thing. She thought of their lovemaking the night before and blushed. Tag definitely had an imagination. Imagination and endurance. She'd have to include those attributes in her next romantic hero.

Michelle's shoulders slumped. She might as well get used to the fact her only heroes from now on were going to be the ones she invented. She had to tell Tag the truth. Today, after she had a chance to get her things together so she'd be ready to leave the minute Tag threw her out.

"Ready to go?" Tag brought Nitro to a halt a few paces from Michelle and Chief. "Ramón says he'll bring Dandy and Daisy down with the rest of our stuff in a couple of days, so we can just enjoy the ride home." He looked up at the gathering clouds. "That is, if we don't get soaked before we make it back to the ranch."

He drew closer and leaned over to kiss Michelle fully on the mouth, right in front of Ramón and the other hands. "I don't know about you," he whispered against her lips, "but I'm lookin' forward to that great big bed waitin' for us. Not that I haven't enjoyed sleeping real close together...in fact, last night was downright inspirational." He straightened up, winked, whistled to Bob the Dog. Before Michelle could catch her breath, he turned Nitro around and headed the white stallion down the trail.

It wasn't fair. Just one kiss from the man turned her insides to jelly. Michelle ran her tongue across her lips, tasting him. A single rain drop spotted her jeans and she glanced up at the dark clouds, swirling overhead like an ominous foreshadowing of her immediate future.

Sensing the worst, she closed her eyes against anticipated pain, tapped Chief's sides with her heels and followed Tag home.

COOP HUNG the phone up just as two horsemen crested the windswept hill north of the ranch. He couldn't be certain from this distance exactly who the riders were, but he recognized Nitro and Chief.

"If that's Miz Michelle Garrison riding Chief, then I guess her little research trip has been successful," he muttered with grudging admiration. "That horse can be quite a handful."

"Now Coop, you promised." Lenore walked quietly into the room and laid her hand gently over his shoulder. "Who was that on the phone?"

Coop sighed. He'd almost hoped Lenore hadn't heard the damned thing ring. "That was a fella name of Mark Connor. He's Miz Garrison's New York editor. He's over ta Will's right now. Came out here as soon as the police called him to report Miz Garrison missing. Will suggested he call here since I'd helped pull the car out of the river. The man's worried sick about her."

"Oh no. You didn't tell him she was..."

"That I did. I'm tired of all the lies, Lenore."

"You promised me you wouldn't say anything to Tag."

"Doesn't really matter now, does it? He's gonna find out soon enough." Coop stood up and slapped his hat down on his head. "They're just ridin' into the yard. I'm goin' out to meet 'em." He leaned over and kissed Lenore on the cheek. "I promise not to say a thing about Lee's real name just yet. It'll take that Connor fella at least half an hour to get here, what with the directions I gave him. Maybe by then we'll think of somethin'."

Lenore smiled understandingly and patted his hand. Coop bowed his head. "I couldn't do it, Lenore. I couldn't lie to her editor. For all I know, the man loves her. He was real worried."

Tag and the woman dismounted near the corral just as Coop stepped off the porch. Coop wasn't quite sure how to think of her, as Lee Stetson or Michelle Garrison. For all he knew, she really did have amnesia. Maybe she still thought she was a cowgirl. If that was the case, he didn't want her any more confused than she already was.

She certainly sat a horse like a real cowgirl. Her Stetson perched real pretty on her dark red hair and she didn't look bad in a pair of tight jeans, either. As Coop walked closer, he noticed something else.

Damned if Tag wasn't looking at her with his heart on his sleeve.

This wasn't going to be easy.

Coop had been right about one thing. Her editor had told him Miz Garrison had come to Colorado to research cowboys.

Considerin' the request Tag made for the damned rubbers, the research had gotten pretty thorough. Coop practically forced himself across the yard. He needed to talk to Tag, get a feel for how things were settin'. He wanted to sit down with the boy and tell him the truth right now, and he would, except Lenore'd made him give his word. Damn, that woman could frustrate a man.

"Hey Coop, you old buzzard!" Tag straightened up from loosening Nitro's cinch, but instead of the usual thump on the shoulder, he enveloped Coop in a tight, emotional hug.

Oh Lordy. Coop awkwardly hugged him back. This was worse than he'd imagined.

"Hi Coop." Lee, busy loosening the cinch on Chief's saddle, smiled tentatively over the horse's back. "It's nice to see you."

For the life of him, he couldn't welcome her. Instead, Coop tipped his hat. "Ma'am," he said. She stared at him, her green eyes sad and understanding. Coop felt like he was reading an open book. She knew. She knew who she was, but she hadn't said a word to the boy.

"I'm going up to the house for a minute," she said, holding Coop's gaze a moment longer. "Do you mind taking his saddle off? I'll come back and brush Chief after I've seen Lenore."

She kissed Tag full on the mouth before she left. The boy absolutely glowed. Coop felt like a pile of horse manure.

Tag watched as Lee quietly left the barn, Bob the Dog trotting along at her heels. Rain fell steadily now, after the intermittent showers they'd had on the way home.

Lee'd been unusually silent all the way down the mountain, but after the time they'd had last night, she had every right to be tired. He grinned. Just thinking about her made him hot. "It has been an absolutely incredible two weeks," he said, spinning around to face Coop. "Remember what you told me, Coop? Before the wedding? If I played my cards right, something might just work out for real? Coop, this woman is my royal flush."

"Now Tag, there's somethin'..."

"I know." Tag felt like all the air'd just been squeezed out of his lungs. "And you're right. It's a pretty big somethin'. I haven't told her the whole truth yet. I don't know how I can tell her and not lose her."

Tag slipped the saddle off Nitro's back while Coop grabbed the one off Chief. They carried the equipment through the barn and on in to the tack room at the back.

This was just the opportunity Tag had hoped for, a chance to talk to Coop without Lee around. He might be almost eighty years old, but Coop never seemed to run out of ideas. Right now, Tag figured he needed all the help he could get.

MICHELLE WAS half way across the muddy yard when she admitted to herself she was running away. Avoiding the truth wasn't going to make it disappear, especially since she was almost certain Coop knew her true identity. He'd had questions written all over his weathered face.

More important, Tag had been honest with her. The least she could do was be honest with him.

She reached down and patted Bob the Dog, then turned on her heel and headed back to the barn. It took her eyes a moment to adjust to the dark but she followed the sound of Tag's voice to the tack room at the back of the building.

She heard her name and halted, uncertain whether to go on in or slip quietly out the back. The unhappiness in Tag's voice kept her feet planted.

"She still thinks the marriage was set up to get Gramma to quit matchmakin'," he said. "I just haven't been able to tell her the truth, that this whole mess was a scam to get the Double Eagle. If I tell her, she's gonna leave. I know it. She's an honorable woman, Coop. I don't think I could stand..."

"Don't worry about the ranch, boy. That's the least of your problems. Your grandmother's already deeded that over to..."

Michelle felt like she might throw up, right there in the middle of the barn. This whole thing was a rip-off, a marriage of convenience to defraud a dying old lady of her ranch! Anger boiled deep and hot, blinding her to anything but Tag's duplicity. To think she'd been so upset about not telling him her real name once she knew it! Her lies were nothing compared to what Tag and that old man were up to.

Fuming, she clenched her fists and barged into the tack room. "I can't believe what a low-down, dirty, rotten, scheming..."

"Now sweetheart," Tag spun around, his hands held out in supplication. "I was gonna tell you the truth, honest."

"Don't you 'sweetheart' me. You lied to me. You said you just wanted to stop her matchmaking, not steal her ranch. You've turned me into a thief! And you..." She rounded on Coop just as Lenore rushed into the barn. "You're just as bad, knowing Tag was swindling the woman you claim to love. Men!" she sneered. "You're all a bunch of lying, thieving..."

"That's enough, Michelle." Lenore's calm voice took the wind out of her sails. Michelle went hot and cold all over, but this time it was humiliation, not anger.

"Michelle? Who's Michelle?" Tag asked.

Lenore merely placed a paperback romance on top of a bale of hay. She flipped it open to the back page. Absolute silence filled the small tack room.

Michelle Garrison's perfectly made up face smiled eerily back at the four of them.

"Lee, that's you. You're Michelle Garrison? You're a writer. Why on earth are you pretending to be my wife? I don't get it?"

"She's out here researching cowboys," Coop sneered. "How's it feel to be a research project, Tag? I'm sorry boy, she put one over on all of us."

"How can you say that? That's not true," Michelle said. She turned to Tag, but his face was set and unreadable. "I didn't know who I was, not at first. I was in a car accident." She swung around to face Coop. "That must have been my car you pulled out of the river. Most of my memories have come back, but I don't recall a thing from the time the car went off the road until just before you picked me up during that storm. You have to believe me."

Coop snorted. Gramma Lenore didn't say a word.

"When did you know?" Tag asked. He leaned casually against the stack of hay and folded his arms across his chest. His stance might have appeared relaxed to someone who didn't know him.

Michelle knew him much too well. His hands gripped his elbows so tightly his knuckles turned white and the muscles in his arms bulged in protest. His midnight blue eyes glinted darkly, the dimple she loved was nowhere in sight. His jaw could have been cast in granite.

"Not until that night," Michelle whispered. She swallowed, blushing. Her gaze flickered from Coop to Lenore, then back to Tag.

"What night?" Tag demanded.

He was relentless. He knew what night. How could he do this? "The night we made love," she said. The words caught in her throat, threatened to choke her. "That first night you made love to me I remembered everything. Most of all, I remembered I came from New York. I'm a city girl, Tag. Exactly what you told me you don't want."

"You're damned right," he snarled. "I don't want a city girl and I certainly don't want a woman who'd lie to me."

"Well you were lying, too," she said, finding her backbone and facing his implacable anger. She turned to Gramma Lenore, standing off to one side with a stricken look on her face. "I'm so sorry," she said. "I guess you know we're not really married. I never would have agreed to this charade if I'd known he was trying to do something illegal. Right after the wedding I started remembering little bits of my past. Which I immediately told Tag," she added, jerking her head around to glare at him.

His expression didn't change. She wondered if he was thinking of that first night in the cabin, when they'd shared a bottle of champagne and tried to figure out exactly who she was.

"Anyway," she said, turning back to Lenore, "we were trying to figure out my identity when I mentioned to Tag I'd heard you were..." She automatically turned to Tag for help. His stony expression didn't change a bit. "When I told him you didn't have much time left, well, Tag was really upset. He convinced me we had to keep up the deception to make you happy."

She clenched her fists, realizing now he'd duped her just as he'd fooled his own grandmother. "Please forgive me. You have enough to worry about without all of this horrible mess."

This time it was Lenore who blanched and looked away. "I, um, didn't realize you knew about my, uh, impending demise," she said. She glanced at Coop out of the corner of her eye. Michelle almost cried again at the look of sadness on the old man's face.

"The truth is," Lenore said. Everyone waited. "The, uh, truth is, well, we're all dyin' you know. Every last one of us, from the moment we're born, we're dyin'. If you want to look at it that way." She fidgeted, folding and unfolding her hands. Tag stared at her, his expression one of anger and hope.

Coop just looked furious. "Are you tellin' me, woman, you are not dying? Are you tellin' me you're as healthy as a horse?"

"I'm as healthy as a seventy-eight year old horse, for what it's worth." She held her head high and smiled beseechingly at Coop.

He flushed a deep red. His eyes narrowed under his busy white brows and he clenched his fists. "That's it. I've had it! I have gosh-danged had it with all the lyin', the pretendin', the...why I don't even know what to call it!" Coop stalked out of the tack room, spun around and stomped back inside.

He pointed one bony finger at Tag, then at Michelle. "For the record, that was a real weddin', with a real preacher and you two signed a real marriage license. Duly witnessed and recorded, I might add. So you'd better quit your bickerin' and act like adults, or figure out how to file for a divorce in the great state of Colorado, because for all intents and purposes, you two are legally married.

"And you," he shook his finger under Lenore's nose. "You take the cake, woman. I have loved you all my life without really knowing you. Maybe we were better off when it stayed unrequited." He carefully enunciated each syllable. "I can't believe you would tell me you were dyin' when you weren't. I can't believe if you really loved me, you would treat me like that, put me through that kind of pain, all to get your own way. I am tired of being manipulated, I am tired of being used, I am fed up with playing your games and I am out. Of. Here."

When Coop stalked out of the small tack room, he took the air and the energy with him. Lenore stared after his retreating figure, her hand pressed to her mouth, tears streaming down her face.

Tag looked equally shell shocked. Michelle couldn't tell whether it was anger at her, relief that his grandmother was all right, astonishment at Coop's violent response, or absolute disbelief over the whole situation.

Somehow, some way, she had to get out of here with her dignity intact. "Don't worry," she said, swallowing her tears and facing Tag. "It can't possibly be a real marriage. I signed the license with a false name. There is no Lee Stetson. She's merely a character in a book I wrote. A book, I might add, that my editor chose to reject. No, there's just a romance author named Michelle Garrison, out here researching the great American West."

She might be shattering inside, her heart splintering into a million tiny pieces, but damned if she was going to let this hard headed cowboy know how she felt. She brushed a few bits of straw off her jeans and looked directly into Tag's dark, unreadable eyes. "Maybe I should thank you for your excellent instruction."

She held his gaze, knowing she still loved him, would always love him. Knowing he felt nothing more than hatred and disgust for her.

Tag didn't try to stop her when she turned away and left the tack room. She could feel him watching her, feel his dark eyes boring into her back. The pain kept her tears at bay. She held her head high as she walked the length of the barn, then out into the pouring rain.

The thought flashed through her mind that she could cry now, if she wanted. The rain would hide her tears. But she didn't cry a single tear, not until a nondescript rental car skidded into the driveway and a very familiar, handsome blond man climbed out.

There were tears on his face. She tried to smile but couldn't control her trembling lips. Mark opened his arms to Michelle. Sobbing, she tumbled into his embrace.

Chapter 12

TAG WATCHED in disbelief, stunned as his worst nightmare materialized right in front of his eyes. He'd followed Lee, or Michelle, or whoever the hell she was, not quite sure what he intended to say, but knowing he couldn't let her leave like this.

Not until they resolved a lot of things between them. Now she was hanging on to some good-looking guy in a suit, both of them hugging and crying like they were a couple of rediscovered long lost lovers.

Damn. She had been hiding a husband. Tag slumped against the barn, unable to take his eyes off the pair even though the sight of his woman in another man's arms just about tore him to shreds.

A terrible thought occurred: she said her memory had returned two weeks ago. That meant she'd known about this guy when she and Tag...no, not that. The image of himself undressing Lee the last time they made love, the smooth silk of her skin beneath his rough hands, the cute way her butt had looked covered in his plaid boxer shorts.

How it felt to slowly peel those worn cotton shorts down her unbelievable legs.

The rain fell unabated, the two of them stood out there hugging and crying, and Tag couldn't get that image of Lee out of his mind. Knowing she wore his flannel boxers instead of her own little silky things when they were working had kept him hot most of every day. Watching her now, knowing she wore another pair of his shorts under her tight-fitting jeans...watching her hang on to another man...damn! Tag didn't know if he wanted to kick something or give thanks for getting out of this mess before he got in too deep.

Who the hell was he kidding? Any deeper he'd be comin' out the other side of something.

He felt a warm hand on his shoulder. Expecting Coop, he was startled to see his grandmother standing beside him. "His name's Mark Connor. He's her editor from New York. Coop talked to him earlier, said he's been worried sick about Michelle. From the look of things, they're a lot more than just business associates, if you get my drift," Lenore said. "The blurb on the jacket said she was single, but it was an old book."

"What're you talking about?" Tag couldn't take his eyes off the pair. "What blurb?"

"The paragraph about Michelle Garrison on the back of her book. It says she's single and lives alone in a New York high rise apartment over Central Park. It was written about five years ago. She may have gotten married since then."

Tag thought about that a moment, about the woman who, over the course of the past couple of weeks had taken his simple existence and turned it upside down and inside out. That woman would never cheat on a husband. He was certain of it.

She wasn't married, because she would have told him.

All evidence to the contrary, he wanted to believe she didn't love the man she was hugging so tightly. In fact, Tag was almost certain she loved Tag himself.

What he wasn't certain of was what to do about it. When he thought of marriage and commitment, his blood ran cold. When he considered spending the rest of his life with Lee...Michelle, his temperature shot up a good ten degrees.

Grinning self-consciously at his own foolishness, Tag covered Gramma Lenore's hand with his own. "She's not married," he said. "To him, anyway." He studied his grandmother for a long moment. "For what it's worth, even if it means I've lost the ranch, I'm sure glad you're okay. It was awful, thinking you were sick, that you might be dyin'" His eyes stung and he recognized tears not so far away, but at least he'd told her how he felt. "C'mon, Gramma. Don't you think we ought to go meet our visitor?"

"Are you sure, Tag? Don't do this for me." Lenore grabbed a handkerchief out of her pocket and wiped her streaming eyes. "I have to tell you something important. Tag," she grabbed his wrist to stop him.

He waited while she seemed to search for the words. "I love you," she said. Words, he knew, that didn't come easy to either one of them. "You've been more a son to me than your father ever was. The ranch is already yours," she said, very quietly. Then Lenore held her head up, the grandmother he remembered from his youth reappearing, defiant even as she apologized. "I had the title switched months ago. It's always been yours, if you'd just thought about it. You've given more sweat and love to this place than either your grandfather or your father. I am sorry, though, for the mess I've made."

The earth should have moved when his grandmother told him the ranch was his. It didn't. He smiled at her, then gave her a quick hug. "I'm not doing this for you, Gramma. I'm not doing it for the ranch, either. In fact, I'm not really sure just what I'm doing, but whatever it is, I'm doin' it for me...for me and," he hesitated over the strange name, "Michelle."

His grandmother studied him silently for a moment. Her blue eyes glistened with tears, but she looked hopeful when she smiled back at him.

She looked hopeful until Coop stormed out of the ranch house with a beat up leather case slung over his shoulder. He paused for a moment and stared at Michelle and her editor, still entwined in a rain-soaked embrace, tipped his hat briefly to Michelle, then approached Tag.

He didn't spare so much as a glance for Lenore. "I'd like to borrow the truck, if you don't mind," he said. "Will's got a place for me at Columbine Camp. I'll fetch my stock in a day or two, once the weather settles. You can hang on to Goldie until the colt's ready to wean."

Tag wrapped his arm protectively around his grandmother. He felt her trembling, her brief flash of defiance gone. What he really wanted to do was knock some sense into his stubborn foreman, but instead he merely nodded his head. "Take the truck," he said. "I won't be needing it."

Coop spun around and left. In less than a minute he was wheeling the old pickup out of the yard, flinging a rooster tail of mud and water as he raced away from the Double Eagle.

Lenore let out an anguished cry, pulled free of Tag's embrace and ran for the house. Michelle glanced up with a stricken look on her face and spun out of her editor's arms to chase after Lenore.

Tag and the tall blond stranger faced each other through the pouring rain. The other man made the first move. "I'm Mark Connor, Michelle's editor," he said, holding out his perfectly manicured hand. "I hope you can tell me what's going on here."

He'd introduced himself as her editor, not her husband, not even her boyfriend, certainly not her lover. Tag couldn't help himself. He laughed, loudly, and shook hands with the man. "Tag Martin," he said. "I run..." he paused, suddenly aware of the implications of his grandmother's act of generosity. The Double Eagle really was his. The ranch he'd been willing to lie and cheat for belonged to him.

"Actually," he said, correcting himself, "I own the Double Eagle."

The earth still didn't move, even though he'd waited what felt like a lifetime to say those words. Instead, they left him feeling empty. Later, he thought. Later when he had time to really think about what this would mean to his future.

Maybe then he'd feel more like celebrating. "Let's get inside out of the rain," he said, clapping Mark on the shoulder. "If you've got time for a pretty unbelievable story, I've got one to tell you."

"Oh, I'm always up for a good story." Mark glanced in the direction Michelle had run. "Always."

They hung their wet coats on the rack by the door, Mark's suit jacket looking very out of place next to Tag's oiled canvas greatcoat. In the kitchen, Tag handed Mark a dry towel then grabbed the bottle of sipping whiskey from the cupboard. He held the bottle out in a silent offer. Mark nodded and Tag poured each of them a glass of the amber liquid.

It was barely noon, but Tag couldn't think of a time when he'd needed a drink more than now.

The two men had just taken their seats across from one another at the kitchen table when Michelle walked into the room. She'd slicked her wet hair back into a ponytail tied with a rubber band. Tag thought she looked about fourteen...and even though she'd obviously been crying, absolutely beautiful.

"I've got your grandmother settled down," she said. "She's very upset about Coop. You should probably check on her before long." Tag noticed Michelle was avoiding eye contact, staring instead at her hands. He wondered if she realized she was spinning her wedding ring?

"Thank you for helping her," Tag said. Michelle gave him a quick nod then turned to Mark. "I'll get my things together. It should only take a few minutes. I want to get at least as far as Montrose before it gets too late."

"You want to leave already?" Mark gazed longingly at the drink Tag had just set in front of him. "I just got here."

"Well, I've definitely overstayed my welcome. I'd like to leave as soon as possible."

The kitchen door opened and Coop stepped into the room. "You're not going anywhere, missy. Not for awhile, anyway." He took his hat off and shook the water from the brim. "Road's washed out, that entire low section across from the front gate. The river must'a come up real fast. The way this storm is blowing in, I doubt county crews'll even get to it a'fore Monday." Coop shoved the hat back on his head. "If'n you don't mind, I'll be out in the bunkhouse. In my old room." He glared at Tag, as if in challenge, then tipped his hat to the three of them and left.

Tag bit his lips to keep from smiling. Not only was Coop back where he belonged, everyone was stuck here until Monday. He figured he could put up with Mark Connor that long, especially since it gave him at least four days to figure out what he wanted to do about Lee...er, Michelle. He'd have to get used to that name! When Tag was certain he could keep his elation to himself, he chanced a glance at her.

She was looking uncertainly down at Connor. Tag might as well not have been in the room.

"Don't worry, sweetheart," Mark said. "I'm sure Tag's got some place we can stay."

"I don't want to stay, Mark. You have no idea what I've gone through in the past few weeks. I want to go home."

"C'mon now, Michelle." Tag might have been addressing Michelle, but he aimed every word at Mark Connor. "It hasn't been that bad. You said you came out here to learn about cowboys and the west. You've been here barely three weeks and you can already ride a horse, you've worked a round-up, spent quality time with a real cowboy..."

He let that one just hang there while he grinned at Michelle, knowing full well she loved his smile. She'd told him exactly how much, often enough. Generally somewhere in the context of their lovemaking.

It pleased him no end to see her blush a deep shade of crimson.

It also pleased Tag to see the questioning look on Mark Connor's face. The man wasn't certain, but he knew something was going on, knew there was a conversation taking place on another level, one that didn't include him.

Tag had always thought of himself as a straightforward, honest man. He knew that was why all the subterfuge with the fake wedding had bothered him so. The next few days, though...well, this was different.

He'd always been a man who appreciated a challenge. He grinned, suddenly aware of a streak of deviousness he'd never expected of himself.

Of course, the stakes had never been quite so high before. Tag met Michelle's curious gaze with a level stare of his own. Her green eyes narrowed, as if she tried to figure out his game plan. Then she rested her hands on Mark's shoulders with disconcerting familiarity and nodded her head.

"I guess we don't have much choice," she said. "If you gentlemen will excuse me, I'm going to my room." She patted Mark's shoulder, turned and left the kitchen.

Tag studied Mark as the editor turned and watched Michelle leave. The frankly appraising look in the other man's eyes was enough to make Tag want to punch him right in that perfectly straight nose of his. When the door closed behind Michelle, Mark turned around in his chair and grinned knowingly at Tag.

"She's something, isn't she? I adore that woman. Thanks for taking such good care of her for me." He took a sip of his drink. "Now, about that story." He paused, his expression suddenly sober, and stared into the whiskey glass he held at eye level. When Mark finally spoke, his voice was so low Tag wondered if the words were actually meant to be heard. "You have no idea what the past few days have been like, receiving that phone call from the state police that Michelle's car was found in the river, waiting to find out if they'd located her body. I wasn't certain she was actually alive until I held her in my arms."

He closed his eyes and shuddered. Tag almost sympathized with the man. Suddenly Mark seemed to pull himself together. He raised his head, took a deep breath and grinned at Tag. "I hope you're going to explain why my favorite author literally dropped off the face of the earth three weeks ago."

"Yeah," Tag said. "It's a little involved." He gazed at Mark Connor with a new perspective. Tag didn't think Michelle was in love with this guy, but she trusted him, might even have some kind of history with him. Obviously, though, she didn't have a clue how her editor felt about her. Tag took a long swallow of his whiskey and told himself it didn't matter.

If only his feelings for her weren't so confused.

She was gorgeous, she was intelligent and tough and sexy as hell and she had a great sense of humor. She was also a city girl who'd lied to him more than once. He didn't need the kind of aggravation a woman like Michelle was certain to cause in his life.

Of course, life with Michelle Garrison would never be dull.

An author! Hell, why would an author want to live in the middle of Colorado? Why would a famous, probably wealthy woman, want to tie herself down to a stubborn cowboy in the middle of nowhere?

Because she loved him? He'd never put much stock in the emotion, not since his parents' untimely death. They'd loved hating each other more than they'd loved him. Tag knew he had some serious thinking to do. Of course, he had until Monday to figure out what he really wanted.

He took another sip of his whiskey. "Well," he said. Mark gave him an encouraging smile and took a swallow of his own drink. "It all started with a marriage of convenience, the deed to a huge cattle ranch and a beautiful redhead with amnesia."

MICHELLE QUIETLY opened the door to Lenore's room, expecting to find the older woman asleep. She'd left Lenore in bed crying, totally devastated by Coop's rejection.

Instead, Gramma Lenore was seated on a bench in front of a small dressing table, carefully applying her make-up. Her hair was neatly styled and she'd changed into a flowing house dress in a vivid shade of blue that did wonders for her eyes.

Michelle could hardly tell she'd been crying. "Are you okay?" She slipped on into the room. "I was worried about you."

Lenore scooted over on the low bench seat and patted the space next to her. "I'm fine," she said. "But what about you? Do you want to tell me about that good lookin' man sittin' out in the kitchen sharing a drink with your husband?"

Michelle sighed and sat down next to Lenore. "You and I both know he's not my husband. Tag doesn't want to be married, especially to a woman from New York. You know how he feels about his mother and father's relationship."

"Jim and Maggie are not Michelle and Tag." Lenore's knowing gaze trapped Michelle's in the lighted mirror. "You love Tag, don't you? You've loved him from the start." It was a statement, not a question.

"I loved Tag before I knew him," Michelle said, knowing exactly how true it was. She laughed softly at her own foolishness. "I think all romance writers fall in love with their heroes in every book they write. Tag's the hero in my last book. The minute I saw him, I knew who he was."

"Well, what are you going to do about it?"

"Nothing." Michelle looked down at her hands, at the gold wedding band on her left ring finger. She carefully removed it and set it on the table. "He doesn't want me, Lenore. He wants this ranch but not me. At least not forever." Michelle turned and touched the older woman's shoulder. "I think Tag loves me a little, but not enough to risk a permanent future. I love him too much to stay, knowing it won't last."

"You said he was your hero, the one you imagined," Lenore said. "If he's everything you want, aren't you willing to fight for him?"

"The book got rejected, Lenore. By Mark Connor. That should tell you something." She shrugged her shoulders, stood up and paced restlessly around the room. Rain splatted against the bedroom window and the wind howled around the ranch house. Michelle shivered even though the room was warm.

"Ah, your editor. Is he in love with you?"

Michelle paused to think about that for a moment. "I think Mark's occasionally in lust with me, but only because he knows I'm safe. I don't lust back." She smiled, thinking about the disagreements and conversations the two of them had had over the years. "He's been my editor for years and my friend just as long. I've talked him through two divorces and any number of failed relationships. No, Mark doesn't love me, not that way. Sometimes I think he's actually a little afraid of me."

"I wouldn't tell Tag," Lenore said, carefully applying her lipstick. "Might help the boy make up his mind if he thinks he's got a little competition to deal with."

Michelle thought about that for a moment. Lenore might just know what she was talking about. There'd been a rather possessive gleam in Tag's eyes when she'd casually rested her hands on Mark's shoulders.

She didn't like the idea of using Mark's friendship to get Tag's attention. On the other hand, she was still peeved that Mark had rejected her western. Of course, now she'd experienced western life and real cowboys, she had to admit he'd been right not to accept it as written.

Thunder rumbled high overhead, lightning flashed outside and the bedroom lights flickered, but stayed on. Thank goodness she and Mark hadn't tried to leave in this storm. "What about Coop?" Michelle asked, hugging herself. "He's out in the bunkhouse, probably reading one of his romance novels. Are you going to try and patch things up with him? Is that why you've got yourself all fancied up?"

Lenore stiffened, then slowly turned to face Michelle. "What did you say?"

"I asked if you were going to patch things up with Coop."

"No, not that. You said Coop's here? I thought he went over to Will Twig's. I thought he was gone."

"Coop's in the bunkhouse. He came back because the road's washed out from the storm. No one can leave until at least Monday, I guess. I thought you knew."

A huge grin split Lenore's face. "No, sweetheart, I didn't know." She turned back to her image in the mirror. "It's getting late. I should probably go start something for supper. I'm sure that old cowboy is pretty hungry after the day he's had."

"Do you think he'll come up to the house to eat?" Michelle asked. "He still seemed awfully angry."

"I hope not." Lenore winked at Michelle. "I'd much rather deliver his supper in person. It's impossible for a man to throw a woman out of his room when she comes bearing food."

"I'll remember that." Michelle turned to leave, then stopped at the bedroom door. "Lenore," she asked, wondering if she had a right to ask. "What's it like, to know a man loves you enough to wait for you for sixty years?"

The silence stretched out so long, Michelle wondered if she'd just made the ultimate social blunder by asking such a personal question. Then Lenore rose quietly to her feet, walked over to the window and stared out into the gloomy storm.

"It's exhilarating and frightening and terribly sad at the same time," she said. "I never had a clue how Coop felt, but even if I'd known I'm not certain I would have done anything differently. I was so afraid of being poor and Ed had so much money and power. Unfortunately, I never realized how much I'd be giving up when I married him."

She turned deliberately, walked across the room and grabbed both of Michelle's hands in hers. "I am such a coward, Michelle. A selfish, self-centered coward. Coop has every right to be angry with me. I can only pray he'll forgive me. I didn't stop to think about his feelings when I told him that stupid story about dying. It was selfish and unfair and cruel and I will be apologizing to that wonderful man for the rest of my natural days. I am not, however, going to let him get away. Not when I've just found him. I had no idea, none, what it was like to be loved by a good man until Cooperton Jones came to me and to my bed. That's a sad state of affairs, young woman, to have to wait almost eighty years to find out what real love is."

Lenore took a deep breath and exhaled. She looked enraged,

about to explode in anger. "Don't you dare waste what you've got with my grandson," she warned. "Don't you dare."

Speechless, Michelle stepped aside as Lenore swept by her and barreled out the door. The older woman's parting words hung in the air.

What, exactly, did she have with Tag?

A marriage, maybe? A real marriage? Without considering the consequences, Michelle walked back to the dressing table, grabbed the plain gold wedding band and slipped it on her finger. It definitely looked right, like it belonged there. She wondered what Mark would say when he finally noticed.

She wondered what she would say when he asked.

Then she decided she'd leave the explanations up to Tag.

Smiling at the potential for a really good scene in this convoluted plot, Michelle headed back to her room to dress for dinner.

MICHELLE BARELY heard the light tap on her bedroom door. Expecting Tag, it was all she could do not to rush to open it. First she tightened the belt on her robe then fluffed her hair back from her face. She cracked the door open a couple of inches. Mark stood in the hallway, a self-conscious smile on his face.

"May I come in?" he asked.

Michelle stood aside and Mark stepped hesitantly into the room. "I've just heard a pretty wild story from Martin," he said. His voice sounded strained, as if he controlled some powerful emotion. "It's got all the elements of the worst romance novel ever written and if anyone would know, it's me. More clichés and stupid plot twists than..."

Michelle didn't think she'd ever seen Mark looking as confused, distressed even, as he did at this moment. She placed her hands on his forearms and smiled. "Mark, it's not..."

"God, Michelle. Do you have any idea how worried I've been?" Before Michelle had any idea what he intended, before she could begin to resist, Mark was holding her, kissing the side of her neck, muttering unintelligible somethings in her ear.

Shock and surprise gave way to indignation. "Mark. Stop it!" She pushed against his chest, managed to create a small gap, and finally shoved hard enough to get his attention. "What do you think you're doing?"

He looked almost as shocked as she felt. In all the years she'd known Mark, he'd never once even made a pass at her. Their relationship had been businesslike and professional, though Michelle had long ago begun to think of him as her friend as well as her editor.

She smoothed the front of her robe, carefully closing the gap that had opened above the belt. The only other time Mark had ever seen her in a robe was when he'd stopped by to drop off a couple of cans of chicken soup and her galleys when she'd stayed home so sick with the flu she could barely see straight.

He'd made her cook her own soup and demanded she have the galleys proofread and corrected and back the next day.

"What was that all about?" She glared at him, wanting answers, explanations...definitely not wanting to anger him too much. He was after all, her editor.

Good editors were hard to find. She certainly didn't want him mad at her.

He took a deep breath. So deep his chest expanded, drawing Michelle's attention to the broad musculature visible even through his tailored white shirt. She immediately compared Mark's carefully sculpted build with Tag's rangy, lean muscles.

She almost licked her lips, thinking of Tag, not Mark. "Well?" she insisted.

"I'm sorry, Michelle. It's just..." He ran his fingers through his carefully styled blond hair and rubbed the back of his head in obvious frustration. "A week ago, I expected to hear from you. You didn't call and I figured, okay, she's just really mad at me for sending her off on this trip and she's going to make me worry about her, just to teach me a lesson.

"So, I thought, two can play this game. I didn't call you, either." He began pacing, back and forth across the small room.

Michelle sat on the edge of the bed to get out of his way.

"Then I started to get worried, so I casually dropped by your apartment, figured I'd catch you hiding from me, I'd give you a bad time, maybe forgive you...we'd have a good laugh. Obviously, that's not what happened. Your neighbor was down by the mailbox, collecting your mail and hers. She said no one had heard from you, that you were almost a week overdue from your trip."

He stopped pacing and stared despairingly at Michelle. "I think that was the precise moment, standing there in that little foyer, that I realized I loved you. I loved you and you were gone and no one knew where you were."

"Mark. I..."

"Let me finish." He grinned at her, the self-deprecating look of a man not used to dealing with strong, most likely unwanted, emotions. "It gets better, believe me. I raced back to the office and my phone was ringing. It was the Colorado State Police calling to report that your car had been dragged out of the river, but you were missing. There'd been no report of a body."

At that point, his face crumpled. Michelle fought every impulse she had to throw her arms around him and give him comfort. She couldn't...she wouldn't.

Not after what he'd just said. She sat quietly and listened.

"I had to come out here," he said, pleading with his eyes, his words. "I had to find you, tell you how I felt. Michelle, when Will Twig put that old codger on the phone and he told me you were alive, I figured it was an omen. It was telling me you'd been saved because I loved you, because you love me, and we were meant to be together."

He grabbed her hands in his and knelt before her on the worn bedroom carpet.

Michelle thought he looked terribly out of place in the old-fashioned room. Terribly out of place and way off base. "Mark," she hesitated over his name, wanting nothing more than to pull her hands out of his grasp.

"Mark," she repeated. "We've been friends for a long time, good friends, but..."

"Michelle, sweetheart, don't say it. You've had a terrible couple of weeks and..."

"It hasn't been all that terrible," she said, tugging her hands. He grasped them tighter. Suddenly he frowned.

"What's this?"

"A wedding ring. Tag told you the story, about the marriage, right?"

"Well, it's not a real marriage." Mark twisted the ring and tried to work it over her knuckle.

"Mark, don't," she said, finally pulling her hands free. "Didn't Tag explain? It is a real marriage, recorded and everything. We signed a legal license, said our vows in front of a real minister." She gave him what she hoped was a convincing smile and tried to forget that just a few hours ago she'd told Tag it wasn't real, that since she'd signed a false name it would never stand up in court.

Mark sat back on his heels and scowled. "Tag said it was a sham marriage, that the two of you only pretended to be married."

Mark's blunt words cut, deeply, painfully. Michelle took a deep breath, successfully finding control. "Tag was pretending," she answered honestly. "I wasn't. When I signed the license, I didn't know who I was, but I really thought we were married. I wanted to be married. Until we get it all straightened out..." She stood up, distancing herself from Mark.

He didn't take the hint. "You can't honestly be in love with that," he paused, as if searching for the perfect disparaging description. "That cowboy. Good Lord, Michelle, you've lived in New York since you were eighteen years old! You love the plays, you go to the opera. You're a writer. You can't expect him to just up and move to New York City, can you?"

"Sneering is so unbecoming, Mark." Michelle glared at him. "Why would he expect to move to New York? The obvious thing would be for me to live here." Who was she kidding? Michelle could literally feel her heart sink. Tag didn't want her here. He didn't want anything to do with her.

"Has he asked you?" Mark wasn't sneering, but Michelle knew the sound of triumph in a man's voice when she heard it.

"No," she said. "He hasn't. Yet."

"Well don't count on it, Michelle. That man's country through and through. You're not. The only thing he's interested in is that deed to the Double Eagle his grandmother just handed to him out there in the kitchen. He was so busy drooling over it, I doubt he even knows I left the room."

"So," Michelle said, as much to herself as to Mark. "Tag's finally got his ranch." Which meant he didn't need her any longer. Of course, he hadn't needed her from the moment Lenore learned of the whole charade.

"I have to dress for supper," she said. It wasn't easy, but she held the tears at bay and looked straight into Mark's pale blue eyes. At least he had the decency not to gloat. "I'll be there in a minute."

"Michelle." Mark gently caressed her shoulder. She couldn't help but think of the shock of contact every time Tag touched her. The sizzle.

There'd be no sizzle with Mark, but he was a good man. He was her friend, even if she didn't love him the way he wanted her to. He represented everything familiar, everything she'd always known, always done.

"Think about what I said, Michelle. I know it's probably come as a shock, but I do love you. We have a lot of history, you and I.

Marriages have succeeded with a lot less."

"Are you proposing? Are you saying you want to marry me?" For a romance editor he certainly wasn't much of a romantic.

"I'm just asking you to think about it." He leaned over and kissed her very lightly on the lips. She wanted to feel something, anything besides the warm pressure of his mouth on hers.

No sizzle.

She couldn't meet his eyes. "I'll keep an open mind," she said. She turned away, her hands waiting at the knot holding her robe together. She didn't untie it until she heard the bedroom door close softly behind Mark.

She untied it, but it was a long time before she found enough energy to take the robe off and slip into a clean pair of Tag's old boxer shorts, a worn pair of jeans and a warm sweater.

It was another half hour before she motivated herself enough to head down the hallway to the front door, across the yard and out to the barn.

She'd check on Star and Goldie first. Then, maybe, she'd have the energy to face Tag.

Chapter 13

TAG RAN the comb through Goldie's silvery mane, unwinding more with each steady stroke. Concentrating intently on the occasional tangle, he felt his tight muscles slowly begin to loosen and relax. The rain beat a hypnotic tattoo against the tin roof, the horses crunched and munched noisily through their daily ration of grain and Star slurped and grunted as he suckled and occasionally butted his nose against the placid mare.

Dandy hung his head over the side of the stall and nudged Tag's shoulder. "Your turn next, big guy." Tag scratched between Dandy's ears, then returned to the job of combing tangles out of Goldie's mane.

This was the place that brought him peace, usually. This barn, these animals. This was the one spot in all the world where he'd always found the answers.

Why couldn't he find them today? Sighing heavily, Tag finished with Goldie, grabbed the brush and curry comb and moved over to Dandy's stall. Dandy nickered and moved aside so Tag could open the door. A moment later he whinnied as a quiet footfall sounded nearby.

Startled, Tag spun around.

"Tag? I'm sorry, I didn't know you were out here." Michelle moved into the pale light cast by the single bulb Tag had left burning. "I came out to check on Star. It's storming so badly, you've been gone for so long, I was..."

"Star's fine," Tag said, surprising himself with the ease with which his lips formed the words. His mouth was suddenly dry as cotton, his heart hammered as if he'd drawn a killer bull and he wanted to hold Michelle so badly it was all he could do to keep from grabbing her up in his arms. "How are you?"

Her head came up, her green eyes filled with surprise. Good. Her turn. She'd certainly thrown him a surprise or two today.

"I...I'm fine, actually. In fact..." She might have been blushing. It was so gloomy inside the barn he couldn't be sure. "I'm glad I caught you out here, alone. I thought you'd like to know..." She clasped her hands in front of her, hesitated, then appeared to draw strength from somewhere deep inside herself.

"I wanted you to know I started my period today, a little while ago. I'm not pregnant. The first couple of times we..."

Her voice drifted off and she looked away, almost as if she regretted...? No, that couldn't be. Tag reached his hand out to her, dropped it back to his side. He wasn't quite certain how he felt. He guessed he should be pleased their irresponsible actions hadn't made a baby.

He wasn't. Instead, he felt deeply, inexplicably saddened by her news. He wished he could tell her he'd imagined her growing round with his child, wondered what the two of them, he with his dark hair and blue eyes, she redheaded and green-eyed, would produce. "That's good, I guess. Lee...Michelle..." He laughed, a short bark that sounded awfully strained even to himself. "I guess I need more practice to get it right."

"Why?" She turned and stared at him. Her eyes, usually so bright and loving, glimmered like dark pools in her face.

"Why what?" he asked.

"Why would you want to practice getting it right? I'll be gone once the road's open. You'll never have to say it again."

He hadn't considered that. Hadn't really thought of her leaving. Had only thought about her somehow deciding to stay on at the Double Eagle indefinitely. Now that they didn't have to pretend, why couldn't she just stay awhile, see what happened....

He said as much.

"You know what'll happen," Michelle said, straightening her spine and showing her first spark of fire since she'd walked into the barn. "We'll end up in bed having absolutely exquisite sex, but nothing will ever be settled. You'll go off and do your cowboy thing, expecting me to wait here until you come back, never knowing what the future holds, never..."

"Exquisite, huh?" He grinned. She glared back at him. Maybe he'd better wait and come back to that topic later.

But not too much later.

"I wouldn't expect you to wait here," he said. Where had she gotten an idea like that? "I'd want you to come with me. You've gotten really good on a horse, Michelle. You were a lot of help on the round-up. More than I ever expected, that's for sure." He thought of the laughter they'd shared, the long talks far into the night even when they knew they had to be back to work at dawn. The touching, the times spent holding each other, not making love, just holding each other tight and falling asleep.

The sex, though. Now that had been special. *Exquisite.* He couldn't think of a better way to describe what they'd shared. He wished he could explain how it had been for him, how far above and beyond any physical intimacy he'd ever experienced with anyone. He really wanted to say something about it, but she didn't look as if that would make any points with her right now.

"Yeah," he said after only a brief hesitation, "for not knowing a thing about cows or horses, you did fine." He gave her what he thought was an encouraging smile.

"Gee, thanks."

He wondered how difficult it was for her to talk through that clenched jaw of hers. Why, when it had been so easy for the two of them to communicate during the past couple of weeks, was he having such a terrible time saying the right things now? "Are you sure you don't want to stay on...just for a while longer?"

"Sorry, Tag. I don't think so. Mark and I plan to leave as soon as the road's open." She averted her eyes and turned to go.

Tag's chest felt as if someone had clamped a vise on him. "Michelle." He stepped out into the passage between the stalls. "At least for a few days?" God, he was begging. He'd never begged a woman for anything, but he needed a reason, any reason, something that would keep her here until he figured out exactly what to do with her.

About her.

"We still have to get this mess with the marriage untangled," he said, grasping the first thing he thought of. "I won't know if we're married or not until I can check with the county registrar. You can't leave until then."

She gave him a look as if she thought he was the biggest jerk on the face of the earth. "Tag, you got your ranch, exactly like you wanted. Your grandmother is healthy, Coop's back in the bunkhouse where he belongs. I'm sure you can figure out how to untangle one simple little marriage of convenience without me here to help."

She spun around and was gone before he could think of an answer. At least an answer other than the one he couldn't bring himself to say aloud...*Stay for me, Michelle. Stay because I can't imagine life without you anymore.*

THE LAMP flickered, then glowed steadily. Curled up in the big old leather couch in the front room, Michelle flipped through the pages of the Western Horseman magazine, the one with the article about Tag and Will Twigg and his sister Betsy. Every time she reread the pages, more of her erroneous memories made sense. She'd absorbed everything she'd read, added some of the plot from her unsold manuscript, mixed the memories together and recreated her past. Unbelievable.

She stared at the photo of a smiling Betsy Mae and wondered how she could ever have imagined actually knowing her. Could have believed she belonged here, in the hills of Colorado. A fire roared in the huge stone fireplace, the wind howled and whistled outside and an occasional flash of lightning split the gloom.

At the opposite end of the couch, Mark fiddled with an ancient Rubric's cube. Michelle knew he periodically glanced in her direction, but she'd done her best to ignore him. Lenore banged and chopped and stirred out in the kitchen, preparing, as she'd told Michelle, the meal that would win her man back.

Tag hadn't come inside all afternoon.

The lights flickered again, stayed off a moment, came back on. Michelle looked up from her magazine just as thunder boomed directly overhead. "I'd better get some candles," she said.

Lightning flashed, plunging the room into darkness. "Great timing," Mark said dryly. "Now what?"

"Don't worry," Lenore called from the kitchen. "I've got candles and a couple of lanterns." A pale glow preceded her as she crossed the hallway from the kitchen to the front room. "There's baked chicken and a rice casserole in the warming oven over the wood stove and a fruit salad in the 'frig. It'll stay plenty cold even without the power. I'll leave this lantern here for you two."

Lenore juggled a flashlight in one hand and two heavy baskets in the other. She stopped at the door and smiled at Michelle. "I'm taking a meal over to the bunkhouse for the boys, then I'm going to see if I can locate a certain hard-headed cowboy. With any luck, you won't see me 'till mornin'." Then she winked, opened the door against the howling wind and headed out into the pouring rain.

"Explanation?" Mark asked. "Why won't she be home until morning?"

"She'll be busy," Michelle laughed. *Go girl,* she added silently. At least Gramma Lenore had the guts to go after what she really wanted. "Coop, the old foreman? He's the hard-headed cowboy she's taking dinner to. I think she's intending to spend the night with him."

"But she's so old!" Mark looked as if he didn't know whether to laugh or be ill. "She must be seventy years old if she's a day."

"Actually, she's almost eighty," Michelle said. She grabbed the lantern Lenore had left on the table and stood up. "They've been in love for over sixty years, but it's taken that long for them to finally get together. I envy them what they've found."

Mark snorted in disbelief.

"For a man who deals in romance every day, you haven't got a clue, have you?" Michelle waited for an answer. When none came, she headed for the kitchen and the enticing aromas of chicken baking in rosemary, garlic and lemon.

She set the lantern on the counter, folded her arms and stared into the flickering flame. What was wrong with her? Two men in her life, both of them jerks. Mark as handsome and urbane as could be, in love with himself, but claiming he was ready to marry her if she'd only say yes. Tag, even better looking, trying to hang on to her long enough to figure out what to do with her as long as it didn't include marriage.

Was it so wrong to want a little romance in her life? To want the sizzle Lenore and Coop had discovered after all these years? To want courting and kisses, words of love and promises, a future?

Mark promised the future, Tag had the sizzle. Wouldn't it be great if she could just figure out a blend of some kind?

The image wouldn't jell. Tag and Mark were nothing alike. She'd forget both of them if she could. Start fresh, look for a man who met her expectations.

From past experience, Michelle knew that was impossible.

Did she fight for Tag? Should she risk a broken heart but hope for the best, or open her heart to possibilities and familiarity with Mark?

Michelle suddenly imagined a cartoon strip woman with a bubble over her head, a groan of Aaarrgghhh! in bold type filling the empty space. She giggled. Whenever she'd written a story with a heroine forced to choose between two men, the answers had always come so easily, the solution neatly bundled in a few tightly written paragraphs.

One thing she'd learned on this adventure—life didn't happen in tightly written paragraphs. Life had convoluted story lines with plots and subplots, unsolved problems and complicated emotions. The answers weren't always the ones you wanted, either.

Mark wandered into the room, obviously following the light and his nose, drawn by the rich scent of Lenore's chicken dinner. He looked expectantly at Michelle.

"We might as well have dinner," she said. "Tag could be out all night if the storm causes problems with the stock."

Mark's answering grin might have knocked her socks off. Might, if she didn't already have Tag's lopsided, rakish smile for comparison.

Sighing in frustration, Michelle wondered for a brief moment if Mark was grinning because she'd offered to feed him, or at the thought of an evening without Tag. The way he attacked his dinner a few minutes later, she figured it must be the food.

TAG HUNG his wet coat and hat on the rack by the door, slipped his muddy boots off, then trudged into the kitchen. Michelle and her editor sat across from each other at the kitchen table. Candles glowed between them, each held a glass of wine as if preparing to toast, their eyes were so caught in each other's gaze neither one seemed aware he'd even entered the room.

Michelle noticed first. She glanced up, obviously startled to see him standing in the doorway. "Tag!" She set her wine glass on the table and stood up. "Let me fix you a plate. Your grandmother..."

"That's okay," he said. "Finish your dinner. I'll take mine out to the barn. I've still got some work to do." He knew he was running away, knew he should stay and at least challenge Mark Connor, but damn, it'd been a long day. He was just too tired, and from the way Michelle'd been looking at the man, it wouldn't do him any good anyway.

He and Coop had worked their tails off for the past few hours. Coop was still checking fence along the north pasture and all that time these two had been sitting in here by a hot woodstove, drinking his wine and eating his food by candlelight, making calf's eyes at one another. Grumbling under his breath, Tag washed his hands in the kitchen sink then grabbed a plate and loaded it with enough to last him awhile.

"Did you have any problems?" Michelle asked.

"A few head caught in some low spots. Me'n Coop got em' to high ground, but I'm sure we missed some." Tag grabbed a knife and fork and his overflowing plate, then found a cold beer in the refrigerator.

Inspiration struck. "Coop's pretty tired," he said, looking pointedly at Michelle. "Would you be willing to lend a hand tomorrow? The storm should blow through tonight. It'll be hard, muddy work, but at least the sun should be shining."

"If your grandmother has her way, Coop won't get much sleep tonight, either," Michelle said. At least she was smiling. "Of course I'll..."

Mark interrupted her. "We'll both be glad to help, won't we?" He grabbed Michelle's hand possessively. Tag clenched his teeth and wondered why she didn't pull her hand free. Finally, Mark released her. She quickly grabbed her wine glass.

Tag thought her fingers were shaking, but he couldn't tell, not in the faint glow of candlelight. He felt tight as a coiled spring, so he took a deep breath to release some of the tension. "Can you ride?" he asked Mark.

"Not as well as you, I'm sure, but I did spend a few weeks over at Columbine Camp this spring. I learned a lot more about horses than I expected."

"Will Twig's a good teacher," Tag acknowledged. He'd much prefer a day alone with Michelle, but right now he needed the help. If Gramma Lenore had her way, Coop was definitely out of the question, most of his crew would have their hands full up packing and loading the gear from the round-up, which left the Double Eagle more short handed than usual.

The ranch came first, his convoluted love life, if there even was one, would have to stay way down on Tag's list of priorities. "We'll leave at sunrise. I'll have fresh mounts for both of you in front of the barn." He chanced a quick glance at Michelle, then quickly turned and left the kitchen. The look of pain in her eyes was almost his undoing.

TAG UNSADDLED Nitro and dried him off before brushing the big stallion down. The horse shifted uneasily beneath his touch, obviously favoring his left rear leg. Tag leaned over and propped Nitro's foot against the front of his thigh to check the shoe. A nail had come loose and the iron shoe was damaged.

Tag carefully pried the rest of the nails out of the animal's hoof and removed the shoe. One more thing to worry about in the morning. The storm still raged overhead, but according to the satellite readings he'd checked on the computer earlier, it should blow itself out by first light. Hopefully he or Coop would have a chance to get Nitro reshod in the next day or two, but until then the horse was out of commission.

Tag patted the big stallion on the rump, then sat on a bale of hay outside the stall and wolfed down his supper. Even his taste buds were too exhausted to care what he ate.

Tag looked up just as Coop led his little sorrel cow pony into the barn. Water dribbled from the brim of the older man's hat and his clothes appeared to be soaked clean through in spite of the heavy oilcloth slicker.

In the muted glow from the emergency lamps in the barn, Coop looked twice his age, his skin gray-tinged and the lines around his mouth deeply etched. Dark circles shadowed his eyes.

"Thanks for your help," Tag said. He set his plate aside and took the reins from Coop. The poor old guy looked beat half to death, what with the past couple of hours of work that would have exhausted a younger man. Tag and Coop and a couple of the boys had pulled more than a dozen head of cattle out of flooded low spots near the creek. Hard to believe that lazy little stream could stretch sixty feet across and a good six feet deep at the middle after just one good storm.

Now Coop looked as if he were ready to fold. The two ranch hands were grabbing a quick bite of Gramma Lenore's dinner at the bunkhouse, then heading back out for a second shift. Tag knew Coop expected to go out again in the morning, but if he were a bettin' man, he wouldn't bet Coop could make it to bed on his own, much less back on his horse in less than eight hours.

Thank goodness Michelle and her damned editor had agreed to help. Now, if he could figure out how to convince Coop to take a day off. "Why don't you get some grub," he said. "I'll take care of the ponies. It's been a pretty long day."

"You're darned right it's been a long day." Gramma Lenore stepped into the barn and shoved the yellow slicker back off her hair. "You've had this old man long enough, Taggart Martin. It's my turn."

Coop stared at Lenore, his mouth open in surprise and a twinkle in his eye that certainly hadn't been there a moment earlier. He snapped his jaws shut. "So you say, 'eh old woman?"

"So I say. You're soaking wet, you haven't eaten all day and you look exhausted. Now get your scrawny butt over to your room so I can get some of my good chicken dinner into you before you keel over. Then you're gonna take a long, hot bath and soak some of the aches and pains out of that beat up old carcass of yours."

Tag would've said he was too tired and too miserable to grin, but right now he couldn't help himself. As far as Coop and his grandmother were concerned, they were the only folks in the barn. He felt like a voyeur, watching the two people who'd been like parents to him, knowing their cantankerous arguing was just their brand of foreplay, a prelude to a fine night together.

He hoped they'd have lots of nights together. Coop had been absolutely miserable company over the past few hours, frettin' over how to make things right with Lenore.

Coop took Lenore's arm and guided her toward the back door of the barn that led to his private quarters at the far end of the bunkhouse. "Now, this here hot bath you're talkin' about..." Coop glanced back over his shoulder, grinned and winked at Tag.

Tag waved. "I've got you covered tomorrow," he said. "Don't get up early on my account."

Coop positively beamed. Then he turned his attention back to the woman at his side. "Is this bath one I'll be takin' by myself, or is some sweet young thing gonna crawl in that big tub and wash my back for me?"

"You wouldn't know what to do with a sweet young thing! Anybody besides me crawls in a tub with you, old man, and..."

Their voices disappeared as the door shut quietly behind them. Tag looked down at his muddy boots and thought of the big tub up at the line shack, of the scrubbing and loving he and Michelle had managed to share over the past two weeks.

He wondered what she was doing right now, if she thought of him at all, if she'd worried about him, out checking on his ranch in the storm.

His ranch. He did like the sound of that, even more knowing his grandmother had intended all along that it go to him.

Then he remembered Mark Connor. No reason for Michelle to worry about Tag, not when she had her fancy New York editor here to keep her company.

Until bedtime. Gramma Lenore had found Connor an extra bed in the bunkhouse. Unless, of course, Michelle invited him to stay with her. Tag hadn't even thought of that. Maybe he should have.

Coop's pony snorted and nickered. "Okay, little guy. I'll get you dried off, too." Tag put Michelle and Mark Connor out of his mind, grabbed the brush and an extra towel and went to work on the horses. At least with them he knew exactly where he stood.

MICHELLE WAS applying a bit of gloss to keep her lips from chapping when Mark knocked on the door. She knew it was Mark, recognized his knock just as she had known Tag's hesitant step last night when, much later than she, he'd headed down the hall to his bedroom. She knew the exact moment he paused outside her door, felt the indecision filling his mind, and anticipated his quiet step as he'd continued on to his own room.

She had huddled there in the big, lonely bed and thought of following him, knocking on his door and joining him in the old double bed of his childhood room.

"Michelle? Are you ready to go? It's getting late."

"Coming, Mark." She had to stop thinking of Tag like that. She grabbed a coat and her ratty looking Stetson, jammed the hat down on her head and swung the door open.

She hardly recognized Mark. He stood there, leaning against the wall opposite her door, one jeans-clad knee bent, his worn cowboy boot resting against the baseboard behind him, thumbs tucked loosely in his front pockets. His jeans were faded and fit like a glove, the boots less worn but definitely not brand new. His shirt was a pale blue chambray, the same color as his eyes. He wore a red kerchief tied around his throat.

"My goodness," she said, accompanying her words with a low whistle. "Whatever happened to my fancy pants New York editor? You almost look like a real wrangler." Michelle shut the door behind her and stood in front of Mark, both hands resting on her hips. "There's a side of you I guess I haven't seen," she said.

"What do ya mean, I almost look like a real wrangler. I am a real wrangler. Can't you tell?" He adjusted his black Stetson just so. "If it looks like a cowboy, acts like a cowboy, etcetera, etcetera. I told you that trip to Columbine Camp made a big impression on me." He laughed, shoved himself away from the wall and tucked her hand around his arm. "C'mon, sweetheart. We've got cows to wrangle."

There was something to be said about the familiar, Michelle thought, especially when the familiar came packaged in faded blue jeans and a Chambray shirt. She looked down at her hand, resting comfortably on Mark's arm.

Something, but not nearly enough.

The sun was barely rising over the nearby hills, the air still carried a decided chill and out in front of the barn Tag was saddling Chief. Bob the Dog crouched beside the gate, one ear pricked forward, his body in a state of readiness. He obviously had no intention of missing the fun.

Two other horses waited nearby, one a lanky dark red sorrel

gelding, the other a compact buckskin mare. Tag glanced up as Michelle and Mark crossed the yard. Michelle tried to slip her arm free of Mark's as unobtrusively as she could, but he suddenly tightened his grip.

She glared at him, he grinned back at her and carefully loosened his hold on her arm. "Good morning," Michelle said, stepping quickly away from Mark. "I thought I'd be riding Daisy."

She stroked the thick tan colored neck on the buckskin and tangled her fingers in the black mane as she scratched along the horse's neck. The animal snorted with pleasure.

"Daisy's too inexperienced to work her around the creeks when the water is so high," Tag said. "Marcia's got a lot of..."

"Marcia?" Michelle turned the horse's big head around so they faced each other. "You named a horse Marcia?"

Tag deadpanned. "Old girlfriend," he said. "She had hair about that color. Unfortunately, she was built a lot like the horse; flat chest, skinny legs, broad rump."

"I don't think I need any more details." Michelle grinned. "What's that one's name, or should I even ask?"

"Red."

"Named after...?"

"He's red." Tag looked at her as if she didn't have a clue, but Michelle caught the twitch at the corner of his mouth, proof he was struggling not to give way to that fascinating lopsided smile of his. They held each other's gaze a moment longer than necessary. Then Tag broke the contact.

"C'mon, cowboy," he said, gesturing to Mark. "Let's get your stirrups adjusted."

Mark mounted the red gelding easily, settled into the saddle as if he knew exactly what he was doing, and slipped his feet into the stirrups so Tag could adjust the length. Mark straightened his legs out to check the fit and thanked Tag.

Michelle mounted Marcia. Tag had saddled the mare with the same saddle she'd used for the past two weeks, so no adjustments were necessary. Tag swung his leg over Chief and settled into the saddle, while Bob the Dog barked and ran in circles around the horses. Mark's horse snorted and pranced, Michelle's followed suit and they all whirled about and headed out the main road.

The three horses tossed their heads and fought the bits as Tag led Michelle and Mark across the long valley in the direction of the flooded pasture. "Let's give these ponies their heads and burn out some oats."

Tag leaned forward and Chief practically exploded. Within seconds they were galloping across the flat ground, the easy rhythm of well-trained horses a pleasure at the faster pace.

Michelle laughed aloud, her legs gripped the mare's sides and she felt as much a part of the animal as the leather saddle securely fastened to Marcia's back. Mark cut loose with an Indian yell. Tag turned his head to laugh at both of them.

By late afternoon, galloping was the last thing on anyone's mind. Michelle took a long swallow of water out of her canteen and wiped her face with the back of her sleeve, then realized she'd transferred the mud on her shirt to most of her forehead and across her mouth. Mark sat hunched over in the saddle, his shirt mud-covered and torn and a large bruise from close contact with a calf's hard head marking his left cheek.

He'd probably have a black eye in the morning.

Even Tag looked exhausted, but the missing cattle were almost all accounted for and they'd finished the work before sundown.

Ramón trotted up on his big bay. "Señor Tag, we found the missing cow and calf, the big Hereford you asked about."

Michelle knew this particular cow was a key to Tag's new breeding stock. Her calf, a healthy bull, was one of the few that hadn't been castrated during round-up.

Tag turned and grinned at Ramón. "Why is it I have a feeling this isn't good news?" Ramón shook his head and laughed aloud.

"Because you've been in this business too long, Señor. The pair found a high spot in the middle of the creek. Unfortunately, it's soft earth and appears to be shrinking...other than that, they're just fine."

Tag audibly sighed. "You up for one more rescue?" he asked. Then, without waiting for an answer, Tag turned Chief's head towards the trail Ramón was taking.

"You know, the weekly meetings with marketing are beginning to sound more appealing every minute," Mark said dryly. He took a swallow of water and screwed the lid back on the canteen. "Coming, Michelle?" he inquired, as if inviting her in to tea. Then, before she could answer, he turned his horse's head and trotted after Ramón and Tag.

Bob the Dog cantered along on Marcia's heels as the tiny parade of humans and beasts worked their way closer to a rugged section of river canyon. They toiled their way higher into the canyon, passing huge piles of brush and trees that had washed into the river and formed a series of temporary dams.

The steady roar of the flood-swollen stream intensified as they passed one area where the flood from yesterday's storm had carved a deep fissure through the earth. Rather than the wide flowing stream farther out in the valley, this water surged and frothed through a narrow section of rocky cliffs.

Just above it, standing hoof-deep in the rapidly sinking muddy island, stood Tag's favorite Hereford cow and her calf.

Her white face was spattered with mud and she rested awkwardly on three legs, as if her right front one had been injured. The calf seemed healthy enough, but the water was rising quickly and it was obvious he was exhausted from his long night on their deteriorating refuge.

Tag assessed the situation quickly. The water was too deep to cross on horseback, the surging river too powerful a force to swim. There was a dead tree on the far side of the creek, a healthy live oak on this side. The snag was out of range of his lasso, but not so far that two ropes couldn't be tied together then tied off between the trees...if only he could get one end across the water.

"It looks narrower up above us," Mark said, reading his mind perfectly. "Let me take one end of the rope and see if I can cross. Once it's attached..."

"Let's do it," Tag said. He and Mark raced their horses to the narrow section of the river where a large tree had fallen and partially blocked the flow of water. Mark dismounted, took one end of the rope and crossed the creek as far as he could on the fallen log, then struggled through the swirling water, tangled brush and piled rocks until he emerged safely on the far side.

By the time he and Tag had reached their respective trees, the rope barely reached the distance across the water. Mark looped his end over a sturdy branch while Tag tied his off to the trunk of the oak. Michelle held on to all three horses. When Tag turned back to the creek, she handed him the rope from her saddle.

"Good luck. Be careful," she whispered. Then she kissed him, for luck, he figured.

He almost forgot about the damned cow and Michelle's boyfriend on the other side of the creek.

"Yeah," he muttered. Then he looped the extra rope over his

shoulder, grabbed the one stretched between the trees and walked out into the raging current. The icy water reached his knees, then his waist, sweeping his feet out from under him.

Ramón, Michelle and even Mark shouted encouragement. The cow mooed, the calf bawled and Bob the Dog ran in circles, dipping his front feet in the water then backing out again, barking furiously the whole time. The cow shook her lowered head threateningly as Tag approached, but he managed to loop the lasso over her neck and throw the other end to Ramón.

Tag climbed up onto the muddy outcropping and grabbed the calf in his arms just as Ramón backed his horse up and hauled the cow off her precarious perch. She hit the river swimming, her powerful strokes aided by the steady tug of the rope and within minutes was safely on dry land, calling for her calf.

Tag tucked the frightened, squirming youngster under his arm, looped his free arm over the rope and headed for shore. The weight of the calf helped him keep his feet under him this time. Michelle steadied the rope, then helped grab the calf from Tag and pull it on to dry land.

None the worse for wear, limping only slightly, the cow and calf ambled away as if nothing out of the ordinary had happened. Tag lay on his back in the mud, gasping for breath.

"That was pretty impressive, cowboy." Michelle leaned over him, the streak of mud across her face just adding to her allure as far as he Tag was concerned. "Need some help?" she asked, holding her hand out to him.

Tag grabbed her hand, but didn't try to sit up. He figured this might be the last time ever he'd be lying on his back with Michelle holding his hand, leaning over him, looking as if she cared. Looking like she might be moving a little bit closer, maybe even close enough to kiss?

Mark cried out. Michelle blinked and spun around. Tag sat up, just in time to see Mark completely lose his footing on the fallen tree and tumble into the roiling creek.

Michelle screamed. Tag didn't hesitate. He leaped into the water at a point where he hoped Mark would emerge from the froth. The powerful surge of floodwater tore at his legs and threatened to upend him. Suddenly, Mark popped to the surface, not two feet in front of him. Tag grabbed the other man's arm, but Mark didn't respond, neither fighting him nor trying to help.

Michelle yelled as Tag struggled to hold on to the man. Tag

realized she was wading into the creek beside him, the loose end of the rope grasped firmly in both hands. "Here," she said, "tie this around him."

Tag looped the rope around Mark's waist and with Michelle's help beside him and Ramón hauling with all his strength, managed to get the unconscious man to shore. They stretched Mark out on the ground, turned his head to one side and Tag pounded on his back until he spit out a stream of water.

Coughing, gasping for air, Mark rolled over on to his back and lay still, but his eyes were open, he was alert, he was alive, and he was staring with unabashed adoration at Michelle.

"You saved my life," he said, grabbing her hand with both of his.

"Tag saved your life," she answered, looking directly at Tag. "I just gave him the rope."

Enough rope to hang myself, Tag thought, briefly imagining how it would have been if he hadn't dragged Connor to safety.

Hell, he could never let a man drown, especially this one. He actually liked the guy. Mark Connor had worked his tail off today, put in hard hours like any cowhand. Tag could see why Michelle loved the man. Just his luck, finally to fall in love with a woman and actually like the guy she was probably going to marry.

"Think you can ride?" Tag asked.

Mark sat up, shivering in the late afternoon chill. "I'll be fine, if I don't freeze to death first." He tried to laugh, but Tag could tell he was dangerously chilled. Tag was half frozen, but he hadn't nearly drowned. Mark needed help, and fast.

"Get up on Marcia, behind Michelle, and I'll throw a blanket around you. With her body heat and the warm blanket you should be fine till we get back to the ranch."

Michelle frowned at Tag. Now what could be bugging her? Wasn't he doing just what she wanted, giving her the chance to get close to the guy? Even though it was tearing him up to see them all huddled together under the wool army blanket Tag kept rolled behind his saddle, he knew it was best this way.

He might have fought for her, if Connor wasn't such an obvious match. Michelle was a writer, Mark Connor was an editor. Similar interests, similar lifestyles. Two beautiful, well-educated people who obviously cared about each other.

Silently Tag mounted Chief and grabbed Red's reins. Michelle'd risked her life to help him save her man. Tag wanted to think she'd done it to help him, but he knew the truth. She'd been afraid of losing Mark. She hadn't trusted Tag to do the job.

It was a long, cold, quiet ride back to the ranch.

THE SUN HAD long ago disappeared behind the mountains by the time Tag unsaddled the horses, fed and settled them down for the night and got a change of dry clothes for himself. Michelle had offered to help but he'd sent her in to the house to warm up. Mark had headed for the bunkhouse the moment they arrived and hadn't been seen since.

Coop ambled across the yard, whistling softly. "Evenin'," he said. He propped one foot on the bottom rail of the corral and stared off in the direction of the dark mountains.

Tag grunted. He wasn't in the mood to hear about Coop's terrific day with the love of his life.

"Will called," Coop said, staring off in the distance. "The road's repaired. They finished ahead of schedule." He turned his head. From the sorrow etched in the old man's face, Tag knew what was coming next.

"Michelle and her editor are fixin' to leave in the morning. Thought you ought to know." Without another word, Coop turned away and walked silently back to the house.

Tag blanked the pain from his heart and stared blindly into the night.

Chapter 14

MICHELLE SHOVED the rest of her things into the beat-up suitcase. She set aside one pair of Tag's plaid boxer shorts to wear with her jeans in the morning. He wouldn't miss one pair, she figured. She couldn't bear to leave them behind.

It was going to be hard enough leaving Tag.

A quiet tap sounded on the bedroom door. Tightening the belt around the worn robe, Michelle shoved her damp hair out of her eyes and opened the door.

Lenore smiled sadly and stepped into the room. "Are you absolutely certain?" She took hold of both of Michelle's hands. "He loves you. I'm sure of it."

"He might love me, Lenore. He probably does, in his own way. Unfortunately, Tag's not sure of it." Michelle squeezed Lenore's fingers, then crossed the room to the bedroom window and stared out into the darkness. Lenore's figure and her own reflected back in the clear glass.

Old and young. One discovering love, the other leaving it behind. "I can't stay here and hope he'll figure it out someday." Michelle turned to face Lenore. "I'm thirty-four years old. I never thought of myself as a wife or mother, not until I met Tag. I don't think I've ever been in love before, not when I compare those feelings I've had for other men with how I feel now. But I won't settle, Lenore. I want real love, the kind of love a man declares without any hesitation, without any shame. I want the sizzle."

She blushed, embarrassed she'd actually said it out loud. "I want what you and Coop have, Lenore. The passion, the desire, the need to share your lives. There's no doubt Coop loves you. He's loved you for so long it's like breathing to him. Is it asking too much to want to be the air Tag breathes?" She laughed, a humorless sound even to her own ears. "Sounds dumb, doesn't it? To want to be loved that much?"

"No," Lenore said, pulling Michelle into her arms. "No, sweetheart, it doesn't sound dumb at all. My grandson's a fool if he can't see what he's losing, but maybe you're right. Maybe if you go, he'll realize what he's giving up. Maybe then..."

"I don't see Tag following me to New York." Michelle hugged Lenore back, then sat on the edge of the bed. "I think, once I'm gone, he'll throw himself into running the Double Eagle and before long he'll have himself convinced that what we shared wasn't all that great."

She followed the quilted design on the bedspread with one blunt fingernail, remembering the perfectly painted ovals she'd had when she first arrived.

Had it only been three weeks? She looked down at her hands, at the rough palms seamed and lined with ridges of callus and knew she was a different person in more than appearance. Her three weeks at the Double Eagle had changed her life in more ways than she ever could have imagined.

"I can tell you one thing," she said, feeling new strengths within herself. "Tag Martin may be the master of denial when it comes to his emotions, but he's never going to find another woman like me. He can ignore how he feels all he wants, but it's his loss. I'm not staying. I'm not going to spend my life waiting and wishing for something that's not gonna happen."

Lenore sagged against the wall. "Does that mean you're going to marry Mark? He told me he'd asked you, but you hadn't given him an answer."

Michelle thought about it, about the passion she shared with Tag, the friendship she had with Mark. "I don't honestly know," she said. "I've never really thought of Mark...that way. Maybe, now that I know how he feels..." She sighed. "Let's just say I'm going to leave myself open, okay? Maybe in time, but if nothing happens I'll still have a good friend."

"Don't do anything rash, dear." Lenore's soft admonition wasn't lost on Michelle. This from a woman who'd married the wrong man and regretted it most of her adult life.

"I won't, Lenore. I promise."

Lenore quietly left the room. Michelle paced the confining space for a couple of minutes, then decided on one last trip to the barn to see Star.

She slipped her feet into her boots, wrapped the robe tightly around herself and headed through the darkness to the barn. A few bulbs glowed dimly, the smells of horse and hay filled her senses and Michelle knew an immediate sense of calm.

She never would have dreamed she'd grow to love this kind of life as much as she had, never thought she could so easily give up the familiarity of everything she'd left behind.

Never dreamed how much she would miss it when she finally had to leave.

Goldie munched quietly on her flake of alfalfa. Star slept in the sweet smelling hay, his skinny legs stretched out at right angles to his body, his velvety nostrils fluttering with each breath. Michelle stroked Goldie's soft muzzle and marveled at the miracle of the tiny colt's life. A miracle she had helped to bring about. Her eyes stung, remembering.

Bob the Dog trotted into the barn and nuzzled Michelle's leg up under her robe. "Hey, beast," she said, kneeling down to pet him. "Your nose is cold!"

The dog immediately rolled over on his back, presenting Michelle with a soft tummy in dire need of scratching. She rubbed his belly for a few minutes, wondering how it would be if she got a dog once she got home.

Home. She'd lived at the Double Eagle for a mere three weeks, but it felt more like home than her little apartment over Central Park ever had.

A quiet snort followed by soft whispers caught her attention. Giving Bob the Dog a final scratch, Michelle stood up and followed the sound. At the far end of the barn in the heavily reinforced stall reserved for Tag's stallion, she could see someone moving.

Tag. He appeared unaware of her presence, so intent on brushing and currying the big horse. Michelle placed her hand on the dog's head, signaling for him to be quiet and slipped closer to Tag. She would never have this opportunity again, the chance to watch him unobserved. After tomorrow, she'd probably never see him again at all.

Biting her lips to stop the tears, Michelle edged even closer to the stall. Neither Tag nor the horse could see her, she knew, but suddenly Nitro's big body tensed and he reared up, pulling away from Tag.

Tag grabbed for the halter, crooning softly to the stallion, but the horse's agitation increased. He whinnied, a bellowing stallion's call and flailed his hooves, narrowly missing Tag.

Michelle screamed. She ran forward, wanting to help, not thinking of how, or what, but only that she had to save Tag.

"Get out of here," Tag yelled. "Can't you see what you're doing to him? Get away!"

"Why? What's..." Michelle stammered, backing away. The horse reared again and charged at the stall door just as Tag leaped aside.

"I said, get out of here!"

Sobbing, Michelle turned and ran.

Once Michelle was gone, Tag calmed the big horse with soft words and gentle touches. Nitro whinnied and nibbled at his hay as if nothing had happened. Tag picked up the brush and comb he'd dropped and quietly left the stall.

He didn't want to think of the look on Michelle's face when he'd yelled at her, didn't want to consider how his command might have sounded.

He put the gear away, slowly, avoiding the inevitable. He needed to apologize, he guessed, but she should have known. *No,* a little voice said. *She shouldn't have.*

He found her in the stall with Dandy, her arms wrapped around the big old horse's neck, crying as if her heart would break. Tag figured if she felt anything like him, it already had.

"Michelle?"

She ignored him.

Maybe she didn't hear him. "Michelle?" Tag stepped into the stall and awkwardly patted her on the shoulder. He wanted to haul her into his arms and kiss the tears, he wanted to lay her down in the sweet hay and make love to her, make all the problems go away. He wanted....he couldn't have what he wanted. He couldn't because he loved her and it wouldn't be right.

She raised her head and wiped her nose on the sleeve of the robe. Her eyes were huge, deep emerald pools so filled with longing he thought he might die.

"I'm sorry I yelled," he said, giving in to impulse, framing her jaw with his hands and wiping the tears from her cheeks with his thumbs. "It's just, Nitro, he's a stud. You told me yesterday it's your time of the month. Sometimes, not always, but sometimes that makes a stallion go a little crazy, confuses him, makes him act like there's a mare around."

"Oh God, how embarrassing." She dipped her head, turned away from his hands. "I'm sorry. I didn't know...I never even thought about something like..."

"I know. It's not your fault. I shouldn't have yelled, but he scared me."

"Cowboys aren't supposed to get scared," she said, biting her lips, then smiling at him. "You're supposed to be brave and fearless and always get the girl. At least that's how we're supposed to write about you."

"I've been brave before, don't know about fearless. As far as the girl..." He put his hands on her shoulders and forced her to look at him. "I love you, Michelle. I love you more than you can imagine."

"Oh, Tag. I..."

"But it won't work." God, he hated doing this. Her face crumpled, her lip quivered so that he wanted to kiss her, tell her he was an idiot and somehow they'd make it work.

Uno, dos, tres...damn! He could do this. He had to.

"Life's not a story, sweetheart. It's flawed people and situations that don't always work out the way you want. What just happened in there...doesn't that tell you this isn't where you belong? You're a city girl, Michelle. You're used to a life I can't ever give you. Mark can. He loves you..."

"Oh, so you're just going to generously turn me over to Mark, is that it?" She twisted out of his grasp with an outraged jerk of her shoulders. "Here Michelle. You can fall in love with this guy. He's the perfect man for you. Is that it?"

"I'm just trying to do what's right for you."

"Don't give me that! You coward," she hissed. "You know, Taggart Martin, you're enough to give cowboys a bad name. You're so afraid to open yourself to love you're going to spend the rest of your life denying you ever had a chance to know what it was like. Maybe you're right. Maybe Mark would make a better husband. At least we'll both be in the same town so we can find out."

She gave him a look that would freeze sunlight, whistled for his profoundly disloyal dog and headed back to the house.

Tag watched her go, the mutt trotting along at her heels. He had a feeling he'd just made the biggest mistake of his life.

MICHELLE REFUSED to cry. No way was Tag Martin going to make her cry. She couldn't possibly be in love with a guy as stupid as that darned cowboy. If she didn't love him, he couldn't make her cry.

"Would you care for another helping, dear?" Lenore held the plate filled with tender vegetables out to her. Michelle took it automatically, even though she hadn't even noticed the taste of anything else on her plate.

It took all her concentration not to cry.

Mark, on the other hand, had completely recovered from his dunking in the creek and seemed to be having a wonderful time, thoroughly enjoying his last dinner at the Double Eagle. He'd kept

Coop and Lenore smiling with stories about stories, tales of the crazy stuff he'd read from the slush pile, that bottomless pit where unsolicited manuscripts went when they arrived at the publishing house where he worked.

Tag had decided not to join them at the table, instead opting to make a late evening check of the newly repaired road. *He probably wants to make sure we can leave in the morning as planned,* Michelle thought.

"You look tired, kiddo." Mark's teasing comment snapped Michelle out of her fog. "Rescuing editors must be exhausting work."

"I told you," Michelle said. "Tag's the one who rescued you. I merely handed him the rope."

"You could have let me drown," Mark replied.

"You reject another story of mine, I might just consider it...should we ever be where you need rescuing again."

"Yeah, but then you'd have to break in a new editor and you'll never find one as wonderful and accommodating as I am." He flashed her that hundred megawatt smile that belonged on the cover of a romance novel.

Michelle snorted, falling easily into the give and take teasing they'd shared for years. Mark was likable and when he wasn't telling her how to write her stories, he was fun and easy to get along with.

She could do worse.

I am not going to settle. Wasn't that what she'd told Lenore? Would it be merely settling, to spend her life with a man whose friendship she cherished? A man who might not bring her passion, but could give her happiness and love, children, companionship, a future?

She promised herself she'd think about it. She'd leave herself open to Mark and see what the future held.

"One thing, Michelle," Mark said. "You'll have to admit that, even though this trip didn't quite go as planned, it was a good idea of mine to send you out here. At least now when you write that western, you'll know what you're writing about."

She felt the pain pass through her like the shaft of an arrow. "I guess you're right," she mumbled.

"Of course I'm right." Mark patted her hand affectionately, hesitated, then lifted her fingers and studied them. "You really do need a manicure, sweetheart. Haven't you been wearing gloves?"

She laughed then. Laughed to keep from crying. Snatching her hand out of Mark's light grasp, she waggled her fingers under his nose.

"You're paying for it, sweetheart. You owe me and I want it all. The massage, the hair stylist, the complete makeover. I want a manicure, a pedicure, maybe even a wax job...and you're paying for all of it. This girl's getting a whole new look."

He grinned, but she could tell he wasn't certain if she was teasing or serious.

Tag would have figured it out, she thought. He always knew when she was teasing. She just wished he knew how much she loved him.

TAG HESITATED outside Michelle's bedroom door. He'd been up since dawn, which didn't really mean much since he hadn't slept all night.

He'd actually thought about joining all of them for dinner, but he'd caught part of Michelle's conversation about wanting a whole new look. He hoped she was kidding. He didn't want her to change a thing, but since he couldn't see her eyes, he didn't know if she meant it or not.

He could always tell when she was teasing by the little twinkle she got in her eyes.

He was really gonna miss that twinkle.

He knocked.

Before he had a chance to prepare himself, Michelle flung the door wide.

She was dressed for travel in her good jeans and one of her fancy dress western shirts. The fringe along the yoke was the same green as her eyes.

"Tag?" Her eyes, her beautiful emerald green eyes. She stared at him a moment, her lips parted, her soul wide open to him.

Just as quickly, she shuttered all of it, hid her emotions where no one, especially Tag, would see them. "What are you doing here? It's barely seven."

"I wanted to tell you good-bye," he said, the carefully prepared words nowhere to be found. "I thought it would be easier if we were alone."

He looked away. He couldn't meet those eyes of hers, look into the hurt and know he was the cause. Even though he was certain she'd thank him one day.

"You're probably right. Good-bye, Tag."

He turned back and she was holding out her hand. She wanted to shake his damned hand! He stared at her fingers a minute, those fingers with the blunt nails that were going to be manicured and polished, probably before the day was over. He couldn't stand it.

He grabbed her. He moved so fast he thought she'd belt him one, but she just melted into his arms as if they'd never been apart. Tag stepped through the door and kicked it shut behind him and all the time he was kissing Michelle she was kissing him back, kissing him the way she had up there in the line shack all those nights and days.

He covered her mouth with his, breathing her in, tasting her, needing her so much he thought he might shatter into a thousand tiny pieces.

Her breath came in ragged gasps. She tore her mouth away from his and leaned against his chest, her chest rising and falling in cadence with his.

The front of his shirt was wet. Damn, she was crying. He didn't want her to cry.

"Michelle, sweetheart, please..." He tipped her chin up with his fingers, expecting to see the love shining in her eyes. He saw a fierce determination, a will every bit as strong as his own.

"Good-bye, Tag," she whispered. "I think you'd better leave now." Then she slipped out of his embrace and before he could think of a thing to say, opened the door. "Thank you for everything." Her voice sounded stiff, foreign.

He licked his lips, tasted her on his mouth. Couldn't take his eyes off her. Michelle's throat convulsed as she swallowed, but her tears had stopped and she held her head proudly.

She also held the door open.

He could take a hint, Tag figured. Nodding his head, he left.

MARK KNOCKED on her door a few minutes later. "You okay?" he asked after Michelle opened it to admit him. "I saw Tag race off on Nitro and wondered if he'd stopped by here."

"Yeah, he was here." She grabbed her battered suitcase off the bed. Her luggage, what was left of it, had been washed out of the trunk of her little rental car and was probably buried under tons of mud by now.

"I told Lenore we'd skip breakfast, just have a cup of coffee and get something on the road. I didn't think you'd feel much like eating this early."

"Thanks, Mark. You really are sweet," she said. He *was* sweet. He'd been kind and understanding, everything a friend should be.

He just wasn't Tag. She'd been right to send Tag away, though. If he'd come to ask her to stay, to tell her he loved her and couldn't live without her...well, that would have been one thing.

But he'd come to say good-bye. Privately, so he wouldn't have to say it in front of everyone, so afraid of his emotions, terrified someone might see that her leaving actually meant something to him.

She wouldn't live her life with a man afraid of love. She'd give up the most passionate relationship she'd ever known, but she wouldn't trade love for anything.

Not even the sizzle?

No, she told herself. Not even that.

LENORE CRIED when she said good-bye. Coop didn't cry, but his pale blue eyes shimmered with tears and his embrace was warm and strong. "You come back, ya hear? The Double Eagle ain't gonna be the same without you."

"Thanks, Coop. Lenore, I'm really going to miss both of you, so much. Thank you for everything. If you ever come to New York...?" She left the sentence dangling.

They'd never come. Not in a million years. Why should they, when they had all of Colorado to call home? When they had love and laughter and shared nights for the rest of their lives?

Coop had proposed to Lenore just last night. They'd announced their impending marriage this morning and invited Michelle and Mark to come to the wedding.

Michelle didn't think she could stand another wedding on the Double Eagle, at least not one that didn't include her and Tag.

Mark grabbed her bag and threw it in the trunk, then opened the door for her. Michelle scanned the horizon, hoping for one last glimpse of Tag.

She spotted him, far off atop one of the low hills that surrounded the ranch, a silent silhouette against the morning sky. Her throat tightened as she watched him, mounted on Nitro, horse and man, so much a part of the ranch they seemed to flow up out of the earth.

She wondered what he thought, waiting up there on his hill. She wondered if he knew what a terrible mistake he was making.

"C'mon, sweetheart. It's a long ways home."

Michelle glanced up at Mark's gentle smile, gave Lenore and Coop one last hug, then crawled into the front seat. Her face felt frozen, her eyes dry and scratchy, her jaws ached from clenching her teeth.

Mark started the car, they all waved and she was suddenly leaving the Double Eagle behind. Leaving Lenore and Coop, Daisy and Dandy and Star.

Leaving Tag.

She hadn't quite left Bob the Dog. He bounded along beside the car, his beautiful tail flying in the breeze, his joyful bark out of place with Michelle's mood.

She opened the window. "Go home, Bob," she yelled. "Go home." The dog ran a few more paces then stopped, one ear up, one ear down, his tongue hanging out of his grinning mouth. Michelle thought he looked as if he were laughing at her as the car slowly followed the long drive to the main road.

"I should have known he was letting you get away too easily." Mark's disgruntled laugh startled Michelle.

"What?"

"You ever put an ending like this in one of your books, Michelle, I swear I'll make you rewrite the whole damned thing."

"Whatever are you talking about?" Michelle spun around in her seat and scanned the horizon.

"No, stupid. Over there!" Mark was laughing out loud now, but he gave the car a little more gas and increased their speed.

Michelle looked in the direction he pointed and gasped. Tag, riding low over Nitro's back, galloping in a reckless dash across the hillside in a course destined to head them off before the main gate. The stallion's powerful legs stretched and pounded over the ground, throwing up huge clods of mud and turf.

Tag held his Stetson in one hand, the reins in the other. Michelle held her breath, glorying in the powerful combination of man and beast, the knowledge that Tag was finally, really and truly, coming for her.

In front of Mark, his grandmother, even Coop, he was chasing after Michelle.

Her cowboy hero, racing to the finish for his one true love.

Mark was right. No way in hell could she get away with a finish like this. She was laughing, out of breath, in love, when horse and car reached the same point on the road.

Mark hit the brakes, Tag pulled back on the reins. Nitro reared, his front hooves flailing the sky, his mouth wide open in a stallion scream of triumph.

Tag slid easily to the ground, tipped his newly replaced Stetson to Mark, then opened Michelle's door. "I can't let you do it," he said, gasping for breath. "I can't let you marry him."

"Why?" Michelle asked, unbuckling her seatbelt and stepping out of the car.

"You know why, Michelle. You know damned well why."

"Maybe I do and maybe I don't," she said, laughing for the pure joy of the moment. "Why don't you enlighten me?"

"Because I love you, dammit! I can't live without you and you know it. You've gotten yourself under my skin, you've left bits and pieces of yourself all over the Double Eagle so that every where I look, every place I go, I see you. I finally get the damned ranch and it's not even mine! It's yours." He grabbed her hands and got down on one knee.

Michelle burst into tears.

"I love you, Michelle. I love you more than I ever thought I'd love anyone. I think you love me just as much. I hope you do, because you're gonna have to love me a lot to put up with me once we're really married. You will marry me, won't you? You'll be my wife, have my babies? Help me during round-up," he added, grinning that damned lop-sided grin she never could resist.

She was crying so hard she couldn't answer him. She figured he must have taken it as a yes, because he suddenly stood up, kissed her hard on the mouth and grabbed her hand. "I'm really sorry, Mark," he said. "You're one hell of a nice guy and I like you a lot, but you can't have her."

At some point Mark must have gotten out of the car, because he was leaning against it, his arms folded on the roof. His smile was bittersweet, loving, the smile of a good friend. "For what it's worth, Tag, she never was mine to have. You be good to her, though, or I'll be back."

"You're welcome back any time. You know that." Tag rubbed his hand along Michelle's back. "C'mon, sweetheart. We're going home."

"But Nitro? You said I can't get near Ni..."

"Nitro listens to me," Tag said, tilting her chin up with his finger. "I promise to listen to you. Okay? Is it a deal?"

"It's a deal."

Tag scooped Michelle up in his arms and settled her on the suddenly placid stallion. He mounted behind her and grabbed the reins. "Drive carefully," he said, waving to Mark.

Michelle couldn't think of a thing to say. "Mark, I..."

"It's okay," he said. "You're doing the right thing. However," he added, pointing his finger. "This doesn't mean you quit writing. I want a western from you, Michelle. I want the best damned western you can write. Now get busy." He dipped his head to get into the car, then straightened up again. "Be happy, sweetheart, but don't you dare end the story with the hero racing up on a white stallion to rescue the heroine. That sort of thing just won't fly."

She heard his laughter as he drove away. Michelle and Tag watched until the rental car reached the main gate and turned toward town. Mark waved, they waved back, then Tag clicked his tongue and Nitro calmly headed back to the ranch.

Michelle snuggled into Tag's embrace, fit herself into the valley of his thighs and grinned at the future lying in wait for both of them.

"Yes," she said, turning to kiss Tag on the chin.

"Yes, what?" he asked, kissing her back.

"Yes, I'll marry you." She kissed him once more.

Tag nudged Nitro and the big horse lunged forward. Coop and Lenore waited for them, hand in hand on the broad front porch.

Standing there waiting as if this were exactly the right way for Michelle's story to begin.

Epilogue

MARK CONNOR replaced the final page of Michelle's latest manuscript and rubbed his hand over his face. All he managed to do was smear the tears, so he grabbed his handkerchief out of his pocket and wiped his eyes, blew his nose and did his best to make himself presentable before he headed home.

Thank goodness the office was empty. Anyone with half a brain, or a life, had gone home hours ago.

He'd stayed on, reading Michelle's western. Started it the minute it arrived with the morning mail and hadn't been able to put it down.

She'd certainly gotten it right this time, though Mark wasn't certain if it was the story that touched him so, or the personal note she'd added on the end.

She was taking an unofficial leave of absence from writing for awhile. She hoped he didn't mind too much, had thought she could manage with the baby coming and everything else going on.

Twins, a boy and a girl, had complicated things more than she and Tag had expected, but they couldn't be happier.

Or more in love.

When was Mark coming to visit? She missed him, missed the occasional lunches, the phone calls. She even missed his insults.

Phones worked just fine in Colorado, in case he'd forgotten.

She'd signed it "Love, Michelle," then added a PS as long as the note. Lenore and Coop were fine, Tag sent his greetings, Star was learning his paces. Will and Annie Twigg were expecting a baby come spring, but Betsy Mae's clown had decided he wasn't cut out for marriage. He'd left her at the Durango rodeo and she was back at Columbine Camp, nursing a broken heart and driving her brother and new sister-in-law nuts.

Life on the Double Eagle, however, was absolutely wonderful.

Mark stuck the note in his pocket, tidied his desk and stood up. He glanced at his calendar and smiled.

Just six more months and he'd be out of here. Long enough to get Michelle's book going, long enough to farm his authors out to other editors. Then it was his turn.

He'd been thinking about Colorado, lately. Thinking about horses and mountains, trees and freedom. Thinking about love.

Michelle'd told him he didn't have a clue when it came to romance. He was willing to agree with her, up to a point.

What better place to learn than Colorado? It had certainly worked for Michelle. Whistling, Mark turned out the light and headed home.

~ The End ~

Kate Douglas

Kate Douglas is a sucker for happy endings, but this romance author never makes it easy for her characters to find their own personal paradise. Kate's found hers in the wine country of northern California where she and her husband of almost thirty years live in an old farmhouse in the midst of a hillside vineyard.

When she's not writing, Kate does sports photography for many northern California cycling teams.

Visit Kate's Web site at: http://www.katedouglas.com

Printed in the United States
17426LVS00001BA/62

9 780759 901261